The Night Crew III

Hunting Ground

Brad Ricks

Published by Crystal Lake Publishing
Where Stories Come Alive!

Crystal Lake Publishing
www.CrystalLakePub.com

WELCOME
TO ANOTHER

CRYSTAL LAKE PUBLISHING
CREATION

Writer's note:

This story uses the real town of Mena, AR as its primary setting. Although the town and the forest around it are real, most places within this book are fictional. Directions from one location to another are also fictional.

For the horror lovers and the monster hunters.
May your passion never cease.

1

Dᴀᴠɪᴅ Hᴀʟʟ ᴘᴜʟʟᴇᴅ ʜɪs black 2019 Ford Mustang up to the front of Rebecca Summers' house. The back of his car was packed and ready for the evening. It had taken a week of convincing before she agreed, but now that she had, he'd made sure everything was ready to go.

Rebecca leaned against the frame of the front door wearing jeans and a loose-fitting sweater. Her short blonde hair was tucked into a baseball cap. The moment David opened his car door, she hollered, "You're late."

"Would you believe traffic?" he responded with a grin on his thin face. The entire population of Mena, Arkansas sat just shy of six thousand people. In all of David's twenty-six years of being alive and living in the small town, traffic had not ever been a problem. He'd lost track of time searching for his tent in the garage. He walked around to the other side of the car, opening the passenger door.

She rolled her eyes and shook her head. "You sure I don't need to pack anything?"

"I have everything we need. Air mattress, blankets, tent, chairs, campfire supplies, ice chest, food. We're just camping for one night. I didn't bring a change of clothes. I'm going to wear these same jeans, sweater, and hoodie when we wake up tomorrow."

She closed her front door, locked it, and started down the sidewalk. "It's going to get cold tonight," she said, as she strolled over to him. She tossed her arms around his neck and planted her soft lips on his.

"Don't worry about that. I'll keep you warm." He kissed her again, thinking about the night ahead under the stars.

As they separated, she said, "You'd better. I'm not usually the camping type. My idea of camping is the Holiday Inn instead of the Marriott."

"I'm aware."

She dropped her arms and shuffled into the passenger seat. He closed her door and hustled around the car, sliding into the driver's seat.

David drove them into Ouachita National Forest. He had a campsite picked out far from any other campers. It was just the two of them alone in the woods. When he'd first told her that, she commented how that's exactly what a serial killer would say. He hadn't thought of it that way, but he could see her point. He'd only thought of the quality time they'd be spending together, him sharing something with her that he enjoyed, not the "drag you into the forest to kill you" aspect of how it might appear.

As he set up the tent, he glanced around the familiar setting. The woods were dense. The smell of dirt, oak, and pine filled the air. The trees blocked the wind, leaving only a damp chill in the air. It wouldn't be long before the sun set, and David would lose the last of the evening light. He had to hurry so he had time for everything else.

Once the tent was built, air mattress inflated, blankets and pillows tossed on the air mattress, and the campfire lit, he opened the ice chest and cooked a delicious steak dinner for them. After dinner was done and night took over, the two found their way into the tent and under the blankets.

David had worried that Rebecca wouldn't be able to sleep, that the sound of the forest would keep her awake deep into the night. To his surprise, she laid on her side under the blanket and scooted into him. Within moments of wrapping his arm around her, she was snoring and deep into a dream. He smiled listening to the sounds of the forest.

Wind rustled the leaves, owls hooted, rabbits and deer bound across the ground, all while Rebecca Summers slept peacefully.

He fell asleep to the sound of her rhythmic snoring.

"David," she said, anxiously shoving his arm through the covers. Whispering, she said, "Wake up. Something's out there."

It took him a few moments to realize he wasn't still dreaming, she was actually shaking him awake. He opened his eyes and yawned. It was still pitch black.

"What time is it?" he asked, while his arm searched for his phone.

"A little after two," she said, raising up from under the warm covers. She grabbed her sweater and quickly shoved her head and arms inside, pulling it on. She swung her legs around and began shuffling her pants around her feet.

"What are you doing?"

"Getting dressed. There's something outside the tent."

Now fully awake, he processed what she'd said. He reached out and placed a hand on her arm. "Don't do that. Relax. Animals come sniffing around all the time in the middle of the night. Get undressed, lie down, and curl up with me. You've let out all the heat from under the blankets."

She glared at him. "This didn't sound like some raccoon foraging for...whatever the hell raccoons forage for. It sounded big. Bigger."

She whispered as she spoke, but her voice had a commanding urgency. Whatever she had heard, spooked her.

"In the woods, sounds are deceiving." David yawned again. "But, if you're that worried about it, I'll check. Just lay back down." He rose from the air mattress and tossed his arms around her, giving her a hug and a kiss on the neck.

"You're going to check it out?" she asked.

"Yes." He smiled and slid toward his side of the tent where his clothes lay in a pile.

Rebecca lay back down, pulling the covers up to her neck.

David, still sitting on the air mattress, pulled his pants around his feet, up his legs, and then squatted in the small tent to hike them around his thin waist. He sat down to put his socks and shoes on. Last, he grabbed his hoodie and pulled it over his head, leaving his shirt on the tent floor. He knew he'd be back in a few minutes after shooing away whatever animal rummaged around.

Standing back up, he shuffled to the tent's door. He placed his hand on the zipper. His experience, as soon as the zipper ripped open, whatever had startled Rebecca would take off.

He craned his neck around and saw her lying on the pillow with the blanket tucked around her, trapping her body heat within. "I'll be right..." Before he could finish, he stared at a shadow on the tent wall behind Rebecca's head.

The moonlit silhouette suggested a very large animal. It stood on two legs with a large snout. Large paws with long, sharp nails tipped each arm. Based on the size alone, David immediately knew it was a bear. He was glad he hadn't left the tent yet. With bears, he just needed to stay calm and quiet. They'd look for scraps left around and then leave. It had probably smelled the steak from earlier and had come for leftovers.

"Don't. Move," he whispered, trying not to startle her.

The beast sniffed the air inches from their tent. Suddenly, its head turned. The snout disappeared in the shadow. It was facing the tent. David changed his mind and started to tell Rebecca to come on this side of the tent, when the bear's arm lifted and crashed down. The claws punctured the tent. A loud rip shattered the silence as nails quickly tore through the tent's thin wall. It cut smoothly as a surgeon's scalpel through skin. The other hand came down and shredded the tent.

Rebecca screamed.

As she did, the beast dropped its hand to the ground. It crashed on top of her with its full weight, burying its claws into her sweater. Its snout pierced the tent and leaned forward. Black fur covered its entire body. Its eyes stared into David. Pitch black but for a thin yellow ring around the iris, they held David in a trance. They demanded he wait his turn to become its victim. Releasing him, it dropped its head, and David followed its gaze.

Rebecca lay pinned under its paw. Blood spurted from her mouth. The claws dug into her chest. Dark red inklike blood stained her sweater, pouring from each wound. The further into the tent the animal leaned, the more weight it put on Rebecca, crushing her chest and forcing blood to spray out of her mouth. David heard her sternum crack. In one quick motion, it lifted the other paw above its head and dropped it onto her abdomen. The claws pierced the blanket, her sweater, her stomach. It ripped its bloody hand back, tearing through the fabrics and the contents of her stomach. Deep, dark red spilled from the gaping wound and pooled around Rebecca, covering the tent floor. The air mattress exploded underneath her, showering the tent and David in Rebecca's blood. Rebecca's body violently twitched as the beast buried its snout into her entrails and tore huge chunks of gory small intestines out of her.

Panicked, David reached down to the bottom of the tent, found the zipper, and ripped it open. Halfway up, the zipper caught on the tent fabric and stopped moving. He dropped low and pushed his head through the small opening. As he worked his shoulders, a sharp pain erupted in his side. He spun his head around and saw the bear had climbed through the tent and latched onto him. Three claws raked across his side and back. David rolled away from the pain, trying to squeeze his shoulders through the restricted opening. Just as he finally wriggled free, his other side burst with fire. He glanced down to see the bear's snout wrapped around his stomach, its teeth buried in his abdomen. Blood gushed from his side.

David pounded the bear's head, hoping it would release its grip. He wasn't dying tonight. He refused to become food for some wild animal. He shot his hand out and found his flashlight rolling around in Rebecca's blood. He gripped the silver handle, hoping it didn't slip through his grasp, and banged it into the creature's eye. He felt the clamp around his side release, and he shoved through the tent's zippered front. The top of the zipper scraped down his back, gouging it, but after everything else, that pain was nothing.

Once free of the tent, he found his footing among the dead leaves and ran. He ran through the woods as fast as he could. He knew there was a road not far ahead. Despite the late hour, he hoped someone would be there to help. He stumbled through the foliage as he ran, narrowly avoiding crashing into trees. Blood poured from multiple points on his body. Both of his sides were badly injured, though now was not the time to stop. He felt blood flowing down his back and his legs. Somewhere not far behind him, the bear pursued. He heard paws slapping against the ground. If he stopped now, he was dead.

Just ahead, he saw a hill. He collided with it and crawled up the side of it on his hands and knees. With pain radiating and darkness creeping in, he made one final push. He topped the small hill and stumbled onto asphalt. Tires squealed, and David was washed in lights. Then darkness.

2

SITTING BEHIND THE WHEEL of his blue and white F150, Roy pulled up behind David Hall's black Mustang, stopping a dozen yards away. This wasn't how he liked to spend his mornings, especially Saturday mornings. If it was a weekday, he would have his feet propped up on his desk, a coffee in one hand, and a donut in the other. But a fucking Saturday morning? The officer on duty had woken him up at four in the morning. No four AM call was a good call, especially not on a Saturday.

He opened the door and hopped out of the truck. The moment his feet hit the mud, he regretted the decision to leap down from the driver's seat and not use the small step just under the door. Mud splattered onto his burgundy dress shoes and the bottom of his dark blue suit pants.

"Ah fuck," he said, glancing down at the mess.

Roy slammed the door shut and peered at the side of the truck. Mud covered the sleek decal displaying the Mena Police Department logo. He thought about taking it to the car wash later, but being the beginning of April, he knew he just needed to wait a few days, and it would rain again, washing the mud away.

"Chief," an officer yelled from twenty yards away.

The officer stood on the other side of the police tape circling the camp site. Inside the tape Roy saw a huddled mass of fabric and tarp, a small campfire circle, an ice chest, and two chairs. A handful of large trees lay within the perimeter.

Roy raised his hand, acknowledging the officer, and then marched in that direction. He tried to avoid as much mud as he could, hoping to not add to the mess already on his clothes. He glanced around the forest, soaking in the surrounding details. He had learned a long time ago to keep his eyes open when entering a crime scene. It wasn't very often that he had to visit Ouachita. Their little community stayed quiet. A possible homicide was rare. Except these past few weeks were different. Something was off, and he was afraid he knew what it was.

"Give me the rundown," he said as he approached the officer. He lifted the police tape and ducked underneath it.

"Sure thing, Chief. Well, the tent is over there." The young cop pointed to the mound of fabric. It was primarily different shades of green, similar to every other tent Roy had ever seen. This one had an added color, though. It was covered in bloodstains. The body of Rebecca Summers had been buried somewhere underneath the destroyed tent. Roy knew the medical examiner had already zipped her up and taken her away earlier that morning. "The tech guys are working on bagging it up. It's a mess in there. Joe puked his guts out when he saw her; I've seen that man field dress a wild hog in the heat of summer, and he wasn't fazed."

"What else?" Henderson placed his hands on his belt, pulling back his suit jacket. His white shirt protruded out, stretching around Roy's relatively large gut. He didn't have time to hear about how Joe contaminated the scene by losing his breakfast by a tree. He needed specific details before making his next call.

"Surprisingly, that's it. Well, you know about David Hall. He's at the hospital now."

"Talked to the doctors a few minutes ago. He's still out, scheduled for surgery number two in a few hours. This one for his leg. The docs have already patched up his side and back. Outside of the tent, was anything else destroyed, rummaged through, or torn apart?"

"You mean outside of Rebecca?"

Roy glared at him and the officer shrank, turned his head, and glanced across the area. Yellow crime scene tape moved in the wind. The only people meandering around were those gathering whatever evidence they could find. It appeared most of what they had were pieces of Rebecca and the tent.

"Nothing else. Whatever did this—"

"A bear—" Roy interrupted.

"A bear?" the cop asked.

"Yes, a bear. Continue, though."

Hesitantly, he continued. "The bear went straight for the tent. It avoided the trash and the ice chest. Nothing else looks like it was touched."

Roy nodded his head. He'd hoped for a different answer. He'd hoped the beast went after more than just the sleeping couple. He turned and started back to his truck, reaching into his pocket and pulling out his phone. "Thanks, officer. I look forward to reading the report."

He glanced down at the device in his hand, scrolled through his contacts, and clicked on the one he was looking for.

"We've had another one," Henderson said the moment the ringing stopped.

"Are you sure?"

"Yes, I'm fucking sure. I know a goddamn attack when I see one. I thought you had this handled." He gripped the truck's door handle and swung it open. This situation was escalating. Each incident had been messier than the last. He doubted he could hide this one. The Summers family wasn't shy, and they had tempers. Losing their daughter would cause repercussions.

"I'm waiting to hear from the pack. We don't know it's one of ours yet. Some believe it could be a wendigo."

"A wendigo, my ass. How many more are going to die before you actually do something?" Roy lifted himself into the truck and slammed the door, frustrated.

"At least we know where the hunting ground is. Once I have approval, I'll head that way and put a stop to this."

Roy shook his head. "Hunting ground? I've had two bodies drop in my quiet town, and a third is in the ICU with a bite! We both know what that could mean. And that doesn't count the missing persons' reports that've come in! Six, all leading this direction. Six more bodies are somewhere in this big ass forest. Glad to know until you fucking do something, anyone who's out here is in the middle of a hunting ground. Fucking lovely."

Chief Henderson hung up the phone and resisted the urge to throw it against his windshield.

What a way to start a fucking weekend!

Tuesday nights were Tanner's favorite night of the week. They didn't have much time once he got home from school, so his parents picked up pizza for dinner. Pizza Hut was just down the road from their house. He loved their pepperoni and sausage. She'd pick up a personal pan for him, and a medium supreme for his dad and her to share.

Tonight was no different. Tanner rushed home from Mena Middle School as soon as the bell rang. Fifteen minutes later, he bolted through the front door of his house. He smelled the pizza wafting from the dining room and into the living room. He sprinted upstairs to his room and tossed his backpack on his bed.

"Tanner," his mom shouted from downstairs. "Get changed before you come down. I need to run an errand before I drop you off at scouts. Remember: dress warm. You boys have your hike this evening."

"OK," Tanner responded back. "I'll be right down."

Scouts made Tuesdays his favorite. Sure, the pizza was great, but he really enjoyed scouting. He got to go camping, hiking, build fires, learn to tie knots, shoot bows and arrows, and do a ton of other fun stuff along with friends he'd known forever. He held the rank of Star, which meant he was working on his Life and then onto Eagle. That was his goal. Eagle before fifteen. He'd heard over and over about how once scouts turn sixteen, work and girls get in the way, which was why he had his sights set on fifteen. He had two years to get it done.

Tanner stripped off his school clothes and threw on a pair of older blue jeans. When the troop was going hiking, they didn't have to wear their normal uniform. Instead, he grabbed a blue T-shirt with the scout logo and their troop number on it and pulled it over his head. The most important thing on a hike was footwear. He had learned the hard way when he was younger to wear good socks and hiking boots. His feet had gotten wet and cold. By the time the hike ended, his feet had hurt so badly he didn't know if he'd ever walk again.

With his wool socks on and his boots securely tied to his feet, he grabbed his jacket off the hook on his door and rushed off. Bounding out of his room, he started down the stairs. His feet slammed on every step, sending the loud stomp from his boots reverberating across the entire downstairs.

"Tanner, less elephant, more church mouse, or at least more considerate scout," his dad hollered.

"Sorry, dad," he said, as he leapt over the last two steps and landed on the ground floor. He bent at his knees, stuck his arms out in front of him, and then slowly stood up, dropping his arms to his side. "He sticks the landing, and the crowd goes wild!" Tanner raised his arms above his head, waving to the imaginary crowd. He simulated crowd noises, and then said, "Thank you. Thank you."

"Hey goof, get over here and eat your pizza," his dad said.

Tanner marched down the hallway and into the dining room. The smell of pepperoni and sausage carried him along. He also smelled onions, bell peppers, and olives on his parents' pizza but chose to ignore those aromas.

As he walked into the dining room, his parents sat next to each other on one side of the square table. An open pizza box sat in between them, three slices already missing. His dad, wearing his typical flannel shirt, shoved another bite into his mouth. Tanner's mom had on a gray Razorbacks sweater. The box with his own personal pan pizza sat on his side of the table. There was no plate for him. He preferred to devour his pizza straight from the box, less dishes when it was his turn to wash.

He gripped the top of the brown, wooden chair and slid it away from the table. He draped his jacket over the back of it and sat down.

"Hiking tonight. That should be fun. Working on a particular merit badge?" his dad asked. He grabbed a napkin and wiped grease from his fingers.

Tanner shaved a huge bite of pizza in his mouth. Mouth half full, he said, "The ever-dreaded hiking merit badge."

"I thought you already had that one?" his mom asked.

Tanner grabbed his glass of water and took a big swig. He realized he had to find the perfect balance between hydrating for the hike and not having to stop to pee a dozen times in the woods. "I'm almost done with it. Just have the twenty-miler left. We're planning on that one in a few weeks."

His dad pushed his plate away from him. After his third slice, he was finished. "So, what's Jack planning for tonight's hike?" he asked. Jack Waters was the scout master. He'd been running the troop since Tanner was a Cub Scout. From hearing his dad and his dad's friends talk, Jack had been running the troop since they were in scouts.

"Conditioning. Tonight's only a two mile. We don't have time for much else. Over the next few meetings, we're mapping out the path for the big one." Tanner grabbed the last of his pizza and shoved most of it into his mouth. The savory taste of meat, cheese, sauce, and grease filled his taste buds. He bit hard and pulled his hand back. Cheese trailed from his mouth to the remainder of the pizza in his hand.

After swallowing, he chomped on the last of his dinner and followed it up with the rest of his water. "We're all piling into Mr. Waters' truck. He's dropping us off at Lover's Lookout on 88, and then we're hiking up to Acorn Vista, and then hiking back."

"If you stay on the road, make sure you watch out for cars," his mom said.

Tanner rolled his eyes. "It's not my first hike, mom. Plus, we don't stay on the road. That's not fun. We take off through the woods."

4

AFTER THE WINDING DRIVE to Lover's Lookout, Jack pulled the truck to the side of the road. Tanner sat in the bed of the pickup with five other scouts. Only one, Joey Winslow, was a higher rank than Tanner. He was a Life scout and working on his Eagle. The other four were newer scouts with lower ranks. This meant Tanner and Joey were expected to take on leadership roles. That was part of moving up. The higher up a scout was, the more he was expected to be a leader and a mentor to the younger scouts.

"Joey," Tanner hollered as both boys hopped out of the back of the scout master's truck.

Joey turned his head and strode to Tanner. "What's up?"

"There are two of us, and three of them." Tanner cocked his head toward the other three. He'd known Joey since kindergarten. They'd be the same rank if Tanner hadn't taken his time with a few of the required merit badges for the First Class rank. That was before he set his "Eagle by Fifteen" goal. For the two boys, it had always been an us and them thing, especially now that they were getting to be the older scouts. "How do you want to split them up?"

Joey scrunched up one side of his cheek. Tanner knew it as his thinking face.

"How about this? You take Brady. He's the youngest and only a Ten-derfoot. He'll need the most help. I'll take Scott and Andrew. They're halfway through Hiking anyway and won't need as much help."

"How come I have to watch after the newbie?" Tanner asked.

"Because I outrank you." Although wearing the same T-shirt that Tanner had on and not his scout uniform, Joey tapped the spot where the badge would've been had they been wearing them. "So you get the Tenderfoot."

"He's going to gripe the whole way," Tanner predicted, rolling his eyes in mock-anticipation.

He kicked gravel from the side of the road and glanced at Brady. Brady brushed his short brown hair under his forest green scout hat. He pushed his glasses up the brim of his small nose. His coat fit loosely. Tanner knew Brady had an older brother and assumed the coat was probably a hand-me-down.

"Suck it up, buttercup." Joey moved toward Scott and Andrew. "You two ready for this hike?"

"Whatever," Tanner said. "I'll whip him into shape. Brady, you're with me."

Jack slammed the truck's door closed. He moved to the bed, grabbed a small backpack, and tossed it on his back. Jack had a headful of gray hair and a beard to match. During Christmas, the younger kids enjoyed tugging on it and asked if he was Santa Claus. The only thing separating him from St. Nick was his shape. He was as lean as they come. Tanner had heard rumor that he once was an expert rock climber and even tackled K2.

"Alright, scouts," he said, tightening the pack. "Joey. Tanner. You two know the route. Use your maps and your compasses. The goal is not to use the road but find your way through the woods. Teach the other three as you go. We're building up to the twenty-miler. The big boy. You two are leading the way. I'm going to stay a few dozen yards behind you in case of an emergency. We don't have much daylight left. Do you have a buddy?"

"Yes," Joey said. "Scott and Drew are with me. Tanner's got Brady."

"Then let's start moving."

Tanner shuffled his feet over to Brady. He reached into his pocket and pulled out the map and compass. "Shine your flashlight over here," he said.

"I didn't bring a flashlight," Brady said. He pushed his glasses back up his nose. "I didn't know we'd need it."

"Be prepared. It's the scout motto. Here." Tanner grabbed his flashlight, and Brady held his hand out. Tanner slapped it into Brady's hand. "Now, give me some light."

The Tenderfoot clicked the flashlight to life and shined the beam over the map. Tanner placed the compass down and found their bearings. He pointed in the direction that Joey, Andrew, and Scott were already treading.

"We're going to go that way. Did you see how I figured that out?"

Brady scratched his hand and pushed his glasses up. "I think so."

"Good, now we need to catch up." Tanner grabbed the map and compass, shoved them into his pockets, and started to jog, hoping to catch up with the rest of the scouts.

"Tanner, don't run," Jack hollered. "Uneven terrain and dark. If you jog, you'll twist an ankle. Brady will need to carry you back to my truck. Brady, are you up for that task?"

Tanner glanced at Brady shaking his head. Of course, Brady wouldn't be able to carry him back. Tanner had a good twenty pounds and six inches on him. Reluctantly, he slowed his pace. He knew what that meant, as well. Joey's group would get further and further ahead. He and Brady would be in the middle somewhere. Their scout master would be somewhere behind them.

"I didn't think so," he continued. "Tanner, slow it down. I trust you know what you're doing. I'll go ahead of you two and catch up with the others. When they reach Acorn Vista, we'll take a break and wait for you."

Despite telling Tanner not to jog in the woods, Jack picked up his pace and hurried to make up some ground between them and the other three. Joey's group had cleared the next hill and disappeared on the other side of it, falling completely out of sight. Within a few minutes, Jack had cleared the same incline and also fell out of view.

As Tanner and Brady started their way through the woods, and up the first incline, Tanner felt the weight of the evening's darkness. It was just the two of them alone in the woods. Although it was the open area, the forest felt claustrophobic. With the sun below the horizon, the trees seemed to creep closer together. Brady stood closer to him than he typically would've allowed, but right now, he didn't exactly mind.

With each step, the leaves crunched under their feet. The sound echoed off the trees. Broken limbs crackled as his hiking boots landed on them. Sound from around him seemed to be transported a few yards away, as if the trees were ventriloquists, tossing noises from one side to the other. Tanner's breathing increased. He wanted to panic but needed to keep a calm exterior for the younger scout. Veterans like him couldn't get scared.

That was, until Tanner heard a loud, high-pitched sound. It happened a few times in succession and then stopped. He quickly turned as he heard the sound of feet quickly running at them, explosively slamming off the ground and stampeding in his and Brady's direction.

Panicked, Tanner and Brady ran. Tanner hoped to catch up with the rest. He didn't know what was behind them, what was chasing after them, but he didn't care. He completely forgot about Brady and pulled ahead of the Tenderfoot.

As he ran, his hiking boot caught on a branch, and Tanner collapsed onto the ground. He fell so hard and so fast he didn't have time to toss his arms in front of him to stop the impact. Instead of having the opportunity to break his arm, he heard the snap of his ankle as it twisted. His face slammed into the ground, and blood filled his throat, washing down from his broken nose. Stars erupted in his eyes.

Tanner rolled onto his back as he saw his predator quickly approaching.

5

Three deer stampeded directly toward Tanner. They had sprinted around Brady as if he wasn't there at all. One of the deer barreling down on Tanner leapt over him, and the other two veered around, disappearing beyond the trees in the dark. Brady ran and slid on his knees to a stop next to Tanner.

"Are you OK?" he asked, gasping for air. "Holy crap, did you hear that noise? It was like something died."

Tanner reached up to Brady's shirt collar, grabbed the front of it tight, and pulled him close to Tanner.

"Get...help..." Tanner struggled to say. "Ankle...nose...broken."

He let go of Brady and clasped his hand over his nose, pinching it closed. Blood coated his throat. His tongue explored his mouth, and as he pushed on his front teeth, thought one of them might be loose. All that paled in comparison to the pain shooting up his leg. Unbearable pressure from the constriction of his boot told Tanner that his ankle was already quite swollen. He wanted to rip it off but knew it was supplying stability.

"Tanner, I really don't think I can carry you out."

"Get...help..." Tanner repeated.

"And leave you here alone? We aren't supposed to do that. They'll be back soon." Brady shifted his head from left to right, searching the woods.

"Go!" Tanner tried to shout, but it came out as a cough of blood and spit.

Brady was frightened to leave through the woods on his own. That was obvious. And after whatever had screamed and sent the deer running, Tanner was equally terrified about what could be lurking in the dark. He didn't want to be left alone, but he needed help. The pain was excruciating. Plus, the scout master said the group would wait for them at Acorn Vista. They weren't going to stop and come right back. They would wait until they figured out something must be wrong.

Each passing second felt like an eternity.

Finally, Brady stood up. He stepped with one leg and turned back to Tanner.

"That way?" He pointed in the relative direction that everyone went.

Tanner leaned onto his side and grabbed the map, compass, and flashlight out of his pocket. He handed all three to Brady. With his nose still pinched and sounding like Mr. Snuffleupagus the Muppet, he said, "Yes, that way. If you need to, stick to the road. Hurry. Go. My foot hurts bad."

Brady angled the direction of the road instead of the woods. Honestly, Tanner couldn't blame him. He wanted Brady to go as fast as possible, but he didn't want the boy to get hurt either. The uneven terrain of the woods was dangerous. Tanner had become his own example. Hesitantly, Brady moved away from Tanner. With every few steps, his pace increased. Within a dozen yards, Brady was running for the road and help. Tanner also knew the odds of Brady running into someone before he reached the Scout Master weren't high, but hope springs eternal.

The reality of his situation hit Tanner hard. He was alone, in the woods, in the dark, injured, and relying on a baby scout to relay his location. Every time he thought about moving, a fresh wave of pain reinforced how bad of an idea that was. But as he sat on the damp ground, tasting the metallic saltiness of blood trickling down his throat and lining his mouth, he was suddenly aware of the stillness and quiet of the forest. Like Brady had mentioned, something had screamed and sent the deer fleeing past them.

Tanner listened to each breath as he pulled it into his lungs and tried to calmly exhale. All the expected sounds from the forest were absent. He'd camped out in these woods often and knew how much noise the forest made. Normally, night was an orchestra of sounds that lulled listeners to sleep. Even the wind had disappeared. The evening's darkness wrapped around Tanner, suffocating him with fear.

A twig snapped somewhere in front of him. He peered through the dark, searching for what had caused the unholy sound.

"Brady? Joey? Mr. Waters?"

The quiver in his voice confirmed to himself how frightened he was. His broken ankle grounded him in place. If not for it, he would've scurried away as quickly as he could. Even with his busted ankle, he wondered how hard it would be to crawl back to the road. He wasn't certain how far he'd run before he fell, but it couldn't have been that far. Maybe he could drag himself along the ground until he reached the road. As soon as he got back home, the first thing he planned to do was pester his parents into letting him have a cell phone. He had a gut feeling persuading them just got a whole lot easier.

Leaves crunched under a heavy footstep. Tanner's heart raced. He couldn't see what was moving, but that sound was unmistakable. Some-one - or something - was close by.

"Hello?"

He wished he'd kept the flashlight.

Where the hell is everyone?

A growl tore through the dead night air. Suddenly, Tanner's blood went cold as soda from the freezer. Every hair on his arm stood upright at once. He held his breath, hoping that he could stay as quiet as possible. If he didn't appear as a threat, if he didn't appear at all, hopefully whatever had growled would leave him alone. Most forest animals were more scared of him than he was of them. At least that's what they were taught. Stay calm, remain still, and the animal would wander off. Except he was wounded and had dried blood on his face, hands, and clothes.

He thought about every animal in the woods that would or could growl. How many of them would be attracted to the smell of blood? And how many of them would enjoy pouncing on wounded and slow prey?

Tanner needed to move away from his current position. He leaned on his side, sunk his hands into the damp earth, and pulled, scooting his body forward a few inches. Red hot pain screamed from his twisted ankle. He bit down on his lip, stifling any noise. Better to fight through the pain of his ankle than become food for whatever wolf, bear, or mountain lion lurked in the dark.

He repositioned his hands on the ground and pulled again. This time, he bent his good leg at the knee and dug his boot into the dirt. He pressed forward with his leg as he pulled and shot forward another two feet. That was progress he could be proud of.

His ankle pulsated, still radiating waves of pain up his leg. Fresh tears erupted from his eyes. He didn't want to scream out, so he continued to bite his lower lip, hard enough to break skin. Fresh, sticky blood dripped down his chin. Tanner ignored the pain in his lip, his nose, and his leg. Instead, he shot his arms out again, bent his leg, and dragged himself forward. He wasn't going to quit. He couldn't quit. Quitting meant he wasn't going to get Eagle by the time he was fifteen. Quitting meant giving in to whatever animal growled. Quitting meant...

Tanner pulled himself forward and heard the growl again, this time it was closer. He accelerated his movement, crawling across the ground at a quicker pace. After a dozen yards, his shoulders added their own voice to his pain. His muscles ached, but he couldn't stop. He closed his eyes, reached out with his hands, and suddenly froze. Instead of the damp ground and leaves that his fingers dug into it, he found a wet, sticky fluid. He eased his eyes open and slowly turned his shaking hands toward his face.

Dark red blood, almost black in the dark, dripped from his palms and fingers. He glanced ahead and saw two paws covered in thick black fur. A series of long, sharp claws tipped the end of each paw. As Tanner tipped his head back, he followed the paws to the large legs and then to the body of the large black beast standing over him. The creature held a deer in its massive arms. The deer's body was bent backwards as if the monster had folded it in half. The deer's torso was ripped open. The creature's snout was buried in the deer's chest. It ripped its head out of the deer, flinging blood and entrails across the ground. Its snout dripped with deer intestines.

The creature glared down at Tanner as Tanner met its yellow-eyed stare. Its eyes went to the inside of the hollowed-out deer and then back to Tanner. Paws tightened on the deer, gripping the deer's chest with one and its pelvis with the other, and pulled, splitting the deer in half. The deer's flesh separated from the body. The ribs broke from the backbone. Every organ still inside of the carcass spilled onto the ground, leaving a mess of gore a foot from Tanner's face. He almost puked from the sound it made as it splattered against the dirt. Being frozen with fear was the only thing that kept him from completely losing whatever pizza was still in his stomach.

The beast held the mutilated deer above it as the remaining blood dripped onto its head. The dark red was barely noticeable against the black fur. The creature tossed the carcass away and took a step back. Tanner had a full look at the beast. It stood over six feet tall and was covered in black fur as dark as the night. Its sharp teeth were caked in deer guts. The only colors on the creature were its yellow eyes and white claws coated in dripping blood. The creature turned its head to the sky and howled.

Tanner felt a warm sensation fill his crotch and travel down his leg. All he could hope was the creature was too full from eating the deer to bother with him. That would be the only way he made it back to the road, made it back to his parents, to ever have pizza again, or to reach Eagle Scout at all much less at fifteen. He hadn't even thought about life beyond that. If this monster chose to eat him, he'd never have the opportunity to think about life beyond the next thirty seconds.

As Tanner broke from his frozen terror and reached a trembling hand forward, hoping to pull himself further along, the monster bent down and wrapped its fur-lined, blood encrusted hand around Tanner's. With ease, it lifted Tanner off the ground. He dangled in the air more than a foot. Gravity's downward pressure on his ankle reawakened the pain. The heavy boot added to the weight on the ankle. Tanner felt his shoulder pulling apart as the creature suspended him. As he stared straight ahead, he glared into its eyes. Tears fell from his own eyes. He knew his fate.

With one sudden movement, the creature's other hand disappeared into Tanner's chest and returned holding the boy's heart. Everything in Tanner's body went limp as life immediately vanished. With as much care as the beast gave the deer, it tossed Tanner's body into the woods and feasted on his heart.

6

Michael stood in a forest flanked by tall oak trees. Darkness blanketed the whole area, enveloping everything around him. Trees stretched high into the midnight sky. Even with his superior night vision, he wasn't able to see the tops of them. Dense foliage blacked out the moon and stars. Scents of wet wood and musty soil hung in the air. Dead and rotting leaves clung to his feet. As he took a step, the leaves didn't crunch as dried leaves would have. These were mush under his toes.

He glanced down at his feet and not his shoes. He was barefoot. Mike had no idea why he was barefoot or where his shoes were. For that matter, he had no idea where *he* was.

Heavy dampness embraced him, sending goose bumps scurrying across his arms. As he peered down, a hand crossed his body and brushed small droplets of moisture from his arm. Not only was it not his hand, he had no control over it. He hadn't told this strange arm to bend or move. It just did, independently. Sensations that he remembered as cold traversed his body; things he hadn't felt since he'd died.

Disorientation swept over him. His stomach flipped, and he felt nauseous. Nothing was right. Some things he experienced as if he had control, but then the control vanished. Sensations came and went. Whoever owned this body fought his intrusion; an intrusion he'd had no intention of causing. His head — this head — spun around him. The world tilted on its axis, and he disconnected from the strange form again.

Forest sounds bombarded him. Crickets made their nightly mating calls. Insects dug homes into the wood of dying trees. Invisible birds squawked above. Bats clicked within the trees. Somewhere in the distance, a stream flowed over a bed of rocks, projecting the sound of a cascading waterfall. Each and every sound filled his head as if the volume was dialed up to the highest possible point.

Michael's breathing increased and shallowed. He'd seen people with panic attacks before and would've sworn one was coming on.

Could vampires have panic attacks? That would be a question for Thomas later on if he survived this. Right now, it didn't seem to matter. Whether they could or not, he was certain he was having one.

He tried to think through what had happened. He remembered being in his room in the Night Crew headquarters in Dallas. He remembered sitting on his bed, meditating. Then moments later, he was in somebody else's body in the middle of a forest. Dallas did not have dense woods like this. He'd have to travel hours away toward east Texas before finding anything even remotely resembling this. In fact, he wasn't sure he was even in Texas anymore. As far as he knew, whatever happened could've transported him to a remote forest in Europe. He'd heard meditation referred to as a journey, but he didn't think this was what people usually meant.

The pounding of his heart filled his head, adding to the cacophony of other noises.

Just as Michael felt like he couldn't take it anymore, an aroma focused his attention. Blood. Immediately, his stomach ached. Hunger rippled throughout his body. He used the sensation to ground himself and seize control of this foreign body. Hunger was something he was used to, a sensation he related to and could capitalize on. It was still something he fought daily to control. When he wasn't careful, hunger consumed him. It had only heightened after he'd sunk his teeth into Niki three months before.

I had to do that, he reminded himself. His Night Crew teammate had been dying within the nightmare Lilith had created. It had been the only way to free her.

The taste of blood directly from human veins was like no other. It put the medically-enclosed blood bags to shame. Drinking from a person was an intoxicating rush, an extremely powerful drug. He'd never tried cocaine, meth, or heroin, but the way those who had talked about it, there was a similarity between the feelings.

He was in total control of this body. It wasn't his, but he could use it like it was. He shifted his head, tracing the smell. The predator within him focused on it. He knelt down and placed the palm of his hands on the damp leaves. He slid the leaves aside and gripped the muddy earth. Vibrations ran from his fingertips through his hands and up into his arms. Someone was running. Blood blended with sweat as whomever it was sprinted through the woods. Not just one person. A few. He wasn't sure how he knew, but he did. The knowledge was inside of him; his very nature was made to know. He used the hunger. It was the only thing that felt solid.

Another smell trailed behind the blood and sweat. Fear. Fear soaked the runner. Whoever he tracked was already being chased by something (or someone) else.

Ignoring his barefoot astral body suit, Michael sprinted toward the smell. His feet slammed into the moist, leaf-covered ground. Twigs broke beneath his heels, but he barely registered them. He ran like he'd grown up in these woods and knew them well. He avoided trees, dodging them at breakneck speed. As he ran, the canopy of leaves opened, revealing a full moon. Somewhere far off, wolves howled. Their bays filled the night sky, providing the perfect soundtrack to this midnight hunt. The call almost summoned him, but he ignored it and latched onto the siren's spell of blood instead.

A stream of water lay ahead. The sound of water flowing over the rocks intensified. As loud as it was in his head, he expected the stream to have roaring rapids. It sounded like the waters rushing over the drop of Niagara Falls. Once upon the stream, he realized how heightened his senses were dialed. It was a shallow stream, no more than ten feet across. Water from a recent rain shower flowed at a brisk pace. No rapids, no waterfall. With one leap, he bounded over it and landed on the other side.

Within moments, his feet had propelled him beyond the woods and into an open clearing. The area was encircled by trees, giving a surreal setting to an already confusing night. A log cabin sat on the opposite side of the clearing. Even though he was a hundred yards away, Michael could tell no one had lived in it for decades. The windows that weren't broken were coated in thick layers of dust and cobwebs. The front porch had rotted through, and the door sat skewed within its frame. Holes potted the roof.

A field of tall grass lay between Michael and the log cabin. Thick dew coated the green blades, glistening in the moonlight. The reflection illuminated the surrounding area, basking it in natural moonlight. Normally, he would've found the area tranquil and calm. Instead, right now in its current state, the image reminded him of horror movies instead; a lone, moonlit cabin hidden in a remote forest. A discolored section of grass cut through the clearing. The dew was missing, creating a darkened trail bisecting the field and leading straight to the cabin.

Michael saw the bloodied man as he approached the abandoned home. The man reached the rotted front porch and started around to the back. He stumbled his way to the side of the cabin, placing his hand against the wooden walls, bracing for support. As his hand came away, a bloody print was left behind. Terror coursed through Michael as he recognized the stranger.

"Jax!" he yelled.

Michael opened his eyes, gasping for air. He was in the dark of his room, alone, sitting on his bed.

7

Henderson eased back in his leather chair perched behind the small wooden desk in his office. Mena was a small town with a small police force. He'd served as the Chief of Police for the past twenty years, and for almost all of it, it'd been an easy job. There'd been the occasional breaking and entering, usually teens blowing off steam. The E-Z Mart had been robbed a few times. The last time was by a local tweaker, and that had proved to be the most excitement their town had had in a few years. Mena was quiet, serene, and surrounded by a beautiful forest. Those who lived there wanted it to be quiet. It was part of its charm.

But, the past few weeks, it'd been anything but quiet. Each year, a hiker or two got lost in the woods, but eventually turned up. For the most part this happened when the hiker wandered off the trail to take a leak and got turned around. After a day or so, they typically found the highway and made it back to town. Starting three weeks ago, there'd been at least two missing persons' reports each week, not counting the mauling of Rebecca Summers, the attack on David Hall, and now the slaying of Tanner Johnson.

Roy rubbed his face with his hands. He had to deliver the news to Rebecca's and Tanner's parents. Telling Rebecca's parents had been tough. Their grief had been reflected in anger, and they had lashed out at David, as if he'd been the one to personally attack her. As soon as Roy had declared it an animal attack, they signed for her body and started funeral arrangements. They wanted to move fast. He imagined it was to get the hard part behind them as soon as possible.

Telling her parents had been tough, one of the hardest things he'd ever had to do. That was until he delivered the news to Tanner's parents. It didn't matter how many years he'd been doing this job, nothing could've prepared him for the grief and heartache that came with telling a mother and a father their only son, who hadn't a care in the world, who had dreams and aspirations that were only just forming, would never come home to them again.

He tried as best he could to spare them the most gruesome details, but small towns talk anyway. The scout master and a handful of scouts had found Tanner. One of the scouts recounted what happened. Through sobbing tears and a constantly bursting and reforming snot bubble, the kid told him about hearing something scream, the deer running past them, Tanner breaking his ankle and nose, and all but ordering the kid to run ahead and get help. The boy was the last one to see Tanner alive.

It took a good deal of convincing, but Henderson finally talked them into believing in the animal attack story, similar to how he explained Rebecca's death. He grabbed his iPad, opened a web browser, and clicked the favorited link for "The Polk County Pulse", the local newspaper. The top headline read "BEWARE THE BEAR". The news article accurately regurgitated the story Roy had told them. There was a wild black bear in Ouachita National Forest killing hikers and campers. Residents should avoid the forest until the US Forestry Service could track and eliminate the bear.

Roy reread the story, knowing full well that it was entirely bullshit. He knew what had happened to the missing hikers. He knew what had killed Rebecca and Tanner, and he knew what had bit David. He also knew what that meant for David.

As he leaned forward and placed his iPad back on his desk, his chair cried out a loud squeal. He placed his elbows on the hard wooden surface and folded his hands together in front of his face. After the boy's body was found, he had placed another call, reiterating what he knew was the truth. A werewolf hunted in his forest. There was no way it was a wendigo. That was an excuse they could shove up their ass. The pack was supposed to handle this. It was their responsibility to make sure this didn't happen. In all the years Roy had been a police officer, then sergeant, and now chief of police, it had never happened. At least it never happened that he was aware of. Something must've changed.

A knock at his door startled him out of his rabbit hole. He glanced up to see one of his officers, Dylan, a young guy with short black hair who'd grown up in Mena and joined the force just two years ago, standing at his door.

"Chief?" Dylan said. He hesitantly leaned into the office.

Roy unclasped his hands and gave a brief motion with his fingers, telling Dylan to come on in.

"What can I do for you, son?" Roy asked.

Dylan's head turned to the station's front door and then back to Roy. "You need to come out here. I think we're going to be in for some trouble."

As Dylan said that, Roy heard the front door swing open, and a number of voices speaking all at the same time. The voices were loud and angry. This wasn't something he'd experienced himself before, but he had an idea of what it was.

"Fuck," he said and pushed himself back from his desk. He stood up and grabbed his suit jacket from the back of the chair. He almost wished he had worn a more official uniform. Something told him he would need every ounce of official he could muster to quell what was brewing. His badge sat on the corner of his desk, and he scooped it up, placing it squarely into his suit coat pocket. "Any other officers here?"

"Sergeant Lowell, sir," Dylan answered.

"Get him as well, just in case this turns ugly."

As Dylan disappeared around the corner, heading for Lowell's office, Roy stepped around his desk and passed the two guest chairs. The voices grew louder as he moved closer. He took a deep breath and marched into the bullpen. A wall separated the bullpen from the front entryway, creating a security vestibule, just in case. A window made of bulletproof glass sat in the wall, allowing Roy to see what was happening. The only way for anyone to get into the bullpen was for the person working behind the bulletproof glass to hit a button under the desk to unlock the door.

While crossing the handful of desks they called the bullpen, Henderson counted a dozen men standing in the lobby. He recognized a mob when he saw one.

When the Pulse interviewed him, he had already feared this would happen. But he had to give the interview and hopefully ease concerns. If not, they were going to run with their own version of things, and Roy *knew that* would've been way worse.

Tragically, reality was still the worst option out of the lot. Reality was a nightmare. An out-of-control werewolf devouring hikers, campers, and children in the woods was the stuff of horror movies. It wasn't what happened in his small fucking town. This wasn't Derry or Haddonfield. Fuck, it wasn't even Camp Crystal Lake.

Dylan rushed through the bullpen and stood in front of the glass. Sergeant Lowell stepped to the doorway of his office.

"Carl, stay there," Chief Henderson said. "I'll talk to them, but I want you to hang tight just in case."

Carl Lowell was in his mid-forties. He had a sprinkling of gray hair on his head and his mustache. Both stood out against his dark black skin. He nodded and crossed his arms.

Roy sauntered up to the door, gripped the handle, and opened it. Immediately, the cacophony of voices quieted, and all dozen men turned to the Chief of Police.

He recognized most of them and tried to lock eyes with each person. As his eyes scanned the faces, they fell on one person in particular. Someone who he had hoped wouldn't be involved.

Troy Johnson, Tanner's dad, stood front and center. His bloodshot eyes screamed with unspoken anger. Instead of wallowing in grief, his anger burned bright. The chief knew, however, that the anger was usually only a defense mechanism to block out the soul-crushing sadness. He'd seen it many times before, and seeing it again in Tanner's dad nearly broke him.

"Good afternoon, gentlemen," Roy said in the most cordial, professional voice he could muster. "Quite a crowd for a Thursday afternoon. What can we do for everyone?"

Troy spoke up with the might of his fellow townsmen behind him. "Justice. We want justice for Tanner. And for Rebecca."

"I've called in the Forestry Service. They have someone on their way who has been trained in these situations." Roy tried to avoid speaking directly to Troy although his eyes continued to be drawn back to him.

"We don't need anyone from the Forestry Service. I have dozen guys here with me today and can have a dozen more by the weekend, if not more. We'll hunt this thing and have it strung up before it can do to anyone else what it did to my son." The father's voice wavered on those last words.

A rumbling of approval rippled through the crowd behind Troy.

"Troy, I'm sorry about what happened to your son, but we don't need two dozen vigilantes swarming the woods looking for this thing." *Especially since your rifles and shotguns won't do anything but piss it off,* he wanted to say but couldn't.

He had to figure out a way to defuse the situation and keep that part under wraps. "I want to minimize any incidents. That's why I spoke with the Pulse. So everyone would be warned about the bear and will stay out of the forest for now. It wasn't so a mob could swarm the area. Sure, one of you might get lucky, but there's a better chance of it taking a few of you out as well. I want less death in our community. For now, stay in town. No more hiking or camping. A professional will be here to handle it."

"What about the guy who was attacked? What do you think he'll want?" Troy asked. Rage still spread across his face.

"The last time I checked, Mr. Hall was still in a coma following his injuries. Hopefully, by the time he wakes up, it won't matter. This issue will be behind us. Now, gentlemen, please go home. Mr. Johnson, you especially. Go home to your wife. She needs you right now, more than ever, and you need her. I will personally make sure this manner is handled. I do not want anyone else in my town dying at the hands of that bear or because someone makes a mistake in the forest.

"As for the rest of you, you go home, too." Roy motioned his arms, ushering the guys back through the front door.

Reluctantly, they slowly turned and filed out the door. Troy was the last one. As he was about to leave, he turned back to Henderson. "I want this thing killed, and I want the hide." His lip quivered and tears welled up in his eyes. "It killed my son, Roy. It broke him and ate his heart. I heard how he was found. People talk, and I heard."

The chief bit his lip and placed a hand on Troy's shoulder. "I'll personally make sure."

As Troy left the station and hopped into one of the trucks parked in the small parking lot, Roy Henderson turned away from the door. Dylan sat behind the bullet proof window. Roy nodded, and the door buzzed.

Roy hoped once David did finally wake up and gave a statement, the pack would have no choice but to send someone and handle their issue. Sure, he knew it was a werewolf, but the pack wanted to point blame everywhere else. It was every other monster killing people before it was one of their own. He knew he had put off the inevitable long enough. He had another number he could call, and as he made his way back to his office, he already had his phone out of his pocket, dialing. This number he had hoped to never use. This number was going to piss off the pack, but if they weren't going to help, it was time to call in someone else.

8

EVEN AFTER TAKING ANOTHER hot shower, Mike's world hadn't fully righted itself.

It had been hours since he came out of the dream, yet he still felt unsteady. Every sound that he had learned to ignore and suppress seemed too loud — the hum of the ventilation system, the faint tick of the overhead lights, the drip of the final droplets escaping the shower head.

He hoped being immersed in the hot downpour would tether him back to reality, that breathing in the steam would cleanse his senses, but the smell of mud still clung to him. He still felt the forest pressing in on him every time he blinked.

The special gift he lived with, his UltraNet, caused weird events to happen inside his head his entire life. Slipping into the past was something he'd grown accustomed to. Each time, it was vivid and alive. Well, as alive as a memory could be. But this dream felt...different. It didn't feel like a dream. He didn't know if it was something that had happened, was happening, or going to happen.

Mike drifted down the hallway, heading to their conference room, wandering like he was chasing ghosts. The place was half-dark, the industrial lights buzzing above in tired rows, but that didn't matter to him. He saw everything with crystal clear precision. Somewhere off behind, he heard a gentle waterfall. Nate and Niki used the ambient noise each night to sleep.

As he stepped into the conference room, Josh was there, as was usually the case. He sat behind the long metal table, a mug of coffee cooling beside his elbow, the wheels of his chair locked at an angle so he could reach the screen in front of him. His hair was a mess, his stubble catching the light in uneven patches.

Michael stood there a moment, watching him work. Josh's concentration was almost supernatural on its own, fingers moving across the keys in a blur.

"Josh," Michael said finally. His voice came out lower than he meant, gravelly.

Josh startled slightly, spinning in his chair halfway around. "Jesus, Mike. Fucking vampire stealth. You move like a damn ghost."

"I am kind of a ghost," Michael said dryly. He tried to smile, but it didn't take.

Josh looked him over. His expression shifted from annoyance to concern. "You look like you lost a fight with the sun."

Michael rolled his eyes but decided to ignore the jab. He was pale, even by vampire standards. The circles under his eyes were bruised dark, and his shirt hung damp against his back. "You heard from Jax lately?" he asked, too abruptly.

Josh frowned. "No. Not since he checked in a few weeks back. Why?"

"A few weeks back," Michael repeated. He moved closer, resting both hands on the edge of the table. The metal was cold enough to sting. "Where was he?"

Josh leaned back in his chair. His brow dipped, just slightly. Most people probably wouldn't have noticed the shift, but Mike did. Suspicion inked across his face. "Pennsylvania, I think. Still chasing leads about the Council. They've been gone for almost six months."

"Has it been that long?" Mike remembered how all this started as if it was yesterday. Brit's murder, Silas, and then everything that's happened since.

"Based on the growing unrest, it's been too long. There have been skirmishes across the globe. Fortunately, it hasn't spilled into the civilian world yet. Alphas arguing over who will become the new Council members. Some have turned quite violent. It won't be long before things descend into utter chaos. I just hope Jax, Thomas, and the others find out who's behind this and restore order."

Michael's jaw tightened. "And you're sure Jax is OK?"

Josh squinted at him. "Fairly certain I would've heard if he wasn't. Why? What's this about?"

"Just checking," Mike said. He forced the words through a dry throat. The urge to sink his teeth into a blood bag became unbearable.

Josh wheeled closer, eyes narrowing. "Just checking, huh? If it was one of us, I'd get it. But Jax? What gives?"

Michael's mouth opened. Closed. He tried to find a version of the truth that wouldn't sound insane. "I...had a dream."

Josh blinked and then barked a laugh. "A dream? You don't even sleep like a normal person."

"Not usually," Michael said, his tone flat.

"All right. What kind of dream?"

Michael shook his head. "Doesn't matter. Just... It had been something about Jax."

"That's vague as hell." Josh turned his chair sideways, one wheel squeaking faintly. "You two have some unfinished business I don't know about?"

Mike met his gaze, eyes darker than the room around them. "I just need to know where he is."

Josh didn't answer right away. He reached for his mug, grimaced when he realized the coffee was cold, and then pushed it aside. "He's still looking into the Council's disappearance. He won't check in until he's found something worth bragging about. Why are you asking? Spit it out."

Michael hesitated. The question felt heavier than it should have.

"I saw him," he said before he could stop himself.

Josh frowned. "You saw him? When? Where?"

"In the dream. It just felt...real."

Josh leaned forward on his elbows. "Real how?"

Mike shrugged. "Like I was physically there."

"Maybe it's your vampire brain playing tricks on you. Did you slip a little something into the blood bags?" Josh said, half teasing but with an edge of unease. "Too much blood deprivation, not enough Netflix."

"Yeah, that must be it." Mike smirked, but it didn't reach his eyes.

Josh's tone softened. "You know, if you're worried about him, just say it. No shame in it."

Mike glanced away. "I'm not worried," he lied.

Josh snorted. "Sure. And I don't need legs."

That earned a small huff of air from Mike, the closest he was going to get to a laugh. "Joking about the legs, now?"

"Someone's got to. You're too broody for your own good. When's the last time you left headquarters anyway?"

"Not something I'm interested in doing. Prefer to meditate as Thomas suggested."

Josh spun his chair back toward his laptop, the glow washing his face pale. "Well, if I hear from Jax, I'll let you know. But I think he's fine. "Probably knee-deep in trouble, but fine."

"Yeah," Michael murmured. "Fine. Do me a favor. Keep this between us. I don't need a lecture from Thomas."

"Or ribbed by Niki?"

"That too."

He stood there a beat longer.

In his head, he heard the crunch of leaves, the rasp of Jax's breath, a heartbeat that wasn't his own. Finally, he turned and walked away, meandering back to his room as quiet as the ghost he was when he entered the room.

9

DAVID SLOWLY OPENED HIS eyes, as if coming out of a dream. Stark, white lights pierced his vision, and he recoiled, snapping his eyelids closed. A mix of sensations coursed through his body. His legs and his entire left side were numb. His arms ached similar to his last intense arm workout. Everything else gave off a weird tingling sensation. He tried to move his legs, but they wouldn't budge.

He shifted his shoulders and discovered he was in a bed. A single, repeating beep rang out next to him. As he grew more aware, he heard conversation happening around him.

"Nurse, I think he's waking up," a male voice said.

Nurse? David thought. *Am I in a hospital?*

Recall kicked in, and images flashed through his head. Memories of what happened: running, growling, headlights, fear, horror.

He fought past the harsh lighting and forced his eyes open. He was lying in a hospital bed. The room's curtains were open, letting natural light spill inside. His left leg was in a cast. Bandages wrapped round his stomach all the way up to his chest. An IV tube came out of his arm and draped around the IV stand next to him. He raised his free hand and touched his face. A nasal cannula sat in his nose and stretched across his cheeks. His mouth felt dry. He wanted to talk but wasn't certain he could.

A man in a dark suit stood next to him. He had graying hair and a mustache. His arms rested on his hips, pulling his suit coat back. David noticed the badge attached to his belt. As he thought back to what happened, it didn't surprise him a detective would be standing over his bed.

David licked his lips with the sanding block known as his tongue, but it didn't help. His dry tongue scraped chapped lips.

"How...long?" David croaked out in barely a whisper.

A doctor in a lab coat nudged the detective out of the way and drew close to the bed. He had glasses and held a tablet in his hand. He pulled up a chair and sat next to David.

"Good afternoon, Mr. Hall. It's nice to see you awake. Do you know where you are?"

David took a deep breath. His throat also felt like sandpaper. Slowly, he choked out, "Hospital."

"That's right." The doctor glanced up. David shifted his eyes and followed the gaze to a monitor above his head. The doctor notated on the tablet. "Your vitals look good."

"Water?" David asked. He moved his hand to his mouth and ran his finger across his cracked lips.

"Of course. Nurse Mitchell, grab David some ice chips, please. Those should help with the dryness and ease your throat. Right now, you're lying down. We can raise you if you'd like."

David nodded his head. He had to crane his neck to see what was around him. It'd be much easier sitting up. He hoped that would also help him regain his bearings. He obviously hadn't eaten in a while, giving his already thin frame a skeletal appearance. He adjusted his blanket and saw bruises on his chest that disappeared under bandages.

The movement of the bed stretched his back muscles, awakening a fresh wave of pain, and causing him to grimace.

The nurse stepped into the room, grabbed the bed tray, placed the cup of ice chips on it, and moved it in front of David. He gripped the cup with one hand and took out a piece of ice with the other, popping it into his mouth and sucking the moisture.

After half the cup was gone, some of the sandpaper started to leave his throat. He used a few chips to moisten his cracked lips. His tongue still felt rough but at least it wasn't a dried rock in his mouth anymore. He cleared his throat, letting out a raspy cough. "Where am I?"

"You're at the Mena Regional Hospital." The doctor glanced at the monitor and notated his vitals. He never left the chair. The detective hovered over him, anxiously awaiting his turn.

"How long have I been out?" David asked, finally circling back around to his first question.

"It's been close to a week since the accident, Mr. Hall."

"Doctor," the detective said, interrupting whatever else the doctor wanted to add. "Is Mr. Hall in a place where he can answer a few questions?"

The doctor turned away from David and stared up at the detective, still remaining in his seat. To David's surprise, the doctor answered as if he wasn't awake in the bed.

"Chief Henderson, he does seem to be cognitively aware, although I'd imagine he's still adjusting to his surroundings."

David nodded at that. As he thought back to the night of the accident, his heart started to race. He felt the pounding grow more intense.

"Talking will be difficult for a little while. We had a breathing tube down his throat while undergoing his surgeries."

"Surgeries?" David asked. He was still trying to figure out everything that'd happened to him. He saw the cast and all the bandages. But surgeries?

The doctor turned back to him. "Yes, David, you had a few. Your left leg was the most severe. It was shattered in multiple places. We had to insert a number of pins to hold the bone together. There will be a good bit of physical therapy in your future. It's not going to be easy, but we have a great facility to help get you back on your feet."

He hated the thought of physical therapy. He wanted to ask if he'd ever be able to hike in the forest again but refrained. He'd only been awake maybe twenty minutes and hadn't heard a shred of good news yet. He didn't want to ask too many questions. He didn't need to. Every time he closed his eyes, images of that night flashed inside his head. The blood spraying the tent as the air mattress exploded.

David struggled to catch his breath. His chest felt tight. He wasn't sure if he was having a panic attack or a heart attack. An alarm went off somewhere above his head, adding to the panic. He fought for every breath.

"Nurse!" the doctor yelled.

Immediately, the same nurse that brought him ice chips rushed in with a syringe and went straight to David's IV bag. She stabbed the needle into a valve on the tubing and depressed the plunger.

"What's happening?" Henderson demanded.

David felt his head swoon. His chest eased, and he caught his breath again. The pounding rhythm of his heart slowed. An overwhelming sensation of euphoria passed over him, and he closed his eyes, taking it in.

"I imagine the memories of what happened made their way back to the surface and sent him into panic. The medicine we gave him is going to knock him out for another hour or two. We'll let you know when he wakes back up. You can try to speak with him then. For now, rest is the best thing."

DAVID GLANCED DOWN AT the green Jell-O. It was his third since waking up. The discarded remnants of the other two were stacked together on the edge of the tray. On the other side, a gray thermos with a straw protruding from the top was full of ice water. He had to remind himself to slow down or he'd have to go pee. Eventually, he was going to have to figure that out but hoped for a little time beforehand.

He scooped the last of the Jell-O onto his plastic spoon and gobbled it away. As he did, the door to his room opened up. The same gray-haired man in the same dark suit came in. Since becoming more lucid and relaxed, David knew it wouldn't be long before the questions came. He guessed now was as good a time as any.

"Mr. Hall," he started. "My name is Chief Roy Henderson of the Mena Police Department. I just spoke with your doctor, and he gave me the all clear to ask you a few questions about what happened that night."

He grabbed the chair the doctor had used earlier and wheeled it next to David's bed. Roy sat on it and took out his phone.

"I've stopped by just about every day checking on you. Glad to see you're awake."

"I'm feeling much better," David said.

A subtle soreness lingered in his throat, but thanks to the ice water and Jell-O, he felt a lot better. Not just his throat, either. His nurse showed him how to use the special button attached to his IV drip. If the pain became too much, he could hit that button. David hadn't felt the need to do that at all. He guessed it was residual from the last dose of pain meds he'd had, but he was really feeling good.

"Great to hear," Roy said. "You're looking a lot better than you did earlier. Your face has more color in it."

"Hospital Jell-O. They must put some great healing medicine inside of it. And just call me David."

"Of course, David. So, how much of that night do you remember?" Henderson swiped on his phone and hit a button. David assumed this conversation was being recorded.

He took a deep breath and gathered his thoughts. "I think I remember most of the evening. Some parts are a little foggy still, like how I ended up here exactly."

"Let's start with what you do remember. What can you tell me about the beginning of the night? Maybe that'll help to clear away the fog. Better yet, tell me about your relationship with Rebecca Summers."

Roy pulled the tray table away from David, leaving the water jug within reach. He placed his cell phone on the table with the microphone facing the patient. David could see that he did indeed have a voice recording app running.

"I've known Rebecca for a few years. We have...had mutual friends. A few weeks ago, I found out she was single and asked her out. We've gone out pretty steady since then."

David thought about the first date he'd had with Rebecca. She had insisted he meet her at the restaurant instead of picking her up. He'd arrived early, but somehow she still beat him there. As she'd sat across from him, he couldn't help but stare into her blue eyes. She spent the evening talking about her realty work. He'd complemented her on how the yard signs didn't do her justice which elicited a wide smile, and she had brushed her shoulder length brown hair behind her ears. He could've died and gone to heaven.

David grabbed his water jug and took a long sip from the straw. He placed it back on the tray table and finally asked the question that'd been bubbling just beneath the surface.

"Am I a suspect here? Should I have a lawyer present?"

Roy reached over and stopped the recording. "No. I need your statement about what happened so the right people can be here to hunt the bear. You're the only surviving witness."

"Only surviving witness," David repeated. The thought of what that thing did to Rebecca haunted him. "I still can't believe she's dead. As soon as I get out of here, I need to pay my respects to her family."

"Rebecca's parents are upset right now."

"With me? I loved Rebecca."

"They want someone to blame besides the bear. You survived, and she didn't. As soon as the autopsy was done, they took custody of her body and had her funeral."

"Before I was even awake?" David asked.

That news hurt almost more than his injuries. What happened wasn't his fault, and now, he wasn't even able to say his goodbyes to her. Tears welled up in his eyes. It was like he was losing her all over again.

"I'm sorry, David. I wish I could afford the time to break it gentler or to let you grieve. I need to ask these questions, so I can fill in the blanks of what happened that night. I saw her body. I saw the crime scene. I saw your injuries. The sooner we get through with this, the sooner you can get on with healing. More importantly, hopefully I'll get some information I can use, and you can hopefully begin to process."

David wiped at his face with his hand, brushing away the tears ready to erupt from his eyes. He thought about what Henderson said. Just get through this so he can move on to healing...and processing.

"Fine. Let's get this out of the way. You can start recording again."

Roy gave him a nod and touched the phone's screen.

"So, you two had been dating for a few weeks. How did you wind up camping? Whose idea was that?"

11

AFTER TWENTY MINUTES OF relaying what he could remember, David stopped at the point where everything went dark.

"The car hit your left side, shattering your leg, as the doctor told you," Roy said. "You're fortunate they were going as slow as they were. If they hadn't been, your skull probably would've done more than just bounce off their hood. Despite everything else, you're pretty lucky to be alive."

"Some luck," David said.

He wiped tears from his eyes. As he had recounted what had happened to Rebecca, he had broken down twice.

"The family called 9-1-1. They were heading back from visiting relatives and trying to make it back home without stopping. You put a wrench in their plans. The mother is a nurse in Hot Springs. She helped stop your bleeding until the ambulance showed up."

"Did they see the bear? Are they OK?"

"They heard something in the woods but didn't see anything other than you. Of course, they weren't really looking either. They were focused on keeping you alive. Guess they wanted to make sure they didn't kill you. Startled them pretty good. I called earlier and let them know how you're doing. They're grateful they could help.

"Regarding what happened in the woods, all in all, your story matches what a lot of the physical evidence shows. Your tent is shredded like a bobcat was looking for a squirrel that had talked bad about his mama.

Other animals devoured most of your supplies. We towed your car back to the station. We think that a black bear has gone berserk. There was another incident after yours. A young boy. The town is in a state of panic after this as you can imagine for yourself. Do me a favor and don't add to it. If the Pulse or any other news comes around, don't talk to them. Let us handle this first so I can tamper down the growing unrest here."

David nodded. He didn't have much else to say. He was drained and had nothing left. He knew he would have questions of his own later, but right now he couldn't summon up the energy or care to think of them.

"Well, I'm going to go back to the station and write up a report. I'm sorry about what happened to you and to Rebecca, and I'm also sorry about things with her family. Give them time. People process grief in a myriad of ways." He waved his hand from David's head to his plaster-encased legs. "You focus on getting better. Physical therapy is going to be a bitch."

"Thanks, Chief."

Roy stood up from the chair, placed it by the sink, and walked out of the room.

David leaned his head back. He closed his eyes, but every time he did, he saw the deep black pupils and the yellow irises of the bear as it tore into Rebecca.

His hand clawed at the blanket and found the special little button connected to his IV. He pressed it, hoping it would take more than just the physical pain away. Maybe it would help keep the dreams away too.

12

"Dad," Cristy Ward hollered from the pullout couch. "Edmund won't stop kicking me!"

Matt Ward opened his eyes to the half-dark of the RV. The ceiling was low, claustrophobic, the air thick with the smell of old fiberglass and stale heater air. His head ached from the constant hum of the generator. Beside him, Heather lay on her side, facing the wall, wrapped in a blanket like a cocoon.

Their bed sat at one end of the RV. Further down, the sleeper sofa bisected the living space. Once extended, the foot of the bed butted up next to the kitchen. The fiberglass door with the aluminum steps sat next to the kitchen, and the driver and passenger seats a little further up from there.

The kids' arguing echoed through the narrow space. Under their shared blanket, ten-year-old Cristy and seven-year-old Edmund seemed to be wrestling with their legs. The quilt twitched and danced from one side to the other as Cristy kicked Edmund and then tried to quickly hide her leg to limit his ability to retaliate.

"You are both kicking each other," Matt said.

He nudged Heather. She lay on her side facing the wall. He couldn't tell if she was asleep or not, but if he had to guess, she was awake but acting asleep so that he'd have to deal with the kids. "Honey," he said as he pushed on her shoulder. "Are you asleep?"

Her shoulders slumped, and she exhaled harshly. He wasn't sure if it was possible to hear an eye roll, but he was fairly certain that if it was, he now knew what it sounded like. Without seeming to move at all, she said, "Stop kicking each other." She spoke in that tone that only mothers can, driving fear into the spine of any child or husband in earshot.

The RV went still for half a heartbeat.

Then, Edmund's voice rose, thin and complaining. "How much longer do we have to stay here?"

"This is only a weekend trip," Matt answered. "We get back tomorrow night."

Matt flopped his head back onto his pillow, staring at the ceiling's faint texture — a beige pattern like dried riverbeds. He wanted this trip to feel like the ones from his childhood: simple, quiet, a chance to escape the city's grind. He preferred the small weekend trips over big ones during spring break or summer.

For this trip, they'd left Friday from Oklahoma City. Matt had parked the RV in Bentonville on Friday night, and they had visited the Walmart Museum on Saturday morning. Then, they had loaded up and driven to the Four Seasons RV park outside of Mena. Matt had always loved Ouachita National Forest and enjoyed sharing, or forcing them to share, this love with his family. Tomorrow morning, he'd load them up for a drive to Crater of Diamonds and then book it right back to Oklahoma City in time for the kids to get some rest and be ready for school on Monday. One big fun weekend adventure.

If only Cristy and Edmund had the ability to get along for more than five minutes at a time. If they weren't sitting in front of the Xbox playing Minecraft, they were fighting with each other. Siblings doing what siblings do.

Matt was an only child, so he'd missed out on that experience. Heather had tried to warn him. She had told him stories about the knock-out brawls and historic shouting matches that she'd gotten into with her younger sisters.

"In an RV, those two are going to have to share a bed," she had said as they had shopped for their RV. "My sister and I shared a bed. She moved around so much at night, she'd wake up perpendicular to me with her feet across my stomach. In self-defense, I was forced to frog her every morning. She never learned but that didn't stop me from trying to teach her. If you want to go forward with this, just be prepared."

He'd reassured her it wouldn't be an issue. Besides, he'd handle any arguments or complaints that arose.

Lying in bed listening to them fight, he secretly questioned his naïveté, his arrogance, and his intelligence. Not that he'd ever mention that to Heather. He'd never hear the end of it, especially after her warning and as much as *he* had spent on their adventure vehicle.

"Get on your side," Cristy said and pushed her younger brother.

"Cristy pushed me," Edmund said.

Matt sat up on the bed. He exhaled through his nose. This problem wasn't going to fix itself. He balled his hand into a fist and pounded three times on the wall. Both kids sat up in bed.

"Listen, you two," he said, glaring down at their faces. The circles under their eyes clued him into at least part of the reason for their extra bickering. "We didn't have these problems last night. We are going to get through tonight, and then..."

Before he went any further, three thuds slammed against the outside of the RV, as if in response to his own knocking.

He froze. The sound reverberated through the metal skin of the RV — three deliberate, solid blows.

Not wind. Not branches.

Heather sat up beside him, her hair falling into her face, whispering, "What was that?"

"I don't know." His throat was dry. "No one else was parked anywhere near here when we arrived. Maybe someone else pulled up and needs help."

"Wouldn't they have knocked on the door? Who would knock on the side?"

He didn't answer. The silence pressed in, heavy as the woods outside. No crickets. No frogs. Not even wind.

Matt thought about hitting the wall again but decided to wait. It could be someone that needed help, but it also could be some kids messing around. It also occurred to him that it could be a serial killer looking to terrorize an unsuspecting family parked all alone in an RV park, like a bad urban legend from the 80s and 90s.

Even as he dismissed that last thought, he suddenly had the urge to ensure the RV was locked tight. He remembered locking everything, but it didn't hurt to check. He swung his legs out of bed.

Heather gripped his wrist. "What do you think you are doing?"

"Double checking the locks."

"Matt — "

"I'll be fine."

He stood, every board and hinge groaning beneath him, and crept toward the door, watching Cristy and Edmund the entire time. The children had gone rigid, wide-eyed, clutching the blanket under their chins. Matt and Heather yelling at them hadn't stopped their fighting, but fear, pure and undiluted, had frozen them in place. For once, they weren't fighting. He'd have to remember that for the next time they acted up.

"You two," he whispered, "get into the bed with your mother. Now."

They moved in a blur, scrambling under the queen bed covers. Heather wrapped her arms around them, her eyes fixed on him as if she was memorizing his outline.

Once the kids had moved off of their bed, Matt lifted the edge of the sleeper so he could pass by without needing to climb over it. They could've bought the model that had bunk beds for the kids, but that option would've added at least another ten grand.

Since he and Heather were already disagreeing on whether this would be a worthwhile purchase, he had decided on the cheaper option. If things worked out, they could always trade this one in for the bigger model.

He gently sat the edge of the bed back down and shuffled to the fiberglass door. The lock was still engaged. Good.

Matt took a deep breath and exhaled. He glanced over at the bed and gave a thumbs up. As he turned his head back to the door, something in the frosted window caught his eye.

Two faint yellow rings stared at him from the other side. At first, he thought they were reflections from the RV's lights, but then they moved, slowly sliding from left to right in perfect alignment. The window obscured everything else, leaving nothing visible but the two golden circles.

Startled, he stopped in front of the door, peering through the clouded glass.

"What is it?" Heather whispered from the far side of the RV.

Matt Ward didn't answer. Fear kept him locked on the golden rings. They drew closer to the window, glowing faintly through the frost. When they were only a few inches away, he heard a sharp exhale and a streak of fog shot across the outside of the window.

Suddenly, he realized they were eyes and that something huge stood just outside the door. Matt's breath caught in his throat. His body wanted to move, but every muscle rebelled. The thing outside was breathing. Close enough that its breath smeared condensation on the glass.

He took a single step backward, hitting his head on the overhead cabinet.

"Matthew Ward, what's going on?" Heather's voice oozed with the fear that he felt.

He didn't answer. He couldn't. The yellow eyes drew closer, until the glass shivered under the weight of something leaning against it.

The key to the RV sat in the cup holder in between the driver and passenger seat. He no longer felt safe. They needed to leave, and they needed to do it immediately. As he turned his shoulders to the front, whatever was outside hit the side of the vehicle. The RV rocked sideways. The cabinets rattled, metal spoons clinking in their drawers. The whole vehicle swayed on its suspension before slamming back onto the leveling blocks. Heather screamed. The three curled on the bed. Matt braced himself between the front captain seats to keep himself from stumbling.

"Holy shit!" he yelled. "I don't know what's out there, but we need to leave. Now!"

An ear-piercing screech scraped down the outside of the RV. It started by the door and traveled down the back side. It sounded like large knives gouging metal. The kind of sound that went through bone instead of ears.

Cristy buried her face in Heather's shoulder.

Edmund whimpered, "Dad, make it stop."

Matt lunged into the driver's seat, yanking the keys from the cup holder. "We're leaving."

"The power's still hooked up!" Heather said.

"There's no time to fucking care," he responded.

He usually tried not to swear in front of the kids. The fact that he had a few times in the last few minutes showed them (and himself) just how scared he actually was.

"We can rip the box out of the ground or the electrical cable out of the RV. Either way, we're getting the hell out of here right now."

He jammed the key into the ignition. The engine coughed but didn't turn over. The headlights flicked on, spilling pale cones into the trees beyond the windshield. He had a momentary sense of safety, but then something loud slammed onto the roof. The whole ceiling bowed inwards from the impact.

Heather screamed again, pulling the kids close. The concussive noises scurried across the top, covering the length of the RV in just a handful of thunderous explosions. The stampede stopped right above Matt. Then, a fresh wave of silence hung in the air. Shallow and frightened breaths filled the RV. Low sobs came from the rear.

Matt's hand hovered over the gearshift.

He whispered, "Come on..." and turned the key.

The engine roared to life.

As it did, something hit the windshield. Matt darted his eyes and couldn't believe his eyes. He knew he would try to process what he saw later. A hand, black and fur-covered, tipped with claws as long as steak knives. Another hand slammed on the window just above him. The hands slid down the windshield, the muscles under the skin shifting as they gripped the edges. He finally saw the face with the yellow-ringed eyes unobscured by frosted glass.

Those yellow irises encircled deathly black, endless pupils. The pupils stared knowingly. A wet, black snout filled with sharp canines dripped with saliva. It grinned, as if happy about the prospect of its future meal.

"Holy fuck!" Matt screamed.

He dropped the gearshift into drive and punched the gas. The RV's tires spun on the gravel before catching, throwing dirt behind them. The engine screamed, and the vehicle jerked forward. From the bed in the back, all three gasped as they hit the wall. The back end of the vehicle fishtailed as Matt spun the wheel, trying to gain control. He swerved down the narrow road, headlights bouncing over the trees. The creature's claws squealed as they dragged across the glass, then vanished. A heavy thud echoed from the top of the RV.

Heather shouted from the back, "It's on the roof!"

Just above the pulled-out sleeper sofa, two sets of sharp yellow claws tore through the aluminum. The roof peeled like a tin can. The beast clung to the top of the RV and was ripping its way inside. Matt spun the RV onto the highway and jerked the steering wheel back and forth, trying to throw the creature off while praying he also didn't flip the RV.

Every movie he'd ever seen where something like this happened, that was what the characters had done. He prayed it would work here.

"Hold on!" he yelled.

The RV rocked back and forth. Inside, the cabinets opened, and pans clanged onto the floor. Drawers slid out and crashed shut.

Heather, Cristy, and Edmund braced themselves in between the queen-sized bed and the wall. Mena wasn't far away. Even if he couldn't shake the monster off the roof, maybe he could at least keep it occupied long enough to rush into town and get help.

After a few violent twists rocked the RV on its wheels, Matt slammed on the brakes. The creature's claws slipped out of the roof, and it rolled off the top, down the windshield and hood, and crashed onto the road ahead in a blur of fur and limbs. As soon as the monster hit the asphalt, Matt shifted into reverse, stared down at the side mirror, and punched the gas, hoping to add space between them and the beast.

"Dad, look out!" Cristy screamed.

Matt lifted his eyes back to the road in front of them. He glanced up just in time to see the creature galloping on all fours, leap into the air, and smash into the front windshield. Glass exploded inwards. As the shattered glass rained down on top of him, his foot slammed on the gas. The wheel spun out of control, and the RV spun in circles. Needles of glass pierced his skin. The creature's body slammed through the passenger seat, taking the top half with it as the beast crumpled into a ball next to the kitchen.

Matt gripped the steering wheel and tried to reverse the vehicle's momentum. The RV spun in reverse, tires howling, the road slanting downhill. The vehicle tilted onto two wheels and then flipped. Matt fell onto the passenger seat, colliding with the door as the passenger window exploded inward. His whole world became fire and glass.

His shoulder and face slid across the pavement first, sending radiating waves of pain across his body, as the RV skidded down the road. The metal shrieked against the asphalt. A storm of orange sparks filled the air.

When the RV finally stopped, the silence was worse than the noise.

Matt lay against the window, half his face shredded, his arm twisted unnaturally. He couldn't feel his shoulder. Blood pooled beneath him. From the back of the RV, someone coughed and moaned.

"Mommy!" Edmund cried. "Mommy, wake up."

"Edmund..." His jaw barely moved. Words came out wet, garbled. "I'm here."

Matt shakily pushed himself upright with his good arm. His right arm dangled limply, and blood drooled from the right side of his face. Broken pieces of the side mirror lay underneath him. Catching a glimpse of his reflection, Matt sardonically smiled, recognizing the similarity to Two Face.

Skin was ripped open, exposing a large meaty flap of his cheek. His right eyelid was black, singed from the sparks, and swollen. He couldn't fully open that eye. Turning his head to his shoulder, he saw it bent further back than allowed by nature. Pieces of bone peeked through the skin in multiple places. It took everything he had not to vomit from the pain. He forced himself not to, knowing that the pain might cause him to black out.

"Mommy! Cristy!" Edmund cried. "Daddy, help!"

His son needed him.

"I'm here, Edmund," he tried to say.

Instead, it came out in a muffled mess. His jaw didn't work. Could be his brain wasn't communicating clearly, but he guessed that since he could mentally form the thought, the miscommunication had been that his jaw was broken.

Reaching deep into his being, he fought past the pain and the urge to pass out. His only thought was his family. Edmund was at least alive. Matt didn't care about his own injuries. He focused on Edmund.

He could only hope, for now, that his wife and daughter were unconscious.

Once he crawled out of the front seats and into the back, he remembered the creature that had slammed through the windshield. It lay in a ball of black fur. It didn't move.

Good. I hope whatever you fucking are, you're dead. I'm going to taxidermy your fucking head and mount it over my fireplace.

"Edmund!" Matt said, although it didn't come out as that.

"Daddy! My legs won't move." His voice was filled with tears.

Matt rose to his feet. The air was thick with blood and antifreeze. The smell made his stomach turn. His arm, shoulder, and face might be fucked up, but at least his legs still worked. He stumbled past the ball of black fur. The fiberglass door and kitchen were now the bottom. While it felt surreal, Matt knew he had to just keep going. He kept his back bent over and trudged across what was the door. He then took another large step over the oven. Using his good arm, he pulled himself around until he finally could see the queen-sized bed. The mattress was on the ground, forming a right angle to the mounted frame.

Edmund lay next to the frame. If the RV had been upright, he would've currently been under the bed. By the angle of his legs, he must've landed hard enough on them to break. Matt grabbed the mattress and lifted it.

Immediately, his good eye teared up, and his heart broke. At least the mattress had obstructed Edmund's view. Heather lay motionless against the wall. Cristy was beside her, her head tilted at an impossible angle. He couldn't process it — at least not yet. His mind refused to believe what his eyes showed him.

"Are mommy and Cristy OK?" Edmund whimpered.

"We all need help," he mumbled.

He lowered the mattress, covering the two from Edmund's view. Edmund was his main focus now. Nothing else. In order to save Edmund, Matt needed to find his phone. Without help, he didn't know what they'd do next. The last place he left it was on the nightstand next to the bed.

Have we not been through enough, God?

"Need my phone. Hold this."

He lifted the mattress, and Edmund gripped it, holding it tightly. Fortunately, it still blocked the view of Heather and Cristy. If there was any grace left on this Earth, he'd be able to grab his phone and call for help before Edmund ever had a chance to realize what was on the other side of the mattress.

He finally spotted his phone — a black rectangle in the corner, near Heather's hand. Between him and it were bodies. His wife. His daughter.

He crawled, trembling. Blood dripped from his cheek and arm, onto his wife and daughter's bodies as he tried to move around them.

He prayed the phone wasn't broken. He'd splurged on the upgraded, extra-protective case. If there was ever a time the case needed to work its magic, it was now. He reached for the phone, tears burning his eyes.

"Hold on," he whispered. "Just hold on."

He looked down at Heather, and at Cristy's small, broken body. His hand shook as he brushed the hair from his daughter's face.

Why must I see this? Please God don't let me remember this.

He wanted to cry, wanted to break down into a muddled mess, and die alongside them, but he knew he couldn't. Edmund needed him. Edmund needed him to live so they could both find a way forward.

With his good arm, he stretched into the corner, reaching over Cristy's body.

"Daddy!" Edmund shrieked. "It's moving!"

Matt turned.

The black mass in the wreckage shifted. Bones cracked. A wet, low growl like a motorcycle engine rumbled inside the destroyed RV.

"Daddy! Daddy!"

The beast roared. Matt lunged for Edmund as the creature leapt toward the back of the RV. Edmund let go of the mattress, pinning Matt underneath it alongside Heather and Cristy's corpses. He was helpless. He felt the additional weight of the monster as it catapulted on top of the mattress, crushing him, suffocating him below it.

Matt screamed his son's name, but the sound drowned beneath the monster's roar and the tearing of flesh.

Edmund's screams stopped; there was nothing but silence again. A silence so total it was almost holy.

Under the ruined mattress, Matt Ward lay pinned. He couldn't move, couldn't breathe. He saw his son's small, torn shape through the haze of blood. The creature turned its attention on the mattress and Matt Ward beneath it. With a few quick swipes of its claws, the mattress was shredded. Matt briefly saw the carved remains of Edmund still pinned next to the bed frame. The boy's head no longer attached to his body.

The creature slowly and methodically slashed its way to Matt, savoring the fear. The last thing he saw were those yellow eyes, burning like twin candles, as claws ripped through the fabric and into his chest.

13

Michael sat on his bed in quiet meditation. He spent most evenings in the same position, working on controlling his thirst. Some days were easier than others. Since the strange dream of Jax in the forest, he'd been distracted. Blood calmed him. He found himself drinking more than he should. Something wasn't right. He wasn't quite sure what it was, but every sensation in his body told him that.

This time, Mike felt it coming.

An electric tremor crawled beneath his skin, a pulse that didn't match his heartbeat but mocked it. The room darkened around him, shadows bleeding into one another until the air itself thickened. He felt his mind falling into a deep cavern, a tunnel opening just beneath his bed. He barely had time to whisper anything before the pull took him.

His vision tore in half. The world inverted — sudden cold, sudden dark — and the smell of earth filled his nose.

When he blinked, he wasn't in his room anymore. The forest had claimed him again. The air was heavy with rot. Wet bark, mold, and the sharp mineral tang of rain-soaked stone. The darkness wasn't natural; it felt thick enough to choke on, pressing close, wrapping around him like wet cloth. Each breath shuddered through lungs that weren't his own.

He glanced down. Bare feet again. Mud sucking at the soles, cold water seeping between the toes. His body — or rather *this* body — was leaner, stronger, moving with predatory confidence even as his mind reeled. Veins burned beneath the skin like faint blue lightning.

Not again, he thought.

Michael steadied himself. The panic from the first vision clawed at him, but he forced it down. He needed to see. To learn. This wasn't madness — it was a connection, a tether to something real. Somewhere in the waking world, this body was walking the same ground Jax walked. Or would be. He didn't know how he knew, but he knew.

A scent hit him like a blade.

Blood — fresh and iron-rich — mixed with the faint trace of sweat and adrenaline.

Underneath it there was something familiar. Jax. It was Jax's blood. He hadn't recognized it the first time, but now, he remembered. His senses carved it out of the world like a beacon.

The body inhaled deeply, savoring.

Michael gagged inside his own head. That was Jax, not prey to enjoy.

The hunter's body he inhabited didn't listen. Its muscles coiled and released, sending them sprinting through the forest. Trees whipped past in smears of black and silver. Each stride landed soundless, efficient, perfect. The body knew exactly how to move — how to kill.

Wind roared through the canopy, and the forest answered with noise: branches cracking, birds bursting from their nests, distant howls threading through the night. The ground itself seemed alive, breathing underfoot. Michael tried to pull back. The harder he fought, the tighter the body held him. It was like being strapped inside a predator's skull, forced to watch through its eyes as instinct overrode mercy.

Ahead there was movement. Footprints pounded through wet grass, spattering mud. A man stumbling, bleeding, gasping for air.

Jax!

Even through the stranger's senses, Michael saw him clearly. His friend's jacket hung in tatters. His shoulder glistened dark with blood.

Each step Jax took left behind a crimson smear on the leaves. Something deep inside the borrowed body *thrilled* at the sight. The heart in Michael's chest wasn't his. This one thundered with hunger. His borrowed tongue tasted the blood on the air and curled against sharp teeth.

He was hunting his own friend.

Stop, damn it!

He tried to shout, but somehow couldn't.

Michael wrenched at the body's limbs like a man trying to steer a runaway beast. The thing barely acknowledged him. It moved faster, low to the ground, breath steady and controlled. The world blurred around them.

The trees opened into the clearing. The same clearing from the first vision — but something was different now. The scene was deader. The grass was pale and brittle. The moon hung swollen and red above the tree line, bleeding its color into the mist. The cabin waited at the far edge, sagging under years of decay. One window glowed faintly orange, like the eye of something that was only half-awake.

The hunter paused. The body trembled   not in fear but from anticipation.

Inside Michael's head, a dozen sounds collided: water dripping, wings flapping, wood creaking. His own pulse pounded in his ears.

Jax braced himself against the side of the cabin. He stumbled under the blood moonlight, clutching his side. The crimson on his shirt had turned black under the pale light. He pressed one hand to the wound, leaving streaks on his ribs. Even from here, Michael saw his face: pale, exhausted, terrified.

The hunter stepped forward. Every motion was deliberate, graceful, horrifying. Michael's own fear became the creature's fuel. He could feel its teeth ache to pierce skin, could feel saliva gather at the back of the throat.

Michael fought harder, shoving against invisible restraints. As Jax turned, their eyes met across the clearing. With every ounce of strength he could muster, Mike forced his way into the driver's seat. The body came to a halt as Mike grabbed control.

14

JAX NEEDED HELP. THAT much was obvious. While Mike had control of this strange body, he had every intention of helping his friend. He quickly strode toward the cabin.

Jax picked his head up and stared across the open meadow. Instead of reacting relieved to see Michael, his eyes opened wide, and he scrambled around the corner. The skilled hunter disappeared around the back of the cabin.

Halfway across the field Michael realized he'd lost control. It wasn't like when he'd lost control because of bloodlust or when Lilith had controlled him. He had slipped back into a passenger inside this body.

He covered the clearing in seconds and stood next to the cabin. Without making a sound, he crept along the outside. As he passed a window, he glanced inside. The cabin reminded him a bit of *Little House on the Prairie*.

The interior could've been sliced straight out of the 1800s. Nothing electric or gas. By the look of the sink, it didn't have running water either. Dirt and grime layered every surface. A thick, musky odor of rot permeated the area.

Whatever force was in control turned Mike's head away from the window and back to the trail of Jax's blood. As his eyes shifted away, he managed to catch a quick reflection in the glass.

He willed his head to spin back around but couldn't make it happen. He braced for the disassociation of seeing the eyes he currently peered the world through. Instead of his usual short trimmed, brown hair, this person was blonde. Michael's once tanned complexion had paled since turning into a vampire, but the image he saw was olive skinned.

"Jax?" Michael heard the stranger's voice come from him. "You shouldn't be here."

The fingertip of his index finger trailed across the bloody print Jax left, smearing it. He glanced at the blood on the end of it and placed it on his tongue.

"I've heard vampires say that frightened blood tastes sweeter. They aren't wrong. And by the taste, you are very frightened right now."

Michael had no choice but to sit and watch. He had a front row seat to whatever tracked Jax, watching through its eyes. He felt everything this creature felt yet had no control over the body. The creature silently strode to the back of the cabin. Sound had died away except for the howling wolves. They cried out, an alarm system for the dense forest. As Michael passed the edge of the cabin, he spun on his heels.

A large log hit him in the face, stunning him, and he stumbled backward. He glanced up and saw Jax swing the log again like a baseball bat. It hit Michael in the stomach, knocking the wind out of him. Jax spun around and swung once more. The club connected with Mike's chin, and he crashed to the ground, landing on his back.

"Have to do better than that, hunter," Michael heard himself say. He tried to control the body he was in but couldn't wrestle back the reins. The host was strong.

Quickly, he flipped onto his stomach and spun his legs behind him. Before Jax could react, Mike leapt off the ground and grabbed Jax by the throat. He saw the hand gripping Jax, and the arm it belonged to. He wanted to control them, to make them stop. Silas had picked him for his inner strength. Lilith had wanted him for the same. His strength was magnetic, a defining point. Where was it now? He struggled to grasp control, watching helplessly as his friend was assaulted. Worse, he was forced to participate. The hand picked Jax off the ground. As it did, he dropped the club. Jax batted at the hand gripping his throat, fighting to break free of the grasp. Michael threw him into the log cabin. Dust and dirt rained down as he collided with the rotted building.

Through eyes that weren't his own, Mike saw his friend lying against the building. Blood streamed down his face, over the hunter's beard.

Mike's thoughts shot back to the last time he'd heard from Jax. It had been a few weeks since he'd last seen Jax on a video call.

He was still following up on leads regarding the missing council members. Silas's revolution had been thwarted only five months ago.

Although Silas was dead, the council was still nowhere to be seen. Leads were becoming fewer and fewer, and many of the prominent creature families had become aggravated at the lack of answers. Talk of the New Orleans incident had spread.

Mike could tell that Jax had grown more desperate and determined over the past month.

Drawn back by the wreak of fear, Mike noticed that same emotion was completely absent in the hunter's face. He stared with solid determination. Mike realized he was seeing Jax not as a friend, but as the ruthless hunter who had taken the lives of hundreds if not thousands of creatures over the years.

Whatever Jax felt behind the gaze didn't matter. His outward expression showed his resolve. He took long, deep breaths. "I didn't think you had it in you," Jax croaked before coughing up dust and blood. "Chaos was never your thing."

"Not chaos. Simply a new order." Mike took a few steps, bringing him closer to Jax.

"Did you take them all?"

"Only had to take the unwilling."

"Are the unwilling dead?"

Michael felt a smile flash across his face. "Only those needed as an example."

Jax's expression changed from stoic to hostile, and he rushed Michael. Before he could reach the vampire, Michael shoved Jax backward, sending him not just against the wall of the old house but through it. The rotted wood crumbled and splintered. Jax flailed his arms, trying to grasp onto anything that would stop his trajectory. Unable to grip anything, he slid to a stop on the far side of the floor. The rotted boards beneath him also gave way, and Jax crashed through the floor, completely disappearing from view.

Michael strode closer to the hole in the side of the cabin. He placed a hand on the disintegrating wall and glanced down into the cellar below. Jax lay on his back unconscious. A dozen feet away from the hunter's location, a large cage sat on the dirt floor. It was large enough to hold a person. It was a jail cell. As Michael peered into the hole, red eyes framed by black hair stared back up at him.

15

David rolled over in his hospital bed.

He closed his eyes, hoping to find sleep. As he drifted off again, images of the beast roared back to life on his mind's silver screen.

He saw it tear into the tent and rip Rebecca apart. She screamed and reached for him, beckoning him to save her...or join her in death.

But in reality, there was nothing he could do. That black snout and sharp teeth clamped down on his side. She was dead. He would soon be as well. Other images interspersed flashes of the beast. The moon, full and bright, splashed across his view. The beast's paw, dripping in blood, raised high above his head and sliced down.

David shot awake and raised his torso off the bed. His heart raced, and he couldn't catch his breath. The bandages pulled at his side, ripping away hair and tugging at his skin. His pillow and blanket were soaked. He patted his forehead and wiped more sweat away. The machine next to him beeped rapidly. He rubbed his eyes and saw the number slowly descend back to one hundred and then continue down as his breathing slowed.

It was dark in his room. He couldn't see the clock, but based on the lack of sunlight streaming through the window, it was still early in the morning.

A noise came from the corner of his room.

"Is someone there?"

He closed his eyes and listened intently. David held his breath, yet still heard breathing.

"Who's there?" he asked.

A strange scent, one he couldn't quite place, filled the room. Since he'd awoken after the attack, he'd been more attuned to smells than before. Even the slightest smell seemed overpowering. He still felt badly about accusing the nurse of wearing too much perfume. Hospital soap was definitely stronger than his at home.

He reached for the call button.

"You don't have to do that," came a male's voice out of the corner.

"Why not?"

The man stepped out of the shadowy part of the room and strode closer to David.

He wore a gray uniform shirt, green pants, and a badge pinned to his chest. His skin tone and facial features were unmistakably indigenous. His dark brown hair was held back in a simple braid. Hard creases in his face led David to believe the man was in his mid-fifties.

"I didn't mean to wake you," the man said.

"Guessing you're a park ranger?" David asked, motioning his hand up and down. "Does the National Forest Service usually make hospital visits this early?"

The man turned his wrist over, checking his watch. "It's already after five. This isn't early. And when something like what happened to you happens in my forest, then yes, I make hospital visits."

David nodded his head. "I haven't slept much as it is, so I guess five isn't a bad time."

"Nightmares?"

David continued to nod. "Every time I close my eyes."

"The nightmares will fade away as quickly as your injuries will. If you aren't careful, though, new ones can take their place." The ranger moved to the edge of the bed. What little moonlight there was fell across his face. His eyes had an odd color to them, almost yellow.

The nightmarish beast with a hint of yellow around its abysmally dark eyes flashed across his mind's eye.

He felt uneasy and shifted his weight on the bed.

David closed his eyes for a moment and then reopened them. When he did, the man's eyes were hazel. The nightmares must be causing delusions. It was either that or the pain medication that was finally getting to him.

"I told Chief Henderson everything that happened. By the way, I haven't gotten your name."

"Yes, Roy's called us a few times, Mr. Hall. Your statement was irrefutable. I came here as soon as I could to see the man who survived. How are your wounds? I hardly see a bruise on you."

David realized the man hadn't given his name. And he had referred to David as the man who survived like he was Harry Potter. The park ranger left David feeling uneasy.

"I've always been a fast healer," David said, trepidation in his voice. "What did you say your name was?"

The ranger moved closer to the window, glancing out at the dropping moon.

"John."

"John...?" He motioned his hand, trying to pull a last name from John.

"Yes. John." He stared out the window, not paying attention to David. His voice turned thoughtful and distant. "The moon has dipped almost below the horizon. Last night's moon was a waxing gibbous. Most people think there are only four phases of the moon but there are actually eight. The waxing gibbous rises between the first quarter moon and the full moon. It can be seen as a warning — a sign of preparation."

The ranger's behavior hadn't quelled David's sense of unease. John continued to stare out the window in a daze. David's hand hovered over the call button. If this guy got any weirder, he'd press the button as hard and as fast as he could. David double checked, just in case, that he wasn't about to press the medication button by accident.

Finally, David said, "Well, Ranger John, I think I'm going to go back to sleep while the waxing gibbous is still out. I hope I'm not a local attraction. Should I expect other park rangers to stop by? I can't be the first to have survived a bear attack. Have you seen the movie *The Revenant*? At least I didn't have to crawl to find help."

Ranger John turned away from the window and cracked a smile, slowly nodding his head. His eyes flashed a yellow color again before shifting back to hazel.

David rubbed his eyes. It had to be the fading moonlight and rising sun, or his meds.

"Try to get plenty of rest, David. It'll help with your healing."

The ranger moved away from the window. Before David could say anything else, he took a few quick steps and disappeared into the hallway, leaving David's door open. David flopped his head against his pillow and closed his eyes. After a few minutes, he opened them again and stared at the open door. The interaction was so strange, he began to ponder if he had dreamed the whole thing.

The pillow and blanket were still damp with sweat.

With the air conditioner blowing, he should have been cold. Instead, the breeze felt oddly satisfying. He touched his head to make sure he didn't have a fever. He thought he might be a little warm, but it was nothing to be alarmed about compared to the fever of the past few days.

It wouldn't be long before the nurse would be in to take his vitals anyway. If he had a fever, they'd put something in his IV or give him a pill to bring it down.

For now, he closed his eyes and hoped to find sleep that didn't have nightmares of a large black bear killing his girlfriend and mauling him.

Unfortunately, David didn't have that kind of luck.

16

Michael White gasped, sucking in a long deep breath. His eyes sprang open, and he kicked his arms and legs, knocking over the nightstand next to his bed. It crashed to the ground. He glanced down at his pale, shirtless body.

"What the fuck!" he said, bringing his hands to his chest and stomach. He touched his skin, making sure it was actually him.

He bolted upright on the bed, still breathing rapidly. He shot his eyes from left to right, scanning the area, confirming it was his room. Across from him, the refrigerator emitted its low hum. On his right, a dresser hugged the wall. His nightstand, which usually butted up next to the bed, was now turned over on the floor. This was his room.

Footsteps hurried down the hallway. They abruptly stopped just outside his room and were followed by a heavy pounding on the door. "Mike!" Nate said. His deep baritone voice reverberated against the wooden door. "Are you OK?"

He was about to say yes. The word almost escaped his lips, but he clamped his mouth shut before he did. In actuality, he didn't know if he was. A few moments ago, he hadn't been. He'd been back in the forest chasing Jax and using his friend's body to demo a cabin. Was he OK? Mike honestly didn't know.

"Mike?" Nate hollered again, followed by another round of deep thuds against the door. "I'll break the door down."

"Don't do that," Michael finally answered. "I'm here. Knocked over my nightstand. Did I wake everyone up?"

He swung his legs off his bed and stood up. He rocked from side to side, confirming they were his legs. He stood there, orienting himself. Moments passed before the effects of the out-of-body experience dissipated. He placed one foot in front of the other and hesitantly stepped to the door. He stared down as his hand under his control reached for the doorknob and turned it. Nate and Niki stood outside the door.

Nate waited worriedly in only his plaid sweatpants. He stood six inches taller than Mike and his large muscular frame dwarfed the vampire. Niki had a house coat wrapped around her slender body. Her arms hugged the coat tightly, protecting her from the drafts inside the warehouse. Both looked as if they'd just woken up, but they were still more than ready to fight if needed.

"What time is it?" Mike asked.

"Three," Nate said. "We heard you holler for Jax, and then something crashed."

Mike sighed. Was it just a vivid dream or something else? Before becoming one himself, he had thought vampires didn't sleep. They did; they just didn't need to as often or for as long as humans. He could go weeks, only needing an hour or two to recharge, usually while sipping on a blood bag. The more blood he consumed, the less he needed to sleep. All of the rejuvenating energy he needed was contained in the thick, red liquid.

"I had a... I don't know what it was." Mike shifted in the doorway. He struggled to find the words to explain it to them. "I guess it was a dream, but it felt extremely real. It felt like me, but it wasn't me. Something like an out of body experience. I was there but had no control. Even now, it feels strange being back inside my own skin."

"Well, love," Niki said, "right now, you are most definitely you. Pale and brooding. I'd say get some rest, but you don't do much of that. Since we're up, anything we can do to help?"

Mike shook his head. "No, that's OK. I'm going to pick my nightstand up and then give Thomas a call. Maybe this is one of those vampire things and he just hasn't filled me in on it yet."

Vampirism came with unexpected abilities, but also some unexpected side-effects that he was still trying to find his way around.

"Sounds good. Do what you need to," Nate said. He turned and led Niki back down the hallway to their room.

Leaning against the doorframe, Mike scanned the hall. Somehow Josh must've slept through the nightstand crash and his hollering. Instead of worrying with his nightstand, he headed down toward the conference room.

The corridor opened into a larger warehouse area, similar to what they'd had when he first met the Night Crew a few months ago. Back when he was still human and had only planned to be with the team long enough to avenge his late wife. It seemed like ages ago, but that had been last October. A lot had happened in six months.

He stepped around the large table in the center of the conference area, pulled out a chair, and sat down. A laptop sat in front of him. He opened the lid, entered his password, and clicked the icon to start a video call. The older vampire answered right away. That didn't surprise him. He doubted Thomas slept much either.

Thomas's appearance hadn't changed. He still had his long black hair.

His face had a gauntness not unlike the faces in paintings of colonial days. Certain features matched Silas's, reminding Mike of the vampire who had killed his wife and turned him into this immortal being.

"Where's Jax?" Michael demanded.

"Why are you calling in the middle of the night asking me?" Thomas inquired in response.

"You're answering a question with a question." He immediately knew when his friend was being evasive.

"There's a reason why you're asking me that tonight. I can see it in your eyes even through a video call. What happened?"

Michael held Thomas's gaze. "I'm not sure how to explain it. It was almost a dream, but it also was..."

"More real?" Thomas finished.

Mike's shoulders relaxed. Maybe Thomas did know what had happened to him and possibly what had happened to Jax. He'd hoped he'd get an answer. "Yes. It was me, but not in my body, and I had no control over myself."

"Use your gift. Tell me everything you saw."

After a few deep breaths, relaxing into his Ultranet, Mike closed his eyes and replayed the events in his head. As he relived the dream, he relayed everything to Thomas. With the exception of a few clarifying questions about the environment, Thomas tried not to interrupt. He was especially curious about the sounds he'd heard in the forest, the howling wolves, and the cabin itself.

As Michael finished, he opened his eyes and focused on Thomas. "Now, where's Jax?"

"We don't know, but based on your vision, I think we have a better idea."

"Vampires have visions?" Mike asked. "Is that in an advanced level class that I haven't taken yet?"

Thomas shook his head. "It's extremely rare. It only happens through an extremely strong blood connection. If Silas was still alive, it's possible you'd have been able to see a vision he projected. Blood connections are very strong. You experienced that for the first time when you saved Niki."

"What does any of that mean? Was it real?"

"Well, it means that whoever projected the vision is not only very powerful themselves, but also is part of Silas's bloodline. You two share a common bond. Whatever power he's using is tapping into that legacy. And there's no way to know if it was something that has happened and you witnessed, or that they wish to happen. It can be difficult to tell the difference between desire and reality."

"I was there until the woman in the cage stared up at me. Red eyes. Black hair. Who is she?"

"Must have been Valerie. She's on the Council. This is the first time a member has been seen since Silas was killed. If you are correct and she's alive, that's a good sign."

"Why's that?" Mike asked. "Besides the obvious?"

Thomas's lips curled into a half smile. His eyes drifted as if a fond memory played behind them. "Let's just say she's a force to be reckoned with. If they've put up with her for this long, there's a good chance the others are still alive as well, despite what Jax was told.

"I'm going to contact Intel and relay our conversation. He'll want to know as soon as possible in order to reach Jax and follow the lead. It's the best we've had."

"What do you want me to do?"

"Grab a blood bag and meditate. In a few hours, once everyone else wakes up, we'll hop on a call."

Mike's eyes perked up. "Are we searching for Jax?"

"No," Thomas said, shaking his head, "we'll have another team follow up. You have a different assignment. We'll talk soon."

Thomas disconnected the call, leaving Mike sitting in the dark. The glow of the laptop's screen illuminated his chest and face.

17

Sunday fucking morning, Roy thought as he drove his truck up the road toward Four Seasons RV Park.

The early morning sun peaked through the trees, turning the overnight dew into an array of sparkling gems. Some days, this would be a beautiful drive but not today. His third call in just over a week. First, he had the campsite where David and Rebecca were attacked. A few days after that, he had the site where Tanner's body was found. And today, he had awoken to a call about an overturned RV on the ground. Initially, he told the young officer Dylan to contact Sergeant Lowell. Carl could process the scene of a traffic accident without issue. That didn't require him. But when Dylan added details about the family inside, Roy headed out.

The closer he got, the more cars lined the road on both sides. He had to drive the truck at a crawl. A crowd of about twenty stood just on the other side of the police tape strung across the road.

At least no one had started a second incident...yet. Everyone just looked on. Most of the crowd had their cell phones out, lifted high up in the air, taking pictures or video of the wreck.

As his truck drew closer, two officers marched to the police tape, bent under it, and cleared a path in the middle of the road.

Roy inched the truck forward. As the two uniformed officers raised the tape for his truck to drive under, he glanced to his right. Troy Johnson and a few others from the previous Thursday stood in attendance, glaring as the Chief of Police drove passed. Once he was all the way through, the officers dropped the tape back to its resting position across the road, and the two sides of the crowd merged back into one. He pulled the truck over to the side, still over twenty yards from the wreck, opened the door, and hopped out.

The moment his foot touched the ground, he heard the shouts from the crowd.

"How many more need to die?"

"Now, can we hunt it?"

"Let us kill it!"

Roy sighed. If they knew what they were up against, they'd have second thoughts. He needed a little time. For now, he ignored the crowd and marched to the RV.

The vehicle lay on its passenger side. The top of the vehicle had claw marks down it. Multiple holes punched completely through the aluminum frame. The RV's power cable dangled there like a torn umbilical cord. They'd been so frightened they had just driven away hoping to escape the nightmare.

Sergeant Lowell stood on the far side of the RV. Roy marched past the wreckage and headed toward Carl. Drag and scorch marks had been carved into the road behind him and all the way to the RV's final resting place. Roy shook his head.

"Carl, this looks to be some kind of a mess. Fill me in."

"I don't know what to think, Chief." He rubbed the top of his head, scratching at his scalp just under his short graying hair. "I've never seen a bear do something like this. I don't care how high on cocaine it is. This is an insane amount of carnage. Plus, it looks like whatever killed the Wards' did it for fun, not survival."

"The whole family?" Roy asked, although he already knew the answer.

"Well, only the father and son were killed by the animal." He glanced down at his notepad. "The wife and daughter were killed in the crash. When the RV flipped, their heads slammed into the side of the wall and snapped their necks. Based on what happened to the other two, though, they were probably the lucky ones. Rebecca Summers' death wasn't nothing compared to this. You sure this is a bear, Chief?"

Before Roy could answer, another voice spoke up. "It's a black bear."

Both Roy and Carl turned. A man in a Forestry Service uniform approached.

"A black bear is one of the most powerful creatures in the forest. Something is wrong in its brain. It is killing indiscriminately. Think of the worst nightmare you had after watching Jaws, and how you felt about getting in the water, and then realize this creature is on land. It's faster than you. Stronger than you. It can climb, and it can dig. With one claw, it can pierce your throat and slide that claw all the way down to your scrotum, spilling your guts all over your feet, and never flex a muscle." He paused in front of the two men and lifted his hand. "I'm John Kohana, from the US Forestry Service." He gripped Carl's hand first, and then switched to Roy's.

Roy glared into John's eyes. "It's nice to meet you, Ranger."

"Chief, is there somewhere we can speak?"

"Sure. Carl, if you don't mind. Follow me this way." Roy motioned his arm back to the end of the RV.

"I have a lot to write up," Carl said. "You two talk. Glad you're here, Ranger. We need all the help we can get with this bear. People are starting to get restless."

Carl turned away as Roy and John started toward the back of the RV.

"I visited David this morning," John said. "He has no idea what's happening to him, and he's going to turn within a week."

"I'm aware," Henderson said. "It's about fucking time you got here."

"David's statement, his description, left no room for doubt," Kohana said. "The pack was hesitant to believe it was one of ours, but..."

"But? But what?" Roy asked. He tried to keep his voice down, but his anger at everything that had gone on was more than he could handle.

"People leave the pack all the time. We don't make them stay. But two members, two young men in their twenties, recently left. We found evidence which led us to believe they have ill intent."

Roy spun around and grabbed John by the shirt. He leaned close to John's face. As he spoke, fine specks of spittle flew from his mouth. "Ill intent? Do you know how many people have been killed? And you're calling it 'ill intent'?"

"After the Ward family, my count is twelve, so yes, I'm aware. Please, let go of my shirt. I'm here to help, to track them, and to bring them back to the pack for justice."

"For justice? Well, you're going to have competition at that." He released John's shirt and pointed to the crowd just beyond the police tape. "They want justice. One of them is Tanner's father."

Roy started toward his truck, leaving John standing by the wreckage. Once he reached his door, he opened it and hollered over to John. "Also, you took too long. I made another phone call as well." He sat down on the truck's seat.

"Who did you call?" John yelled.

Roy slammed the door to the truck. John ran to Roy. He knocked on the windshield and repeated his question. "Who did you call?"

Roy rolled the window down. "We needed help, and you weren't coming."

John leaned into the window and grabbed Roy's arm. "Who did you call?"

Roy shook his arm out of John's grip. "The Night Crew."

18

MIKE WAS ALREADY AT the conference table, waiting on the others. Niki, Nate, and Josh were in the break room, finishing up their breakfast. Sounds and smells flowed down the hallway into the conference room. Coffee was the strongest aroma. If there was one thing — besides Brittany — he missed most of all, it was that first hit that got the blood pumping. The hot, bitter taste was something he'd once taken for granted.

After speaking with Thomas, he'd remained at the table. Over the handful of hours, Mike had reconnected with his body. There was something about being pulled away from it, residing in another's form, that made him want to feel every fiber of his own again before he could feel comfortable. He hoped that type of vision wasn't going to be a normal thing from now on.

Based on Thomas's lack of reaction, he wasn't counting on it. For now, he just had to wait.

Only had to take the unwilling, the voice had told Jax.

When Jax asked if the unwilling were dead, the voice's answer had sent a chill through Michael.

Only those needed as an example.

Did that mean some of the Council had been killed? Or was Thomas right and he was bluffing?

The whole situation gnawed at him. He wished he had more answers. For that matter, he had hoped Austin would've tapped them to lead the search. Jax was their former team lead. If he was in danger, it should have been them out there, trying to save their friend.

"You alright?" Josh asked.

He wheeled into the conference room. His short hair had started to grow long, and he had the beginnings of a beard. He slid past the table and over to his desk. Josh was the only one who had an actual workstation within the conference space. Anytime the team met up, Mike, Niki, and Nate had sat around the table while Josh would either work at his desk or move to the head of the table.

With his hands perched over his keyboard, Josh tapped a few keys, and his multitude of monitors sprang to life.

"Just lost in thought," Mike said.

He stood up and stretched his legs. He strode to the mini fridge and opened it. From inside, he gripped a bag, removed it from the cooler, and tore the top off. A Yeti cup sat on the counter. Mike took the lid off, poured the bag's contents into it, and replaced the lid. He tossed the empty bag into a trash can and sipped his breakfast, still standing.

"I heard you had another bad dream."

Mike smirked. "Is that what they told you?"

"I'm sure it wasn't as simple as all that." Josh kept his eyes on his screens and clicked through emails.

"Thomas thinks it wasn't a dream but a vision. Whatever I was seeing was tied to someone else I share a bloodline with?"

Josh stopped and turned. "Bloodline? Familial or...?"

"Vampire," Mike answered as Josh started to ask. "Someone else that Silas turned. Thomas thinks we share Silas's blood."

"That's interesting. It wouldn't surprise me if one of Silas's lieutenants had absconded with the Council. Someone he turned and is carrying out his work." Josh turned back to his desk. "I hate fanatics."

Mike sat down his cup and slid behind Josh. He gripped the top of the wheelchair and pulled it down. He held onto it so Josh didn't fall. Instead, Mike stood over him. Josh stared up at the vampire, arms crossed, annoyed.

"You're going to use the word absconded and just turn back around like it didn't happen."

"It felt like the right word. Now, can you set me back upright, please?"

Mike shook his head. While he did, he said, "Tsk, tsk, tsk. Have you increased your reading? Is that why your vocabulary is expanding?"

Nate and Niki stepped into the conference room and headed for their usual seats.

"Nate, love, should we turn Michael over to the authorities for picking on Josh?"

Nate pointed a finger at Niki and then back to himself. "Aren't we the authorities who would have to handle him?"

"Oh yes." Niki tossed her hands behind her hair, leaned back in the chair, and placed her boots on the table. "Michael, we've had to save you too many times to end up having to kill you ourselves."

Mike turned his head toward the two sitting next to each other and started laughing. He raised Josh's chair and marched back to his iron-filled breakfast. "If we're keeping score, I think I'm in the lead."

"First of all," Nate said. "We don't keep score. Part of the job is saving each other. And second, no, you aren't. You had your ass handed to you by a succubus multiple times. You're welcome."

Before Mike could argue, Josh interrupted in a very loud and serious tone, while spinning his chair closer to the conference table. "Good morning, Intel. How are things?"

Mike glanced at the monitor and saw Austin's face filling the screen.

"Just another morning." Austin's eyes danced from one side of the screen to the other. "Glad to see you're all present and accounted for. We have a few things to go over this morning."

"Have you spoken with Thomas?" Mike asked before his old friend could go any further.

"That's the first thing I wanted to cover. He filled me in on your vision, along with his theory about it being a blood tie. A few of the elders question if that's the case, though."

"What do they think it was?" Mike placed the cup on the counter surrounding the conference room harder than he intended.

Intel's hands raised almost to his chest. It was the universal sign of "calm down".

"Mike, let me finish. As Thomas told you, something like that is very rare. Because of that, we're going to send someone to Dallas who can help determine if that's the case. In the meantime, we have sent out a team with the information you provided. We've also relayed details to some of our allies. They're going to assist in finding the cabin."

"Who are you sending?" Josh asked.

"Xavier Morcos."

"Holy shit," Nate said. "Xavier?"

"As the new guy," Mike said, glancing from Nate to Intel, "it's annoying as shit when you do stuff like that. Who is Xavier Morcos?"

"A warlock," Josh said.

"Calling Xavier a warlock is like saying John Madden was an announcer," Nate corrected. "If they're sending Xavier, things are serious."

Mike turned to Niki. "Since when do you have nothing to say? No comment regarding Xavier?"

"Oh, love, I'm staying quiet regarding Xavier. Nate and I have an understanding. He's my hall pass."

"For fuck's sake," Intel said. "Can we get back on task?"

"Sure thing, sir." Mike turned his attention back to the monitor. "How is it you outrank me again?"

A dozen different memories crossed Mike's mind. Each one was an instance of Austin doing something stupid and saving his ass. Hell, he didn't even need to access his UltraNet to do that. Those were readily available.

"Technically, Sergeant, I don't. This is a civilian outfit. I'm just your boss." Then, he added, "And don't call me 'Sir'. I work for a living."

Mike lifted his mug to the screen and tilted his head, acknowledging what Austin had said.

"Xavier won't be available for a couple of weeks. In the meantime, I have an assignment for you. There've been werewolf attacks in Ouachita National Forest in Arkansas. I need you all to find and terminate the werewolf."

The image of a werewolf grabbing Nate and Niki's son flashed across Mike's head. Although he had been able to break the nightmarish cycle forced on Niki by the succubus, it hadn't actually changed history. Their son had still been ripped from the top of that Playscape into the jaws of a wolf and dragged away. A wolf that had been sick.

He glanced at Nate and Niki. They didn't try to hide their feelings about the entire hate-filled story. Their friends already knew. Nate's nostrils flared, and Niki looked as if she'd been punched in the gut. He didn't blame them for their resentment of werewolves, but that same hatred concerned him. Too often, he'd seen people become blinded by rage. It only led to trouble. Michael knew he was his own example in this case. His quest for vengeance made him the creature he was.

"I thought you guys said werewolves police themselves," Mike said, recalling a conversation not long after he had joined the Night Crew.

"Usually, that's the case. The Chief of Police reached out to the local pack, but they were..." Austin hesitated for a moment. "They were less than cooperative, which is why we are sending you."

Josh scooted backward so that he was in full view of the camera. "Intel, we're still at least a man short, which got us into a lot of trouble in New Orleans. Plus, Mike is still learning. There's not another team that can take this?"

Intel pushed down his glasses and massaged the bridge of his nose.

"Don't worry about me," Mike said. "My bloodlust is better. I'm able to control my hunger a lot easier. I wouldn't even call myself a fledgling."

"Love, you'll always be our fledgling," Niki said, letting a smile break through the stark demeanor she'd had since hearing about the werewolf.

"Josh," Intel said, pushing his glasses back up, "I agree about needing another member, and I'm working on it. Since creating the special task force to search for the Council, every team is short. It's not ideal, but it's what we have to work with.

"But as for the werewolf attacks, you are the closest. Pack up your gear. You're heading to Mena. Josh, I'll send you the packet to review on the drive."

The call disconnected.

Mike immediately turned to Nate and Niki. After what he had learned, he needed to know if they were solid.

"Are you two OK with hunting werewolves?"

Nate took a deep breath to brace himself against the pain he knew the topic would bring. He placed his hands on the table and stood up.

"When I," he glanced down at Niki and started over. "When we were recruited, we learned the truth about the world around us just like you did. We learned about the creatures that we'd have to kill. Over the years, we've killed a lot of them. Some were monsters like Silas who killed either for an evil purpose or just because they fucking liked doing it, and we've enjoyed killing those. Others didn't have control for whatever reason and would never be able to find peace, and we've hated what needed to be done."

Nate leaned closer to Mike, his massive arms bulging against the table. "But werewolves? I don't give a fuck how much control they do or do not have. I'll add another notch on my belt for every mutt I put down."

None of what Nate said eased his concerns. Was he going to be able to restrain himself if he had to? And what about Niki? How did she feel about this?

Mike inhaled the last of the blood in his mug and placed the cup down. "I understand anger. After losing my parents, the therapist talked about grief in camps. We called that Camp Anger. Most times, I'm still there when it comes to losing Brittany. I'm still angry at Silas for killing her for no damn good reason. I'm angry at myself for turning into the very thing that killed her. I live in Camp Anger and occasionally visit Camp Depression. Acceptance? Not likely this century.

"But, it was that same anger that caused me to rush headfirst at Silas. I don't want the same for you two. As Josh said, we need another team member. What we don't need, what I wouldn't be able to handle, is to lose either of you. I need to know you are both solid."

The tension in Nate's arms and shoulders eased. Niki, who had been sitting straight up and looked like a rubber band ready to snap, melted.

"We're good," Niki answered. "Killing werewolves gives us a little sense of retribution, but our heads are always in the game. We couldn't do that to the team, to our friends, much less to each other."

Nate nodded as she spoke.

"Well then, it's like Intel said. Gear up. We're heading to Arkansas!"

19

As the sun rose, Mike felt the impact on his strength. He assumed one day he'd get used to the change, and if so, that day couldn't come soon enough. The feeling explained why, in lore, vampires slept while the sun was out. It wasn't that he preferred to slumber at that time as much as staying in the dark helped lessen the impact.

Even though the SUV had heavy tint, the bright orb still blazed in the sky. Sitting in the back, he pulled the top of his hoodie over his head and sunk deeper into the seat. He slipped on a pair of sunglasses. The less exposure, the better.

Nate had driven the entire way while Niki slept soundly next to him. Josh had passed out in the back next to Mike.

With a stretch and a yawn, Josh finally woke up. He reached for his tablet and activated it. The inside of the SUV was dark enough that the tablet's screen illuminated his face. Mike was glad he'd put the sunglasses on ahead of time, because Josh kept the brightness dialed high. He scrolled through notifications, finally clicking on one.

"Intel sent the file," he said.

Nate tapped Niki on the shoulder. She grumbled.

"Niki, wake up," Nate insisted.

"How far out are we?" she finally asked, rubbing sleep from her eyes.

"An hour from Mena. Josh has updates."

Niki reached her arms above her head and arched her back, stretching out whatever soreness sleep had left behind.

"Spill it, love. What's going on with the Hounds from Hell?"

At the mention of "Hounds from Hell", Mike remembered the howling wolves from his vision. He'd been so focused on Jax and on his out-of-body experience, he'd completely forgotten about them. The forest currently surrounding them heightened the memory. He doubted the one he'd seen had been the Ouachita National Forest. That coincidence would've been too much. He wasn't a tree expert; an oak was an oak. However, the trees in his vision seemed taller and fuller, blocking out the night sky.

"So far, there've been six hikers who've gone missing," Josh said, scrolling on his tablet.

"Six missing hikers?" Nate asked. "Why hasn't that made the news?"

"Not only have they been spread out over the past few weeks, but it's a big forest. They've also been spread out over several areas."

Mike picked his head up, focusing on the conversation around him instead of on a vision of a remote cabin in the woods. One where at least one member of the Council was being held captive.

"Over the past few weeks?" Mike asked. "Why are we just finding out? I expected better from Austin."

Josh shrugged his shoulders. "I guess it's not entirely uncommon for hikers to go missing. Only two people have been confirmed dead. One was a kid. Had his heart ripped right out of his chest. The news attributed their deaths to bear attacks which are not unheard of but also not common. According to Intel, the original thought was a wendigo. The dossier was started as such until an eyewitness report. Just over a week ago, a couple were camping just outside of Mena. That night, a 'bear'," Josh did air quotes, emphasizing the obvious, "tore into their tent and killed the woman, Rebecca Summers. Her boyfriend, David Hall, escaped but barely. He was taken to the Mena Regional Hospital.

He finally woke up two days ago. Based on his account, the local sheriff determined the problem wasn't a wendigo but a werewolf."

From behind the wheel, Nate glanced in the rearview mirror, catching Josh's eye. "Why was he in the hospital? Which injuries, specifically, did he suffer? Was he bit?"

Niki's head turned toward Josh as well.

All of this monster stuff was new to Mike. He was still learning more about the powers he had as a vampire, how to control his bloodlust, who was on the Council, what kind of creatures they hunt, how they kill those creatures, and a hundred other things. One thing he was fairly sure of, though, was a werewolf bite created new werewolves. He bounced his eyes from the pair in the front over to Josh.

Despairingly, Josh lowered his eyes. "He was bit."

Nate flared his nostrils and turned his attention back to the road.

"And we're going to the hospital now?" Niki asked.

Nate's eyes shot to the rearview mirror as Josh bobbed his head, affirming their destination.

"To put down the new wolf, right?" she continued.

"He's not our target at this time. The one who attacked him is, the one that has killed."

Nate slammed his fists into the steering wheel. "Why can't we take out both? Just because he hasn't turned and killed yet doesn't mean he won't. It's only a matter of time before he does."

"We have four days to intercede before he does."

"Four days?" Mike chimed in.

Nate answered before Josh could. "Until the full moon. The fucking wolf grows inside them until the first full moon. At that point, it's unleashed. Josh, we've got to take him out before that happens. We stop it now, or the fallout will be vicious. You know they're uncontrollable with the first change."

Mike thought back to when Silas had turned him. He remembered how close he had come to giving into the bloodlust and tearing apart Jax and Niki. He couldn't think beyond the blood coursing through their veins. It had demanded all of his attention. At least he had known what was happening to him. This guy in the hospital - David - had no idea what was going to happen to him.

"Love!" Niki tapped Mike on the leg.

He hadn't realized how much he had spaced out until he raised his eyes and saw her completely turned around on the seat, sitting on her knees.

Nate shot her a side-eyed glance. "If you don't sit back down, you're going to get us pulled over."

Niki rolled her eyes.

"Sorry," Mike said. "Got lost in my thoughts. What did you say?"

"Since you're our fearless leader and have a history with Intel, Nate asked if you could plead our case for us. The poor guy needs to be put down before it's too late." She turned back around and stared out the passenger window. Almost as an aside, she said, "It would've been better for him to have died in his tent."

The conversation was over. Both Nate and Niki had made their viewpoints known. Unsurprisingly, their vote had been for elimination. He wondered if they'd voted the same way when Silas had turned him. Was their previous relationship the only reason he was still alive? Despite everything they'd been through before he'd turned, he knew if it wasn't for Thomas and Brittany's intervention, them keeping Mike from killing Jax and Niki, the team would've taken his head as well.

"Mike?" Josh whispered.

Mike shifted his head toward Josh.

"Intel also sent along applications."

"People apply for the Night Crew? Do we have a listing on Indeed?"

Josh smiled. "Prospects would be a better term. Those who've been impacted by the creatures we hunt. Interested in taking a look before we get to Mena?"

The vampire turned his attention back to the large trees passing them in a blur. The sunlight streamed past the dark window tint. Michael actually wanted to curl into the dark, hiding away from the bright rays. New recruits. New people who had been impacted by creatures. Victims like he had been. Victims like Niki and Nate. Vulnerable. He suddenly empathized with how Thomas had reacted when they had first met. Keeping distant. Not making an attachment. Mike had only been a vampire for a few months, but he was well aware of the vulnerability of his human teammates.

Still staring through the window, Mike finally responded. "Let's wait until after this case."

"Sure thing," Josh said.

Hunger shot through Mike's stomach. He felt his deadly fangs against the inside of his lips. Before they reached the hospital, he'd have to feed. Even still, he hoped the smell of blood would be minimal. As much as he wished his control was better, he was still a fledgling.

He closed his eyes and thought back to a conversation he had with Thomas.

"Why do I still struggle with bloodlust? Shouldn't I at least be a beta by now?"

Thomas had nodded his head. "And if you gave into the thirst, if you fed on living victims each night, you would be. Instead, you fight your instinctive nature. It'll take longer to suppress the hunger. It'll never go away, never be satiated. Only suppressed. In some ways, you are beyond a beta. Your strength and willpower rival betas who've existed for decades. But until you are able to conquer that hunger, that bloodlust, you'll remain a fledgling."

"How will I know when I've conquered it?"

Thomas had delivered one of his signature smirks. "When it happens, you will know."

"How long did it take you?"

He had chuckled, which was rare for the centuries-old vampire. "Don't base it off of me. I didn't fight the hunger."

As THEY DROVE INTO town, Nate slowed down. Up ahead a large gathering clambered around a building.

"Mena Police Department," Niki said, reading the words on the front of the building. "That looks like a sizable crowd of unhappy people."

"I think I know why," Josh said. His tablet's screen lit his face. "Yesterday morning, an RV was found wrecked in the middle of the road a few miles ahead. The Chief of Police, Roy Henderson, is still claiming it's a bear attack. The whole family was killed. Unconfirmed reports of claw marks through the walls of the RV."

"Claw marks in the RV?" Mike asked. "People are believing the bear attack story?"

"Love, if the people want a villain, and the authorities are offering up the bear story on a silver platter, why not take the bait?"

Their SUV passed the angry mob and continued down the road. Nate shook his head. "We're going to need to find this wolf and kill it soon. Angry mobs outside of a police station don't wait around too long for permission before they decide forgiveness is better. If they go hunting for a bear and find a werewolf, there'll be a lot more death in store. It'll be a slaughter."

Nate pulled the dark SUV into the small parking lot. They'd referred to the Mena Regional Hospital as a hospital, but calling it that was certainly a stretch. The parking lot only had a handful of spots in the front. It was barely a two-story building. Not at all what he usually thought of as a hospital. This wasn't multiple multi-story towers.

Once Nate had safely parked them, Mike asked, "Josh, has Austin secured a spot for us to stay?"

"Yes. Small hotel down the road. Technically the other side of town, but you can throw a rock from one side and hit the other, so it isn't that far."

Mike smiled. He knew the type of town. Texas was filled with them. He wasn't at all surprised that Arkansas also had its fair share, possibly more.

"Great. Nate, take Josh there so he can get set up. Niki, you and I will have a conversation with Mr. Hall. Can I trust you to behave yourself while we're in there?"

"Yes, love. I'll leave my silver in the car."

At least that gave Michael some sense of relief. If she kept the lasso with her, he wasn't sure she could be trusted not to do something erratic. He'd seen her reaction every time a werewolf had been mentioned. The last thing he wanted was her to potentially have a way to "accidentally" kill David.

He didn't blame her for hating them. He still reserved that same brand of hatred for Silas. Hell, he probably would still have that same animosity for all vampires if it wasn't for Thomas, for his control, and for him mentoring Mike through his own struggles, teaching him that same control.

Ripping Silas's heart out of his chest was just an added bonus.

From the little he had gleaned, Niki Davis and Nathan Edwards never received the same closure by killing the werewolf that had killed their son. They had transferred that resentment onto every other werewolf instead. Every single one was an avatar for the one that got away. Neither Nate nor Niki needed to tell Mike that. Their pain and resentment were obvious.

"Thank you." He opened his door as Niki opened hers in unison.

Niki hopped out first and leaned back into the car.

"Nathan," she said sternly, "you take care of our Josh. You hear me, love? Do all the heavy lifting."

While talking, she removed the silver belt that doubled as her whip and placed it on the seat. She also reached into her boot, pulled out a long knife and dropped it next to the belt.

"More importantly, take care of these."

"Will do, and thanks, Niki," Josh said from the back seat. "We'll be fine, and of course, I'll make Nate do the heavy lifting. Have you seen his muscles?" Josh waved his hand in front of his face, feigning that he was turned on.

"Of course I have. And those muscles are all mine," she playfully threatened.

"I'm right here," Nate said. Mike sensed the increased blood flow to his cheeks. Although Nate didn't show it, Mike knew he was blushing.

Niki blew Nate a kiss and leaned out of the car.

Mike shook his head at the banter between the two of them and stepped a foot out of the SUV. As he did, Josh grabbed his arm. Mike turned his head.

"Be careful," Josh said.

Mike raised his eyebrows. A confused look spread over his face.

"Thomas avoids hospitals. The air is thick with blood. Whether from those with injuries, the blood supply they keep on hand, medical waste, or even the smallest needle prick from an IV, it's everywhere. We know you're strong. Thomas brags about you. Remember that when all of your instincts want you to feed."

Josh verbalized Mike's worry about the hospital and about himself. He probably did it better than he could have.

Mike dropped his eyes and nodded.

"Thanks, Josh," he said.

Josh let go of his arm. Mike slid out of the SUV and closed the door behind him. After throwing the top of the gray hoodie over his head, he shoved his hands into the front pouch and strolled to the sidewalk alongside Niki. The red of the long sleeve shirt she wore over her jeans complimented her. The black leather jacket only enhanced the look of a hunter. Her long, brown hair was braided down her back. Mike knew one of these days, she'd figure a way to attach a blade to it and use it as a weapon as well. If anyone could, it'd be her.

Nate backed the SUV out of the parking spot and drove down the road.

"Shall we?" Mike asked and motioned his arm toward the front doors.

"No time like the present, love."

She turned so quickly her braided hair whipped around, almost hitting Mike in the face. The pair marched up the sidewalk to the sliding glass doors, inviting them into the small hospital.

The moment the doors slid open, Michael's senses were flooded by the presence of blood. He twisted his head and squeezed his eyes tight, recoiling from the sensory overload. His fangs dug into his lips. Even with his eyes closed, he knew they blazed red. The smell radiated from and through the building. Waves of it hit him like standing in the surf next to a beach. He felt the pulses crash into him.

"I'd say breathe through it, but I'm guessing that wouldn't help. Try to stay focused and think of something else."

Her hand wrapped around his arm, and she gently nudged him forward. Without her help, he doubted he could have pushed through. Josh had warned him. As it was, they'd only drawn close enough to the door to set the sensor off before he started struggling. As she eased him over the threshold, he willed himself along.

I have the strength to do this.

He repeated that over and over in his head.

At one point, it reminded him of He-Man yelling "I have the power!" The thought was a good distraction and brought a smile to his face.

Breathing through his mouth helped... At least helped some. He stopped smelling the blood lingering in the air. Instead, he tasted it with each breath — which wasn't any better.

The lobby looked like that of every other clinic he'd ever set foot in. Chairs were lined up in rows. Some back to back. Others had their backs against the walls.

A few pieces of artwork hung high enough to be above the head of a person sitting down. It was just enough color to break up the bland eggshell-colored walls. All of the chairs were empty. Only a large wooden door broke up the monotony of the room.

The receptionist counter was directly ahead, and Niki marched straight up to it. A portly black woman sat on the other side of the desk. The faint glow of her monitor highlighted her face. Mike picked up Solitaire in the reflection of her glasses. Must be a slow morning.

"Good morning," Niki said. "David Hall's room number please."

"Friend or relative?" the lady asked. Her eyes never left the screen, and her voice screamed completely disinterested. Niki could've said she was a circus monkey trained to give massages and this lady was going to let them in.

"Friend," Niki answered with a smile. Although he doubted Niki realized it, none of her charm would work on the lady behind the counter or was necessary.

"Room 110. Straight down the hall on your right. No more than two guests at a time," she said, her eyes still glued to her riveting game of Solitaire.

Mike wondered what move perplexed her so much, but as she hit the button to open the wooden door, he didn't care.

"Thanks, love," Niki said.

The lady gave a slight grunt of acknowledgment.

21

ONCE THEY WALKED THROUGH the security door and into the main area, fresh panic swept over Mike. The smell of blood was so prevalent in the hospital air, he didn't know how he'd survive it. His breathing increased. He felt his heart beating; that wasn't possible. He feared bloodlust would take over if he didn't divert his attention. He needed a distraction like never before.

The hallway seemed to stretch on and on. A handful of rooms sat to his right. On his left, the wall opened up to the nurse's station. A few nurses were on duty. Two of them sat in the chairs staring at a computer screen, their elbows pressed into the counter, and their hands held their heads up. Another two nurses each worked on a cart, prepping it for the day's patient visits.

Mike searched the hallway for something else. From the smell's intensity, he could see waves permeating the air.

This is nuts, he thought. *I'm turning into a fucking cartoon character and about to just float in the air straight to an unsuspecting victim. Control yourself, Mike. Brit, any help would be nice.*

Her voice remained silent as it had for a while. She'd been increasingly quieter with each passing day. Ever since he'd defeated Silas, she'd given him counsel less and less.

Hidden just behind the smell of blood, though, he picked up something else. His head perked up.

"That'd be the wolf, love."

Mike glanced at Niki. She'd been eyeing him since they stepped beyond the secured door.

"Feel him yet?"

"I couldn't tell when it came to the succubi in New Orleans," Mike countered.

"They weren't freshly turned. They'd had centuries to learn how to mask. How to hide in the shadows. In fact, they were so good at it, the Council truly believed they were dead."

The various smells they'd used to hide themselves washed over Mike. It hadn't been until he was close to them that he could sense their true smell, the rot and decay, hidden amongst the sensual aromas they'd used to camouflage themselves. Even Naomi until she couldn't stand Lilith any longer.

"David doesn't even know his true nature yet. He has no idea that he should hide himself, much less how to go about it."

Mike realized how right she was. Each step closer to the room took him closer to the source of the smell. A shiver ran up his spine. His body rippled. As he focused on the feeling, he finally placed it. It was as if two magnets of the same polarity were being brought closer together. A repulsion that shoved the two creatures apart.

At the room, Niki entered first, but Mike followed closely behind her. As Mike turned the corner, David was already sitting up in bed.

"I'm not sure who you are," David said, "but you should probably leave. I'm about to call the nurse. For some reason, I'm not feeling well." David's heart raced.

"You don't have to call the nurse. It'll pass."

Niki eased closer to the bed. Mike stayed where he was in the doorway. He knew David was feeling the same thing he did.

"How do you know it'll pass?" Beads of sweat glistened off of David's forehead and streamed down his face. "I'm pretty sure you can't just wait out a heart attack."

"You aren't having a heart attack," Niki reassured him. "Just give it a few minutes, and you'll feel better. In the meantime, we have a few questions about the attack."

David rolled his eyes. "Don't you guys talk to each other? I answered questions already."

"We aren't from any government agency," Niki said. "We're with a private group investigating the situation."

Mike shot her a surprised glance. He hadn't expected her to walk right in and tell David about the Night Crew or that he was about to turn into a werewolf. That would be quite the shock for anyone, much less someone who believed he was in the midst a heart attack. At least when he'd shared similar news in New Orleans, it was to the victim's friend and not the victim himself. He felt compelled to jump in, but he trusted Niki. This wasn't her first rodeo. She knew what she was doing.

Before she said anything else, David started rambling.

"A private group? Oh great. Did Rebecca's family hire you? Are they blaming me? Of course, they're blaming me. I blame me. She didn't want to go camping, and I talked her into it. Now she's dead, and I'm alive. From their perspective, I obviously had something to do with her death. And I didn't kill her. What do they think happened? I killed her then hired a trained bear to attack both of us? A bear I couldn't control, so it left me almost dead? Let me guess, they also think I hired the driver to run me over? Fuck! I didn't have anything to do with what happened. I loved her! Do you know they already had her funeral? Cremated her, and they're keeping her ashes. So I couldn't attend the services, and now can't even mourn at a gravesite. What do you want to know, Private Group? I'll tell whomever whatever because I don't have a fucking thing to hide."

Niki moved closer and put her hands at her side, hoping to diffuse the situation and bring David some calm.

"Mr. Hall, I'm so sorry for the confusion. We're not hired by Ms. Summers' family. You two weren't the first attacked by this bear. We're hunters, working to track the animal's location. It is obviously extremely dangerous. It's tasted human flesh, and now that's all it wants."

Niki's quick thinking impressed Mike. She hadn't said the bear was sick or rabid. If it had been either of those, David would've already heard. They'd have tested him a number of times for rabies, which he had obviously been negative for. And saying it had a taste for human flesh wasn't exactly incorrect. The werewolf was hunting for victims in the woods.

The other thing Mike noticed was how well she kept her composure. She knew David was turning into a wolf. He'd worried about how she would respond, but she'd done great so far.

"Why didn't the forest guy mention anything about that?" David asked.

"Forest guy?"

"John."

"Did John give a last name?" Niki asked.

"No, just John. He wore the Forestry Service's uniform. He was really weird."

Niki turned her head to Mike and gave him a confused look outside of David's view.

She twisted back around to David. Niki waved her hand in front of her, brushing off the conversation.

The pause had given her enough time to come up with a story. "Oh yes, John. Anyway, if you have a few minutes to tell us about the location and some of the details about the area, my partner and I will be out of your hair. But first, how are you feeling?"

Mike gazed at David, wondering how much of an aversion David felt compared to Mike's own reaction. The longer Mike stood there, the more the feeling subsided, as if their supernatural polarities figured out how to coexist.

"I'm feeling a little better. My stomach is still a little queasy, though."

David's attention went beyond Niki to Mike. After a few moments, he adjusted his gaze back to Niki.

"Your partner is quiet."

"Yes, love, he does that. He's the strong, brooding type."

"Hmmm, do you smell that?" David asked.

"Smell what?"

"I'm not really sure," David said. "Here recently, I keep smelling things that no one else smells. Right now, it smells like blood and... I don't know how to explain it. Honestly, it smells like death."

"Hospital cooking?" Niki asked and smiled.

David leaned back on his bed and laughed. "You're probably right. I was already slim. I swear they are going to turn me into nothing but skin and bones. I just want a big, thick hamburger. Or even better, a steak. Medium rare with all the drippings."

"Fill us in with the information we need, and I'll put in a good word."

David relayed the information about the campsite to Niki and Mike and answered all of Niki's follow-up questions. Once she had everything they needed, the hunters left the turning werewolf to rest. He was going to need it.

It took Henderson longer than expected to get rid of the crowd in front of the station. Since news of the RV incident had spread, the group had only increased. The other day, a dozen people crowded into the station's lobby. Today, there were at least thirty hovering outside. Troy Johnson seemed to be the de facto leader of the group. Roy wasn't sure if Troy had wanted to be the face of the mob, or if the mob had ended up using him to gain sympathy support. Whichever it was, the group of people wanting to storm the forest was becoming alarmingly large.

Only after he had reassured them there was a specialist from the US Forestry Service onsite handling the situation, did the crowd finally start to quell. As long as people avoided the woods, they'd be safe. No one had been killed in town. He had impressed on the mob the dangers of hunting in the woods, despite the experience of the hunter.

Once the majority of the group had left, Roy jumped in his truck and drove to the hospital. If Troy's grief was fueling the group, he didn't want them adding David's pain into the mix as well. He hadn't seen Rebecca's parents among them yet, but he didn't think it would be long. At their age, they wouldn't have been as apt to join in. Plus, they directed their ire more at David.

If he hadn't convinced her to go camping, she'd still be alive. That was their perspective on it. But David, on the other hand, he'd seen the creature firsthand. He had lost someone as well.

Roy somehow needed to reinforce how important it was for David to not get involved.

He pulled into the parking lot and hopped out of the truck. After slamming the door shut, he wiped his hand through the caked-on mud on the side. His truck was never this dirty. It just showed how preoccupied he'd been lately. Roy shook his head and sighed.

He turned toward the hospital's entrance and started up the sidewalk. Halfway there, the automatic doors opened. A man in a gray hoodie, his head lowered, and a slender woman strode down the sidewalk toward him. Although he didn't know everyone, he at least recognized the majority of Mena's citizens by face, if not by name. These two, though, they stood out. He knew if he'd seen them before, he would've recognized them.

As the two drew closer to him, the man lifted his head. His skin was pale, and his eyes had a red tint.

Roy recalled when he'd first acquired that phone number to a group calling themselves the Night Crew. It'd been close to thirty years ago, if not more. He had been a young police officer in Little Rock responding to a call. A missing girl, Amber, had been found wandering around in a neighborhood that young missing girls don't typically wander around in at night. Roy and his partner at the time, Terry, had slowly driven down the street. It wasn't long before they'd spotted her.

She had been dressed in the same clothes she went missing in. As soon as the lights fell, she'd turned her face. Blood had coated her mouth. But it wasn't the blood around her mouth that had chilled the young Officer Henderson... It had been the look in her eyes. He'd never seen a look as feral as hers before. The look in that child's eyes had turned his blood ice cold. The pupils were wide and wild. A vacant realm of nothing had lain inside them. Her irises had been filled with an eerie deep blood red.

Amber had spun around and smiled. Canines which shouldn't have fit in the child's mouth extended beyond her smile. Roy and Terry had found themselves in the middle of a horror movie. With the car still idling toward the girl, she'd run at the squad car and leapt onto the hood. She pawed at the glass as if confused by the invisible obstruction between her and the officers inside.

"What the hell do we do?" Roy asked.

"Fuck if I know. This wasn't in the training," Terry said. "Stop the car."

Roy pressed on the brake pedal and shifted the police car in park. He reached for the radio but had no idea what to say. Was there a police code for a blood-soaked feral child with crazy long teeth attempting to attack officers?

Terry grabbed his flashlight, opened the door, and stepped out, shining the light directly in the girl's eyes. Instead of shrinking and reflecting the light, the black void of her pupils absorbed it. They were black holes, ready to consume whatever was thrown at them.

"Amber? Your parents are worried about you." Terry had kept the light shining in her eyes. He stepped beyond the door and opened the back passenger door. "Get off the car and come with us. We'll get you help."

Hesitantly, she had straightened her arm out in Terry's direction, asking for help off the hood of the car. Terry reached forward, grasping her hands in his. Suddenly, she clamped down, clutching his hands tight, and pulled him to her. She buried her teeth into his neck, slicing through his carotid and sending arterial blood spray all over the windshield. Roy's view was obscured by a shower of thick, red blood.

Panicked, he had reached for his sidearm and opened his door. He bolted out of the car, gun drawn, and pointed it across the hood. Terry's twitching body, still spurting blood onto the windshield, lay on the hood, but the girl had disappeared.

"Fuck me," he said.

He quickly glanced behind him. He wasn't sure if he hoped she was there or not. Instead of Amber, he saw a man with long hair in a black trench coat. His eyes had that same red tint around them. Without thinking, Roy pulled the trigger, but the man grabbed Roy's arm and aimed it to the sky before Roy could fully squeeze. The shot went high.

"Officer, your firearm won't help. I suggest running. Leave the child to me."

"What are you going to do to her?" Roy asked.

"Give her peace." The man let go of Roy's arm.

Once free, Roy started to run. After only a few yards in front of the car, he stopped and turned around. He wasn't exactly sure what was going on, but he couldn't just walk away. As he turned around, Amber had sprinted from the side of the car, running directly at him. Roy had just enough time to realize what was happening before the long-haired man grabbed her by the hair, only a few feet from Roy. With a quick twist, he pulled a machete from behind his back with the other arm. Needing only one swipe, Amber's body fell to the ground, her head still tangled by her hair in his fingers.

Roy had stood dumbfounded at what he'd just seen. Had he just witnessed *The Highlander* in real life? With a shaking hand, he raised his firearm and pointed at the man.

"Officer, I have some friends you need to speak with. They'll explain what happened. For now, I need to borrow your radio." The man strode back to the police car, leaned into the driver side, and after adjusting the dial grabbed the radio. "Cole. It's Thomas. She's been disposed of. But there's a complication. Two officers responded. She attacked one. The other is standing here, shaking and confused. He'll need a debrief. Over."

That was the day Roy had learned about the real world. About teams of hunters who kill monsters. He'd seen a vampire or two since then, but where he lived werewolves were more common. The man leaving the hospital was a vampire, he was certain.

"Thomas?" Roy asked. He knew the teams changed over the years, but a vampire was still a vampire.

Both the man and the woman stopped and turned to Henderson.

"Did you say something, love?" she asked. She had an Australian accent that took Roy by surprise.

"Are you the Night Crew?"

The two stared at each other before glancing back at the police chief.

"I called you after the pack wasn't responding. My town has a problem."

"We know," she said. "How do you know about Thomas?"

Roy smiled. He knew he had the right people. "That's a long story. We've had a few run-ins over the years. I'm Roy Henderson, the police chief." He held his hand out.

"Niki Davis." She gripped his hand. "This is Mike, not Thomas. Although both do have a pale broodiness about them."

Mike held out his hand. Roy grasped it and felt the coldness within his skin. Mike was definitely a vampire.

Niki clapped Mike on the back. "This just got a little easier. With the police chief helping us out, we won't have to worry about evading local authorities."

"I'm not what you have to worry about. Although the pack hadn't been much help in this case, they're pissed you're here. In addition to that, the town is at a boiling point. The bear cover has helped, but it's also made some think they can take matters into their own hands and hunt this thing. Every time something happens, the crowd grows a little bit more. I don't know how much longer I can keep them out of the woods."

"We saw the mob as we pulled up," Mike said. "We'll start hunting tonight. Do your best to keep everyone away from the forest. We need to meet up with the rest of the team, but we'll keep you in the loop."

"Thanks," Roy said. "I'm going to speak with David. Guessing you just did?"

"You know he's going to turn." Roy wasn't sure if Niki meant it as a question or a statement.

"Yes, in less than a week."

THE UBER RIDE FROM the hospital to the hotel only took a few minutes. Once they were dropped off, Niki checked her phone. Josh had texted her the room number while they were meeting with David.

The hotel was dingy white with a red, metal roof. Pairs of steps book-ended the two-story building, and a third set split it down the middle. The complex was shaped like an L. It was picture perfect for a cheap, sleazy motel. If Mike had to guess, this would be the ideal place for hourly rate meetups. He hoped their room had been thoroughly cleaned. He shuddered to think of the smells that might be waiting for him.

Michael followed the other hunter to one of the rooms downstairs, and she knocked on the door.

"Housekeeping," Niki called out in a fake French accent.

Mike rolled his eyes and couldn't resist a smirk.

Nate opened the door and ushered them inside.

The room reeked of cigarette smoke. Mike choked on the ash-filled air. It was a stark contrast from the taste of blood that had lingered in the dry, hospital air. He guessed it could've been worse, so he considered himself lucky.

The room itself had two queen beds with matching comforters straight out of a 1980s Sears catalog. A small flat screen television perched on top of a three-drawer black dresser. More than one of the golden dresser handles had broken off. Next to it, a small silver desk held

Josh's laptop. Both of his monitors were somehow balanced on the desk. Mike feared if the air conditioner blew too hard, one or both of them would hit the tile floor.

"Mike, this is our room," Josh said. "Nate and Niki are next door."

"Was this all they had?" Mike asked, gagging on the taste of stale air.

"Only thing downstairs with a connecting room. They have an elevator but it's currently out of order."

Mike nodded understanding.

Nate clamped a large hand on Mike's shoulder. "Did you not learn the lesson from New Orleans? Jax would have set us up in the Marriott. You are zero for two now."

"Fuck off," Mike said while shrugging his shoulder, knocking Nate's hand off.

"How was the pup?" Nate asked, laughing. He joined Niki by the window.

A flimsy table with two chairs sat next to him.

"He has no idea what's happening," Niki answered. "I almost felt sorry for him. He still believes it was a bear attack. His senses are dialed up. He could feel Mike. By the time we walked into the room, he thought he was having a heart attack."

"He's very close then," Josh said. "We'll need to keep an eye on him." Josh rolled over to the desk and opened his laptop. "I can tap into the hospital's cameras and keep watch. I'll have police scanners up in a few minutes. Great thing about a small town. The security is never hard to crack."

"We also ran into the police chief. He's in the know," Niki said.

"In the know?" Nate asked.

"He's the one who called Intel. He's going to run interference as best he can with the townies. Everyone wants a new bearskin rug," Niki said with a smile.

Josh shook his head. "Are they bear hunting with silver bullets?"

"Of course, love. Isn't that what every small-town gun store keeps in stock?"

"Just saying," Josh said. "It'll be a bloodbath if they go hunting for a bear but find the wolf instead. This thing has killed. A lot. It's doing it for fun, or to torment, or both. Hopefully, the police chief can keep them safely corralled."

Mike glanced around the room. "It's still early. I'm going to stay here and hang out in the dark. Try to get some rest. We might have a long night ahead of us."

After some discussion, they decided to meet back at the hotel by sundown. From there, they would head into the forest, starting where the Hall-Summers attack happened.

Once Nate and Niki left, Josh wheeled over to the small fridge in the corner of the room, opened it, and tossed Mike a dark crimson bag. He hadn't realized how hungry he was until the bag was in the air, moments before he caught it. If he'd been alone, he'd have sunk his teeth into it and drank it straight from the bag. Instead, he resisted the urge and strode to a cup on the counter.

He removed the wrap blanketing the plastic cup, tore the top off the blood bag, and poured the thick, red liquid into the cup. He sipped it slowly, relishing the sweet, iron taste as it traversed his tongue and filled his stomach.

"How was the hospital?" Josh asked.

He typed away on his keyboard. The room was dark, but the monitors lit it up. It cascaded over Josh as his fingers danced over the keys.

"Didn't know if I'd make it. The moment the doors opened, I fanged out. It was difficult." Mike took another sip, relishing the blood coating his throat.

"You did it, though. Be a little proud of yourself."

"Thanks." Mike stepped behind Josh and leaned down next to him. He waved his finger at the workstation. "I don't think I've ever seen you work with such a small setup before."

"You haven't. I had more in New Orleans." Josh typed on a black terminal screen, inputting code. "I should be tapped into the hospital feed soon."

"You didn't bring much gear. You didn't want anything else?"

Josh craned his neck to the vampire hanging over his head over Josh's shoulder. "We really don't need anything else. This is a wolf hunt. They are about as routine as clearing a den of vampires."

THE OVERWHELMING SCENT OF oak and pine sent Michael back to his vision. They'd waited until nightfall to arrive, which only added to the similarity. The strong forest aromas combined with the moonlight streaming through the surrounding trees called to him. So much so he almost wanted to search the woods for the cabin instead of focusing on their mission. Staying on task was a challenge.

Once they arrived, the three of them stepped out of the SUV as Nate opened the trunk and passed out weaponry.

"Niki," he said and handed her a pistol. She had her silver whip at her hip instead of tied around her as a belt.

"Mike," Nate said next. "Be careful with this." He handed Mike a knife sheathed within its leather pouch.

Mike nodded his head. He knew he was just as susceptible to the effects of silver as the wolf they were hunting. It could be used against him just as easily.

"You sure you wouldn't rather have a gun?" Niki asked.

"If we get into close combat, I'd rather have the knife."

"Oh yeah, Sergeant Michael White, Special Forces. I forget." Nate said, recalling Mike's military record.

Once the knife's sheath was attached securely to his belt, he grabbed an earpiece. He thought back to one of their first missions together at the farmhouse. Thomas hadn't needed to use an earpiece. He'd heard Josh's commentary from everyone else's comms. Mike wondered if he had the ability to do that yet. Although, the three of them weren't going to be in the same location so it wouldn't matter.

"Josh, are you there?" Mike asked.

"I hear you, Mike," Josh replied. "Nate? Niki?"

Both affirmed they heard him.

"Alright, Night Crew..." Mike announced. "We ready for a wolf hunt?"

"After what that bitch Lilith put me through," Niki started, "you bet. I have some pent-up aggression that I need to let out."

"The campsite where David was attacked should be about a hundred yards from you guys. It may still have crime tape around it."

"Thanks, Josh," Mike said. "We'll set up in a triangle perimeter, scouting the area. Josh, assuming you see us on your monitor, guide each of us to the spot we identified. It should give us a good vantage point should the wolf return. This is as good a place as any to start the search. If it doesn't pan out, Josh has identified a few other good locations. He can get us there as well."

"Sounds like a plan," Nate said. "We knew you had that take charge planner in you. That's why we elected you team lead."

Mike shook his head. "No, it's not. It's so one day you can retire from this."

"Ah, love, you should know better. You don't retire from the Night Crew."

He wasn't sure if Niki was unsuccessfully trying to be lighthearted, or if she truly believed what she said. He hoped they'd one day find solace enough to step away. Same for Josh. As far as Mike was concerned, he was the only one now cursed with forever being a member of the Night Crew.

Armed and ready, the trio split up. Mike's earpiece was filled with the sound of their breathing and footsteps along the dirt and fallen leaves. The forest was eerily quiet. He'd expected crickets chirping or owls hooting; something that proved there was life in the forest. So far, on this night, there was only silence.

He glanced up to the sky and saw the moon peeking through the branches. It was nearly full. In a few more days, David would be a slave to its draw. There wasn't anything they could do to stop that from happening. Mike had to take care of this problem first before worrying about the other. The last thing he wanted was a rogue werewolf terrorizing this community and a freshly turned werewolf out of control.

Michael let his vampire senses take hold.

His eyes blazed red, and the forest's darkness faded away. He saw every tree and sprinted around them without hesitation. He occasionally glanced up, wondering how fast he could scale one of the tall giants.

In a flash, he arrived at his spot. He paced an area thirty yards from the tent where Rebecca Summers had met her demise and David Hall had been bitten. Police tape flapped in the light breeze surrounding the location. Although some of it had been torn, he still made out the police-made perimeter.

"At my checkpoint," Mike said. "All clear here."

"Almost at mine," Nate responded.

"Be there shortly, love. Not everyone has super sight in the dark."

Mike smiled. During the day, he had felt weighed down by the sun, but now that it was night, and he was on a hunt, he felt alive. That was the closest he could describe it. Although he had fed before they left, sitting in the dark, he sensed heartbeats not far away. A family of deer. He could leave his position and take out at least one, feasting on its blood. The hunt invigorated him. The night invigorated him. He knew why it was so easy to give in to the vampire instincts.

I am the night, he thought and had to suppress a chuckle. *I'm Batman.*

Focus, White! His drill sergeant screamed in his head.

He heard the voice as though it were right next to him again, and it snapped him back to the mission at hand. He needed to stay focused. He wasn't hunting a human but an animal. A wolf. A supernatural being. Strong, with hunter instincts of its own.

He glanced at the not quite full moon and reminded himself they only had a couple more nights. He hadn't talked to Austin yet about what to do with David. Michael felt sorry for him. It wasn't his fault he'd been bitten. Hell, David probably felt lucky, but his survival came with a curse.

Oh, how much Michael related to David.

As the night crept on and the moon hung directly overhead, he grew anxious. Just waiting in the forest, surrounded by the trees, started to wear on him. The minutes passed by with excruciating slowness. Something needed to happen.

To pass the time, Mike closed his eyes and listened to the forest sounds again. He heard the family of deer, including the soft padding of their hooves against the ground, as they found patches of grass to eat.

While he focused on them, their heart rate suddenly increased. Along with the increased heart rate, all four of them sprinted out of the woods. They were startled. Mike had hunted with his father as a kid. He knew frightened deer when he saw them. Well, in this case, felt them. With the deer spooked, Michael picked up a strange odor in the air. An extremely musty scent caught his attention. It reminded him of a wet dog. Along with the smell, vibrations traveled up his spine. They were the same vibrations he remembered from earlier when he and Niki had visited David. The feeling of two magnets repelling each other washed over him.

The werewolf was here.

25

"IT'S HERE..." MICHAEL WHISPERED.

The wind carried the musty aroma. Michael tilted his head from one side to the other, trying to track where the smell originated. He stood still, holding his breath, listening. Something brushed past a tree limb off to his right. The tingling sensation, the vibrations, shivered up his spine. Their intensity grew as the beast quietly drew closer to Michael.

Leaves rustled ahead of him.

Mike focused his attention through the dense forest. He saw every tree, every branch. The sound tracked thirty yards in front. Like tracking a target with a rifle, he shifted his eyes ahead of the noise and waited for its source to cross. As he stared into the trees and bushes, he finally caught movement.

The beast was bent over, traveling on all fours. It bounded silently through the forest. The werewolf's fur was dark and blended with the night. It had a wolf's snout and large pointed ears. The werewolf easily stood six feet tall.

It might have been bigger, but its posture made it difficult to tell.

This was Mike's first in-person werewolf. The only other time he'd seen one had been in Niki's mind while rescuing her from a succubus. That one had been sick and emaciated. This beast was not that. Its arms were thick and meaty, as were its thighs. Every muscle fiber rippled with each step. This beast was well fed and strong. Mike hoped he would be able to put up a fight.

He slipped his hand to his belt and slid the silver blade from its sheath. With the knife clutched in his hands, he ran for the werewolf.

The moment he did, the creature turned its head, staring directly at Mike. It had black eyes with yellow irises. The werewolf stood up on its hind legs and roared, and then it hit its chest with both hands, like King Kong ready for a fight.

Mike collided with the werewolf. His shoulder slammed into the wolf's chest. As the two met, the beast fell to the ground, landing on its back. The moment it hit the ground, it planted its feet into Mike's stomach and launched him through the air. Not expecting that, Mike nearly lost his grip on the knife as he slid to a stop. The vampire leapt to his feet, brushed dead leaves from his face, and shifted into a fighting stance. With all the years of military training, the position felt familiar. Adding in his new vampire agility, he was ready for this fight.

The moonlight glistened off the silver blade. It shined in the black of the wolf's eyes. Realizing what the knife was, the beast growled at him, then turned and ran. It started on just two feet, before dropping to the ground and using its arms to propel itself forward as well.

Mike followed its movement and sprinted in pursuit.

"I'm tracking it. Damn, the thing is fast!" he shouted.

"I've got your location," Josh said. "How far in front of you is it?"

Mike moved to the left, passing the campsite where Rebecca had been slaughtered, keeping the wolf in his sight.

"He's twenty yards away heading west."

As fast as the vampire ran, the wolf somehow still gained ground. Michael dodged tree after tree. Everything flew past in a blur. He thought back to his days in basic. If he could've run like this in training, his whole unit would've hated him. The drill sergeant liked to make everyone keep up with the fastest person. If anyone puked, they did pushups, then had to catch up with the pack. If only he'd had this stamina then.

"West?" Josh hollered. "Niki, it's heading straight for you."

Mike realized it at the same time as Josh had said it.

He glanced away from the wolf and found Niki. Her flashlight danced across the forest, searching for them.

"Coming up fast, at your two," Mike shouted.

Niki spun as the wolf was ten yards from her. Her light landed on its face. At the same time, her whip recoiled back and sprung forward, catching the wolf in the upper part of its right arm just beneath its shoulder. It yelped in pain, stopped in front of Niki, and released a deep, guttural roar, vibrating the leaves.

The silver whip had torn through its fur. Michael smelled blood as it dripped down the beast's arm.

With her other hand, she drew the pistol and fired.

Unfortunately, the wolf moved a split second before the bullet could impact its intended target. It sprang into the air, claws sinking deep into the oak's bark. Halfway up, it clung there, nails buried like hooked iron, before hurling itself toward the next tree. Its claws punched into the hardwood, and then it launched back again, ricocheting between trunks, climbing higher and higher into the dark tangle of foliage.

Michael had never seen something scale a tree so fast. He had no idea a wolf could do something like that.

Once the creature reached the canopy, suspended nearly forty feet above them, it sprang, slamming into the next tree with a bone-rattling crack. Its claws carved deep trenches through the bark before it caught itself, hanging for a heartbeat like a monstrous spider. Then, with one hand hooked into the trunk and both hind legs braced, it hurled itself onward.

The next tree bowed under the impact, swaying wildly. When it rocked forward, the beast rode the momentum, launching again and clearing several trees in a single, terrifying glide. As its arc began to falter, it clawed at whatever branches it could reach, shattering limbs and tearing long grooves across the treetops. Each tree shuddered under the wolf's massive weight, and each sway became fuel, another violent swing pushing it deeper into the forest's dark heights.

"I can track it," Mike said confidently.

As Mike started to launch himself onto a tree branch, Nate hollered, "Mike, don't!"

The vampire skidded to a stop and rushed back to Niki as Nate made it to her as well.

"Why am I stopping?" Mike asked. After the chase, he expected to be out of breath, but instead, he felt as if he'd only just warmed up. "I could've stopped it."

"Did you see what that thing did?" Nate asked, winded from his sprint. "Holy shit, Josh, you should've seen what this thing just fucking did!"

Mike pointed. "Are you referring to the trees? Yes, it was a nice trick."

"I've never seen a wolf do that before," Nate continued. "Anything that can do that is fucking powerful. As a fledgling, it would've torn you apart."

"I was able to tackle it, but it kicked me off." Mike brushed the remaining leaves off his clothes.

"You're one lucky son of a bitch. That wasn't a new wolf. It's been around for a while."

"That's not our only problem, love," Niki said. She coiled her whip and held it in front of them, shining her flashlight on it.

Mike and Nate both saw the issue before she said something, but for Josh's sake, she had to continue.

"David said it was a black bear, covered in black fur." She pulled the piece of skin and fur from her whip. "Based on the fur and what I saw up close and personal, that powerful fucker was brown. We've got more than one wolf out here."

"I'll update Intel," Josh said. "Get back to the hotel. We might need to change tactics."

"Change tactics?" Mike asked.

"Instead of hunting a werewolf at night," Nate said, "we search for their den. It'll be easier to find during the day, and then we can wait there. Ambush them when they show up for a snack."

"We'll also need to update the Police Chief. If he doesn't know there is more than one, he needs to."

26

IT WASN'T OFTEN WHEN Mike actually fell asleep into deep slumber, but after returning from the wolf hunt, Mike laid his head on the queen bed, closed his eyes, and slept.

He wasn't certain if his body felt drained from the sprint through the woods after the wolf or from staying on guard in his predatory state all evening waiting. Whatever the cause, he slipped into a deep sleep within seconds.

Somewhere in the dark, wolves howled. Michael found himself in a dense forest again. This wasn't a true dream, though, more like his UltraNet. His steel vault, where all his memories were stored thanks to his highly superior autobiographical memory, replayed the vision.

He was among the same trees, the same position of the moon peeking through the dense foliage, and the same eerie silence.

Images flashed within his head. A stream flowed across the forest. He leapt over it, landing on a patch of soggy soil and moist, rotting leaves. Wherever he was, this forest was dying. Leaves blanketed the ground. He focused on one of the oaks and saw bugs burrowing in the bark. In fact, every tree had the same infestation.

Death overwhelmed the area.

Mike no longer smelled the musky, earthy aroma but rotten wood, mold, and decay.

Another image flashed. Baying hounds came along with it. They weren't far off, drawing closer it seemed. The image of Valerie's face stared back at him.

She was the first member of the Council he'd ever laid eyes on. Back when he and Thomas had killed Silas, something else had transpired. The Council, the group holding together the agreement between creatures and humans, the Accords, had disappeared without a trace. Some members of the Council had supported Silas's desire to usurp the Accords and become dominant over the humans.

Those members, corrupted by Silas's manipulative nature, preferred to plunge the world back into a dark age where humans feared for their existence; the way the world was before the rise of Charlemagne, the Council, and the Accords. The way the world was before the first Night Crew teams existed.

Valerie's red eyes stared at Mike. They seemed to permeate through the outer facade, the body that was not his own. Those eyes saw him, the passenger, inside the host.

He wanted to reach into the pit where she was being kept prisoner and pull her and Jax to safety.

The wolves howled once more, singing their cries to the moon, the glowing orb beckoning their calls.

"Michael," Valerie spoke, but her lips didn't move. She spoke into his mind. "I see you. You are known to the Council, young fledgling."

Michael shifted his head away from the pit. The wolves drew closer; their cries grew louder.

"Michael, we are waiting for you," she said. Her voice reminded him of Lilith's, calming and intoxicating.

A voice that spurred him to take action.

"The warlock can unlock the secret."

The warlock? Michael thought. He tried to vocalize his question but nothing came out. Then he remembered the warlock Austin had said they were sending. Xavier Morcos. The rockstar warlock who could assist him with the vision.

A strange sensation trembled through Mike's entire body. When he first realized he was in this forest once more, he'd assumed his UltraNet was just replaying the events of the vision. Now, though, it occurred to him that Valerie had never spoken to him. So, how would he be remembering her voice now?

Mike kicked his legs and his eyes shot open. He sat upright in the bed, trying to process. Josh sat at the computer desk across the room, typing. The glow of the monitors lit his face.

Michael used both hands and placed one on his face and the other on his chest, confirming that he was physically present and in control of his own body. The numbness in his fingers subsided, and the trembling throughout his body eased.

It hadn't been a dream. He'd somehow revisited the vision.

"Good afternoon, sleepy head," Josh said. He never broke his concentration on the monitor.

"What time is it?" Michael couldn't quite believe he'd been asleep. It wasn't something that lately he'd done often.

"Almost fourteen hundred. You were tossing a lot. Said Valerie's name a few times. Reliving your vision?"

"Something like that."

Mike slid his legs to the side of the bed and stood up. That feeling of needing to reconnect with his body, his muscles, his nervous system, flooded him. After a few moments, he marched to the fridge, pulled out a blood bag, and began drinking. The blood rejuvenated him, easing the transition back to this present reality.

"Nate and Niki woke up about an hour ago so you aren't too far behind. I've mapped out the area with points of interest and sent the maps to your devices. As you three are looking for the den, it should give you a good zone."

"Thanks, Josh. It's a big forest so that'll be helpful. While we're out, what are your plans?"

"I'm going to check in with the police chief after I give Mr. Hall a visit. Curious how he's doing."

Mike nodded. "I thought you tapped into the cameras."

"I did, but there aren't many angles, and he hasn't left his room. Also, his charts aren't online yet. His doctor keeps analog records on all of his current patients."

"Ah, analog. The bane of everyone like you. How do you expect to get the info from the doctor?"

Josh smiled. "What's that saying from your neck of the woods? This ain't my first rodeo."

27

Spring in Ouachita National Forest wasn't like springtime Mike knew when growing up in Texas. There, by the time spring officially started, the afternoons approached the eighties if not higher. Here, the forest ground was moist and soggy. Not enough sunlight broke through the tree cover to burn off the previous night's dew. Each time Michael took a step, the ground sunk beneath his shoes, giving the impression of walking on a sponge.

The trio had spread out across the forest. They'd each been given dots on a map that strategically positioned them between the latest kills outside of Mena. The points weren't close together, so the members were a few clicks from each other. They stayed in contact through the comms in their ears. After last night's werewolf encounter, and the new knowledge there was more than one in the area, Mike would've preferred if they'd stayed closer together. The way the wolf had scaled the trees and then flung himself across the forest was superpowers nonsense, not real life. He knew trying to search the large forest as one team would've been time-consuming, but deep down, he felt the protection would've been worth it.

Mike had on his gray hoodie but left the hood dangling against his back. His arms hung loosely by his side instead of tucking them into the front pocket. No one was around for him to feel self-conscious, and not enough sunlight broke through for it to weigh him down. Yet, he kept the hoodie on in case either of those things changed. It was starting to become his protective blanket. He had assumed Thomas felt the same way based on the fact he never saw his mentor without his black leather trench coat.

"How will I know if I find the den?" Mike asked. He stopped plodding along in what he felt was nothing more than a bunch of circles.

"You'll know it when you see it," Nate answered. "Think of a dog pound or kennel, and then amplify that."

"One werewolf wouldn't have a den? Only multiple?"

"It has to do with the wolf's nature, love. One rogue werewolf tends to kill and move on. It'll seek out the easy targets such as a couple sleeping in a tent or a hiker, fill its stomach, and then turn back into a human. But when there are more than one, they start to develop a pack mentality. They drag the kills back to their den and like to stick around in a feeding area. Why leave when your food source is abundant?"

Mike strode to a tree and flopped his back against it. He stared up at the dense foliage high above him.

"All creatures focus on food, don't they? Vampires, werewolves, zombies if those exist. Everything just wants to eat."

"Don't get yourself down, Mike," Nate said. "Creature or human, everything has to eat. I only go a few hours before my stomach is growling."

"All those big muscles require sustenance, love," Niki chimed in.

"That's the whole reason for the Accords. Make sure nothing eats too much."

Mike said, "And without the Council dictating the rules to the various clans, everything falls apart."

"Exactly! Thomas, Jax, and company are searching for the Council, and we make sure those things that go bump in the night don't eat too much in the meantime."

Mike nodded. He'd heard the spiel on what their purpose was more than a few times now, and today's mission for saving the world was stopping two werewolves from terrorizing Ouachita National Forest.

"Niki! Mike! I found something. Get over here."

Mike bounced his back off the tree and grabbed his phone. He pulled up the segmented map Josh had made for them.

"What sector are you in?"

"Five," Nate answered. "About two hundred yards due east from where that kid Tanner was killed."

Based on the map and Nate's information, he estimated the distance between them.

"Niki, how far out from that position are you? I'm five klicks away."

"Half that," she replied.

"Nate, hold. We'll be there shortly."

Before Nate responded, Mike made note of his current location in relation to Nate's. He oriented himself to ensure he wouldn't sprint in the wrong direction. His military experience had taught him how to navigate a wooded environment, and he tapped into that training like it happened yesterday.

He swiftly navigated the forest, running at a good pace. He wasn't moving nearly as fast as when he'd chased after the werewolf, but he was still moving faster than normal.

He maneuvered around the trees, dodging them by only inches. Once, he stopped to make sure he hadn't veered off course. Just over three miles was a long way to run in an unfamiliar environment. Similar to how he didn't trust himself around blood, he didn't yet fully trust his senses to lead him in one direction the entire way.

Mike made the journey over the rugged landscape in just over ten minutes. He could get used to vampire speed. As he approached Nate's area, he slowed.

"Nate!" he shouted.

He popped the comms out of his ear. No reason to hear Nate through it. He needed to hear him in the open.

"Over here."

Mike swiveled his head. Nate stood on the other side of a tree twenty yards away. He wore a black T-shirt and jacket over dark jeans. If it wasn't for Mike's supernatural vision, Nate would've been nearly impossible to spot. Although the sun hadn't started to set yet, the forest did a good job blocking out the light. Anyhow, what little light did permeate through cast shadows among the trees. Nate blended in perfectly.

Mike jogged over to his teammate.

"What do you have?"

"Take a look at this," Nate said, and motioned his arm behind him for Mike to get a better look.

Behind Nate, the terrain inclined. Staring up, Mike estimated from the base of the hill to the top was thirty feet. Nate walked the base of the hill, circling it, and Mike followed. A third of the way around, Nate started up the hill and stopped after ten feet. Broken tree limbs and bushes littered the ground. Mike raised his leg to head up the hill, but Nate shot his hand out and stopped him.

"Stay there. Tell me what you see."

Mike shrugged his shoulders. "Broken tree limbs. A few bushes."

"What else?"

He took a deep breath. Now wasn't the time to play guessing games. "I just ran a 5K, and it'll start to get dark soon. What am I looking for?"

Nate bent down, grabbed one of the leaf-covered branches, and pulled it off the ground. As he did, Mike realized what Nate had seen. The opening of a dark tunnel started to reveal itself. With just that one branch shifted, the camouflage vanished. The tunnel was a small cave in the side of the hill. The layers of branches draped the ground, covering the entrance with various bushes and leaves adding to the disguise.

Quickly, Mike joined in. He grabbed a branch and pulled it away. The mouth of the cave widened. Before Nate had tugged on the branch, the side of the hill had looked complete. A large patch of brush and a pile of branches would keep anyone from walking over it. As Nate and Mike removed the branches, the darkened void of the cave appeared.

With each subsequent branch removed, the cave's entrance grew wider. By the time the two men finished, the mouth of the cave opened up eight feet tall and four feet wide.

With the brush removed, a strong scent emanated from the dark hole. They weren't lying about the resemblance to a pound. It smelled musky but also held the unmistakable smell of rot and decay. Mike lowered his head and pulled the front of his hoodie up at the same time, burying his nose underneath it. The air was thick with the stench, and he coughed, trying as best he could to not taste it but failing miserably. His eyes watered, something he didn't know was even possible. Using the sleeve of his jacket, he wiped his eyes and saw red stains. His tears were blood.

"That's bad," he said. His voice was muffled inside his clothing.

"What did you find?" Niki asked, jogging up and out of breath.

The stench had overpowered Mike so much, he hadn't heard Niki approach.

"Ah, holy fuck, that smell is terrible," she said, still gasping for air. "That's definitely the den. Nathan, did you use your nose to find it?"

Niki shot her hand to her face, pinching her nose closed. She turned away from the cave entrance while trying to catch her breath after her run. Her long, braided hair swung in an arc as she spun. Except for her brown hiking boots, she also wore all black.

"Stepped in the wrong spot coming down the hill and nearly fell in."

Nate marched over to Niki. He grabbed a flashlight from his belt and clicked it on. A beam of light extended from his hand and raced to the hill.

Niki pulled her flashlight from her belt and ignited it as well.

Mike turned to the cave. In another two hours, the sun would drop below the horizon. Once the night fell, the forest would hold its own darkness. One that would assuredly be visiting its den for a late-night snack.

He glanced back to Nate and Niki. "Let's see if anyone is home."

28

As Mike, Nate, and Niki explored the forest searching for the wolf den, Josh stopped his wheelchair in front of the Mena Regional Hospital. Instead of bothering with an Uber or public transportation, he had used the time since the trio had left to make his way from the motel on his own. Mena was a small town and easy enough to find his way around.

After his helplessness in the face of Silas and the succubi, he'd taken every opportunity he could to strengthen himself. He'd kept his body in shape, routinely fitting in over an hour a day of vigorous workouts. His arms, shoulders, and chest had taken on a lot of definition. He had no idea how many times he would need to crawl into a ceiling, but he knew he needed to be in good physical condition, just in case.

His actual preference was to be strong enough to help when needed. Intel had continuously warned of trouble on the horizon as more and more vampires acted against the Accords. Creatures like Lilith, werewolves like the ones here, and other incidents all over the world were becoming more common. Joshua Campbell wasn't going to allow others to fight this battle for him.

The stroll from the hotel to the hospital didn't take him nearly as long as he'd initially thought. All the exercising he'd done helped his speed and stamina. The weather was cool but not cold. It was what you would normally call a beautiful spring afternoon. This was perfect workout weather.

He hadn't grown up in the south, but he had heard horror stories about what the weather was going to turn into as the summer approached. In another month, the temperature at their headquarters in Texas would consistently hit over ninety. It wouldn't be long after that when triple digits would be the norm. Josh wasn't looking forward to those days.

He'd pondered asking Intel if they could move their station. Certainly he could come up with a reason why they needed a winter headquarters in Texas and a summer headquarters in Michigan. The thought brought a smile to his face.

Prior to the final showdown with Silas, the Night Crew hadn't stayed in one place longer than a month. The rogue Alpha had kept them moving almost non-stop. Dozens of places over the past few years had been called home as the vampire had escalated his plan. A plan no one realized he was enacting until it was too late. From what Josh had gathered from Intel, the plan had two parts. Silas had worked on one half of the plan; someone as yet unknown had been responsible for the other. Intel, Jax, and others in the organization hadn't figured out who the accomplice was yet, but he or she killed or kidnapped members of the Council while Silas had built his army of vampires. With no Council, Silas's army would stage a coup and institute him as ruler.

The Council had been a formidable unit. It was composed of the oldest and strongest of all the clans. Whoever was responsible for that part of the plan had to be extremely powerful in their own right.

Josh let his mind wander while enjoying the spring air and laid-back atmosphere of Mena. He reminded himself they had a mission, and that mission wasn't figuring out what happened to the Council or what anybody's plan was now that Silas had been killed. Was there a new plan? Was the secret partner flying by the seat of their pants now? He loved solving puzzles, and this one intrigued him. He wished Intel would tap him for that team, but he also knew how much he was needed on this one. A four-person team wasn't big enough for what they needed to do. Without Naomi's help in New Orleans, it would've been their demise.

As much as he had tried to convince her to stay and join the team, Naomi's only desire was to revisit her homeland. She had talked about coming back one day, but she'd already lived for hundreds of years. One day for her could be in a month or could be in twenty years.

He forced himself out of his head and onto his destination. After crossing at a light, Josh saw the hospital directly ahead. He spun the wheels of his wheelchair a few times in quick succession, speeding him down the sidewalk.

A small truck passed on his left and pulled up in a parking space in front of the hospital. The truck was a forest green color.

On the side, the words "U.S. National Forest Service" were printed. The driver opened the door, stepped out, and strode to the sidewalk just as Josh made it in front of the building. The driver was a Native American dressed in a gray uniform shirt and green pants. He looked as Josh would've thought someone working for the forestry service would look straight down to the hiking boots.

The man stared at the hospital entrance and then turned to Josh.

"Good afternoon," he said. "Or is it evening yet?"

Josh glanced at his watch. It was four in the afternoon. "I believe we can still call it afternoon."

Before Josh could shift his direction from the sidewalk next to the road and turn up the wider walkway leading to the entrance, the man pointed at Josh and continued. "Quite admirable."

"What's that?" Josh asked.

"I've lived in the area all of my life and recognize most everyone in town. I don't recognize you which means you're staying at the motel. A ride share would've dropped you off in front of the hospital and not on the main road. You made the journey on your own. That's quite admirable."

Josh curled his forehead. He'd run into people before who weren't sure how to react around him being in a wheelchair, but this was especially unusual. He wondered if it was a cultural difference. He decided to opt for his usual pleasantries.

"Thank you. I've made it a goal to not let the chair get in the way of being in shape. We all have the ability to rise above our adversity."

He slowly angled his chair so that he was pointed toward the front door.

"My name is John Kohana," the man said and held out his hand.

Josh twisted his chair to John and shook John's hand.

"Josh Campbell. Pleasure to meet you. If I had to guess, you work for the forestry service?" Josh pointed to the truck and then at John's attire.

"That's correct. I grew up in Ouachita. As I got older, working the forest, protecting it, seemed like the only thing that made sense. Been a ranger for almost thirty years now."

"Wow, thirty years. That's quite a long time." Josh's interest was piqued. Thirty years of experience in the forest might come in handy. "You must know Ouachita very well, then. All the best camp sites, hiking trails, forest secrets."

John nodded. "You could say that."

"I heard rumors of animal attacks recently. Chief of Police was quoted as saying a wild bear killed a few people. Heard there was a woman who was camping with her boyfriend, and that he's here in the hospital. Is that something that's happened before here? Or, let me rephrase. How often does something like that happen around here?"

Kohana stared at Josh inquisitively. Josh could tell John was trying to figure out why Josh was asking. Finally, he said what Josh assumed he was thinking.

"Are you a reporter? National Inquirer type looking for some story?"

"You got me," Josh said. "I'm not with the National Inquirer, though. I do freelance reporting and try to sell the story to whichever supermarket rag will buy it." Josh grabbed his phone, opened up a notes app, and acted like he was about to start typing. "So, Ranger Kohana, do you mind if I ask you a few questions? Is it true Bigfoot is lurking in the forest?"

John rolled his eyes. He glared down at Josh and shook his head. "Bigfoot, huh? Is that the theory?" His tone changed, laden with condescension.

Josh plastered the cheesiest, fakest smile he could across his face. "Bigfoot sells papers. At least, so I've heard. Do you have another theory?"

"I believe the official account is a black bear."

"Unless it's hopped up on cocaine, that's not as salacious of a story."

"No, I guess it isn't," John said. "Well, I'm going to check on Mr. Hall. Am I to assume you're here to also speak with him? Convince him that Bigfoot killed his girlfriend and mauled him?"

Josh ignored the ranger's questions, opting to ask his own. "Is it customary for the Forest Service to make hospital visits? That wasn't something I was aware of."

The more Josh spoke with Kohana, the more he realized they were both hiding something. Josh knew he was lying about his own intentions and reason for his visit, but something about John didn't sit right with him. It could be that cultural difference, and John was protecting the forest from an onslaught of reporters and tourists, but a deep feeling in Josh's gut had him doubting that was everything.

"We are a small community. When a tragedy like this one hits our town, we all feel it. I learned growing up that we must take care of our own." John gazed at the hospital entrance again, but his eyes also drifted toward the sky.

"I've heard similar statements from those that grew up on a reservation." Josh placed his hands on the wheels of his chair and rolled forward and backward as he spoke. "If you don't mind me asking, what tribe are you from?"

"Caddo. Although Ouachita is a forest and not a reservation, the tribe stays tight and grounded to the area. The name Ouachita comes from a Washita Indian word meaning good hunting ground."

"Good hunting ground? That's interesting given what's happened, wouldn't you say?"

"Mr. Campbell, I think our conversation is done." He shifted his body, facing the entrance to the hospital. As he did, he raised his left arm across his body and scratched at a large scrape the width of his right arm just below his shoulder. "I can't stop you from speaking with Mr. Hall, but be mindful of what he's been through."

John took a few steps forward.

"That's a nasty cut on your arm," Josh said, spinning his wheelchair to face the hospital as well.

Kohana stood a dozen feet in front of him and paused. He twisted his neck instead of turning around and spoke over his shoulder. "Tree limb. Hazards of the job."

He started toward the entrance again, this time faster.

Josh decided to keep his distance and slowly pushed his wheelchair. "It doesn't look good," Josh hollered, ensuring a good deal of space between the two of them. "Might want to speak with someone and get it looked at."

The park ranger ignored him and strode into the building.

29

Nate and Niki shined their flashlights into the mouth of the cave as they poked their heads in.

"How far back does it go?" Mike asked. He hovered a few feet behind Nate. He'd reached inside his hoodie and pulled his shirt up over his nose, hoping it would dampen at least a portion of the smell. Unfortunately, it didn't.

"Maybe only thirty or forty feet. It's not very deep," Niki said. She glanced over to Nate. "No time like the present."

"Guess not," he affirmed.

With Nate on the left and Niki on the right, the two entered the mouth of the cave. If not for their flashlights, the darkness would've swallowed them. Mike pulled in a large breath, exhaled, and placed his hand on the dirt embankment as he leaned into the cave.

The stench of decay weighed the air down and gave it a thickness. He didn't even want to think about the taste. Blood, bile, and human waste soaked into the floor. Although the ground was flat, the roof of the cave was in an arc. Each side tapered to the top. Mike slid his hand against the hardened dirt walls. Scratch marks scored the cave's interior. This wasn't a natural formation. They'd dug this hole for specifically this purpose. Tree and grass roots covered the walls, jutting through the earth, hanging down, ready to latch onto them if they stood too close.

"This what a normal den looks like?" Mike asked.

"Sometimes," Niki answered. "There must not be a cave in the area so they dug this one."

The ground squished beneath Mike's shoes. He almost glanced down but decided against it. He didn't want to see what was underneath him. The mud wreaked of dried blood. Though the burrow wasn't very far underground, there was still a stark change in temperature. Mike felt a chill in the air, even through his hoodie.

Nate pulled a few feet ahead of Mike and Niki. He bent down next to a pile on the ground.

"Check this out," Nate said.

He reached down and picked up a clump of fabric. It was small with black and white stripes. As Nate lifted it higher, the torn straps, pieces of Velcro, and zipper hung loose. Dried blood caked to the outside of it. Claw marks gashed the fabric into shreds. Once upon a time, it had been a small hiker's backpack.

Nate angled his flashlight across the earthen floor. "There's more over there," he said.

Niki shuffled past him and stopped next to another pile. Mike shifted in between the two, eyeing the rest of the pieces. Everything he picked up and dropped was another torn garment of some sort. Shirts and jackets. Another backpack. Niki's pile was the same thing. Instead of bending down to investigate, she brushed the lump of clothing with her boots. Tacky blood stuck a pair of pants to a shirt.

"Anyone want to count how many different articles of clothing, bac kpacks..." Mike started to ask, then noticed something next to the wall. He bent down and picked it up. "...or shoes with feet still in them, are in this burrow?"

He tossed the blood-covered shoe back where he found it and wiped his fingers on his pants.

Niki moved deeper into the cave, almost to the back wall. "Oh love, I have more than shoes with feet over here. I haven't taken a headcount, but I think we've found most of the missing hikers."

Nate stood up and added his flashlight to Niki's. He and Mike joined her at the rear of the cave. Decomposing bodies, what was left of them anyhow, lay stacked in the corner. Some of the corpses were completely missing limbs. Others had exposed bones gashed with bite marks. Most of the meat had been chewed or gnawed away. The chest cavities were ripped open. Mike didn't go digging through the bodies, but based on the few he could see, all the internal organs were gone.

"They tend to eat everything but like to start with the inside stuff," Nate said, standing over the stack. He turned to Mike. "How are you handling all the blood?"

Mike shook his head. "This is easy. It's all spoiled. It smells horrible. There's nothing appetizing about this at all. It's sickening actually. Add in that the blood is mixed in with dirt, wolf piss, stomach bile, and God knows what else."

"Scat," Niki said.

"What?" Mike asked.

"You said 'God knows what else'. There's a pile of wolf shit in the corner. Pretty sure that's called scat."

Mike pursed his lips and swallowed hard, trying to convince the contents of his stomach to stay where they were. He didn't want to regurgitate his dinner and then have to stave off bloodlust in this cave with Nate and Niki. After a moment, he nodded. "Yes, animal droppings are called scat. Pretty sure I didn't need to know there was a pile of wolf shit in the corner. As if this place wasn't bad enough."

"Watch where you step then."

"Noted," he said. Mike glanced around the rest of the cave. Between the putrid air, the rotting corpses, and the low ceiling, he felt the weight of the cave crushing him. Despite the feeling, he fought through. "I'll lean on your expertise. On a typical wolf hunt, what's next?"

"What's next?" Nate repeated. "We wait. This is where they're returning. If the two werewolves are not hunting tonight, then they're coming back here to eat. They have a fair amount of sustenance built up." He pointed to the pile of bodies, some with meat still clinging to a few limbs. "The moon rises in another hour or so. Then, they'll be out here grabbing a bite to eat or looking for an easy kill. With that Henderson guy telling everyone to avoid the woods, hopefully, that will persuade them to come back here. All we have to do is stay here and wait for them to come to us."

"That's worked in the past?"

"Well," Nate said and dropped his eyes.

"Nathan? Spill it," Mike said, hoping the use of Nate's full first name would help.

"Niki and I have done it once before. Jax was the expert on wolf hunts. He talked about doing this. Remember what we said? Werewolves typically police themselves. We don't get called in for werewolf stuff very much."

Mike glanced from one side of the cave to the other and spun around. "There's only one fucking exit, you know. We have no escape route if shit goes sideways." He took a deep breath and thought through the pros and cons. "There's only one way in and out. Hiding out here, we'll have the element of surprise. I hate this plan, but fuck it."

Josh followed John Kohana into the hospital but stayed a dozen yards back. Josh could tell that the Ranger wasn't being honest with him, and he knew the tree story was bullshit. That injury was in the same spot that Niki had said her whip had hit the werewolf. If it was a normal cut, he'd have healed long before now. But Niki's whip was made of silver. It would take a lot longer for a wolf to heal from a silver injury. He was confident that Kohana was the werewolf from last night.

Without the rest of the team, Josh didn't want to create a scene. He was there to check on David. They didn't have much longer before David would turn. Josh hadn't told the rest of the team yet, but Intel hadn't given them the go ahead to kill David. Instead, Intel had told Josh he had been in contact with the local pack. They were planning to take David in, teach him, and protect him.

It did cross Josh's mind that John could be the pack representative. If that was the case, though, what was he doing out in the woods last night? Why did he attack Niki instead of work with them? Assuming John was a werewolf, Josh couldn't tell if he was friend or foe.

The automatic door slid open, and Josh went inside the lobby. As he did, John turned around and glared at Josh. The nurse behind the reception desk pressed a button, and the door swung open.

"Aaaaahhhh!" someone screamed as the door opened.

Josh, John, the nurse, and the two people in the lobby all turned. Kohana picked up his pace, nearly running down the hallway. Josh spun his wheels quickly, thrusting his chair forward and speeding right past the counter and into the hallway.

"Sir, you need to check in," the nurse tried to say as the door closed behind Josh.

"Fuck, it hurts!"

A doctor and two nurses ran into a room at the end of the hallway. Josh recognized the room number. John stood at the entrance to the room. Josh hurried down the hall and skidded his wheelchair to a stop next to the tall man.

David sat up in bed. His left leg, covered in a white plaster cast, stuck straight out in front of him. His hands gripped his thigh where the cast ended. The white of his knuckles stood out against his tan skin as his fingers pushed into his leg. There was no way he wasn't going to leave bruises.

"David, describe the pain for me," the doctor repeated as he began taking vitals.

"It's on *fire!*" David shouted. "It burns so bad. Give me some fucking pain meds or something."

The doctor looked up at the nurse and nodded his head. "We're working on it, David. You're going to have to remain still while we figure out what's causing the pain. David, can you do that?"

"I'll try," he said. Sweat covered his chest. David wore a gray muscle shirt. The sweat line descended half of the shirt. His face contorted every few seconds, fighting off the waves of excruciating pain.

"They removed his IV yesterday," Kohana said. It took a moment before Josh realized he was talking to him. "If they'd left it in, they could've just injected meds into his IV."

"Is he going to be released soon?" Josh asked.

"As fast as he's recovered, they thought he'd be released tomorrow. Guess that'll depend on what's going on with his leg."

The nurse stood next to David with a syringe.

"Hold still," the doctor ordered.

David's face shook and grimaced, but he held his arm still. With skilled precision, the nurse jabbed the needle into David's left arm and depressed the plunger. She withdrew it and stepped away. David never flinched. Josh assumed the pain in his leg overrode anything else at this point.

"It should only take a few minutes before the Toradol takes effect. Until then, just breathe through the pain."

"Easy for you to say, doc," David said. He glanced at the door and saw John and Josh standing there, watching. "You again?"

Josh shot his eyes to Kohana. The Ranger must have visited David already.

"I was in the neighborhood and wanted to check on you. I heard you were doing much better, although it doesn't sound like it right now."

"Oh, I'm just fucking peachy. Who's your friend?"

"He's a reporter writing a story on Bigfoot. I can send him away, if you'd like." John smirked and shot a sideways glance at Josh.

David rolled his eyes. His breathing had eased a little. "Yesterday I got bear hunters and today a reporter. I'm so fucking popular right now."

"Bear hunters?" Kohana asked. "What do you mean?"

"I mean bear..." he reached down to his leg and scratched just above the cast. "Oh fuck. It died away for a hot minute, but just roared back. It itches like hell, and dear God, it burns!"

The doctor placed his hand on David's forehead. "Nurse, he's burning up. Run his vitals again."

"No shit, I'm burning up. I'm in a shit ton of pain, doc!" he screamed. "My entire leg... God, it burns." David reached further down to his cast and started scratching his fingernails against it.

Josh slid past John in the doorway and drew closer to David's bed. Small plaster shavings fell next to David as he clawed at the cast.

"Get this fucking thing off!" he shouted.

David fell back onto the bed and screamed. As he did, small indentations appeared on the top of the cast. To Josh it looked as if the cast had dimples, as if goosebumps had formed. The white plaster rose up in a dozen places. David screamed again. He thrashed his arms, and his back bucked. He rose at least six inches off the bed, thrusting his chest in the air.

Josh's eyes never strayed from the cast. As he watched, a small circular indentation fell off, exposing a hole. Immediately, a metallic pin shot out of the hole. It propelled over David's right side and landed on the floor in front of Josh.

"What the hell?" the doctor exclaimed. As he did, another pin broke through the cast and hit the exterior wall. More and more pins fired out of David's leg, pulverizing the cast. Each time one left his leg, David's screaming declined, as if each one eased some pain.

"His temperature is at one-oh-three right now. Heart rate over a hundred-and-fifty."

The doctor ordered the nurse to prep a cart, afraid David was on the verge of crashing. She hurried out of the room.

A few more pins hit the bed and floor. Over a dozen small pins, some longer than others, lay on the ground or next to David. The cast on his leg barely held together before crumbling apart, leaving David's bare leg laying on top of the blanket. It was covered in plaster powder and gauze.

The nurse returned with the cart and stood frozen in the doorway. David's screaming slowed until it was nothing more than a whimper as he collapsed back onto the bed. The nurse checked his heart rate again. "Ninety and falling back into normal rhythm." David, covered in sweat and tears, lay comfortably on the bed, passed out from the pain and exertion.

"What the fuck just happened?" the doctor said.

"Are these..." Josh started to ask.

"The pins holding his leg together? Yes," he answered before Josh could finish the question.

Josh reached up to the bed and brushed the remains of the cast onto the floor. Those remaining in the room stared at David Hall's formerly cast leg. Aside from the plaster dust still clinging to it, the leg appeared perfectly normal. There was no sign of surgery. No abrasions from the wreck. No bruising. And most surprisingly, no indication that the leg had just shot out all the pins.

"X-Rays!" the doctor said. "Now!"

MIKE STARED UP AT the evening sky as the first stars appeared. The claustrophobic atmosphere of the den had weighed too heavily. He needed a breath of fresh air. He shuffled his feet, rubbing his shoes into the dirt and leaves. All they could do was wait and hope one of the werewolves stopped in for a snack. Nate was certain at least one of them would.

He sucked in a long breath of cool night air. The forest smelled much better than the stench of the den. Still, it was nowhere near the wonderful taste of blood in the air. Mike wished he had brought something to sip on. He licked his lips wishing there was something to savor.

Michael strolled to a tall oak and leaned his back against it. From what the others had told him, waiting was part of the game. Not every hunt was in a nightclub or crawling through the ceiling of an abandoned school. Sometimes, the monsters had to come to you. Mike hated it. He'd always struggled with patience. Patience and waiting meant his mind had time to wander. That usually meant his Ultranet would kick in, and he'd relive some memory that he really wanted to forget. Rarely had boredom ever conjured happy memories.

Feeling the rough bark against his spine, Mike closed his eyes. As he did, his mind drifted off, pulling up memories of his latest vision. The open field with the rotting log cabin unfolded in front of him.

The moonlight glistened off the dew coating the tall grass. Despite the distance, Valerie's voice echoed in his head.

"We've seen you, young fledgling."

Her voice called to him. The urge to rush off and save her captivated him. Consciously, he had no idea where she was or what he needed to do, although something within screamed that he already knew where to go.

"You are special."

Her red eyes blazed inside his head.

"The others await."

The draw pulled at his soul. With his eyes tightly shut, he felt his existence begin to float. The world was a dream, and it pulled him further away from reality.

"Mike," a voice called to him. "Hey, Mike!"

He opened his eyes.

"Where are you going?" Nate asked.

Mike glanced around him. His back no longer rested against the oak tree. He stood at least fifty feet from where he'd started. The mouth of the cave was barely a shadow on the hill. If not for Nate's flashlight, he wouldn't have been able to see the den or his friend.

"I'm... I'm not really sure," Mike said. His words hesitated from the confusion. He slowly strode back to the burrow.

"Are you OK?" Nate asked.

Mike rubbed his hands across his face. "I don't know. I haven't truly felt like myself since the vision. I keep slipping back." He held his arms in front of him and faced his palms upward, then placed them back down to his side as he spoke. "Being here, in the woods, surrounded by trees? It's just so similar. It's almost deja vu but not quite. This forest is different. The one in the vision is dying. Death is consuming it. But still. There's a draw. I heard Valerie call out to me. I don't know where she is, but I felt this pull. It almost feels like if I could put myself into some dreamlike state, she could lead me to her."

Nate clapped Mike on the shoulder. "Once we get done here, Xavier is going to have a field day inside of that head of yours."

Mike stared at his friend. "I'm not sure if I should be looking forward to it or scared shitless."

"Eh, column A, column B?"

"Story of my life," Mike said. He turned and glanced up at the moon. It wasn't quite full; it still had a sliver to go. Two days remained. He took advantage of one last breath of forest air before marching into the den's stench.

"After a little bit, you don't even smell it anymore," Nate said as the two plodded through the mud-packed hole.

Niki crouched at the back of the den. "He's a lying bastard. This place still reeks. I'm going to need one of the dogs to show up and soon."

"Question to pass the time," Mike said.

"Fire away," Nate responded.

"I thought werewolves only changed during the full moon. Obviously that's not the case, since bodies have been dropping all month long. Where did the whole full moon thing come from?"

"It doesn't matter how young or old a werewolf is," Niki started, "they are guaranteed to change during the full moon. For a new werewolf, during that first change, they have no control over themselves. Think about when you first turned. You tried to take a bite out of Jax and me. They are beasts, pure and simple. After a few full moons, they start to learn how to control themselves. If they can learn control during the full moon, then they'll learn how to change pretty much at will."

"I wonder why it's just wolves they change into," Mike said to himself.

"It's not just wolves. There are all manner of were-beasts," Nate said. "Wolves are most common in the US and in Europe. I heard about some hunters down in Mexico who chased a were-jaguar all the way to

Central America. In Japan, they have this thing called a *kitsune*. It's like a were-fox. Russia has a thing for were-bears. Met one once. Huge fucker."

"Huge fucker?" Mike asked. "You're not a small man, Nate. How huge of a fucker was this thing?"

Nate raised his arm as far as it would reach above his head. "About here."

"Damn, that is a huge fucker. Am I missing anything else?"

"Let's just go with, we get werewolves. There's a huge list to include leopards, tigers, and even fucking dolphins."

Mike shook his head. "Unbelievable."

"That's a word for it, love. Now, will you two stop your gossiping like a couple of girls. The quieter we are, the better. One or both of these mutts can show up at any time."

As Niki was hollering at them, Mike heard sound come through his earpiece. He placed his hand against his ear and tried to make out what Josh was saying, but the static was too much.

"Josh, I can't hear you," he whispered.

"David...bone...forest...werewolf...heading your way."

"I CAN'T SHOW YOU David's x-rays without his consent, and since he's currently unconscious, I don't think he's going to give that at this time."

Dr. Wagner kept the folder held tightly to his chest. Josh, John, and the doctor stood outside of David's room.

"You have no reason to see his chart," Wagner continued. "You're a park ranger, and you're a journalist."

"Actually," Josh said and reached into a side pocket on his chair. He pulled out an identification card. "I'm not a journalist. Dr. Josh Campbell. I'm with the CDC."

Dr. Wagner grabbed the ID and examined it. Josh's picture was in the upper left corner with his name and credentials to the side of it. A blue square held the white letters "CDC". A gold chip was centered at the bottom of the badge.

"You told me you were a reporter," John said with a scowl on his face. His eyes squinted into tiny slits. Josh could tell it took all of the ranger's restraint not to explode.

"You assumed I was, so I played along. I'm certain it wasn't the only falsehood either of us told."

"Gentlemen," Dr. Wagner said harshly, still flipping the badge over in one hand while the folder filled with David's X-rays stayed pressed firmly against his white lab coat. "I don't know what kind of pissing match you two have going on, but I don't want any of it in my hospital." He turned to Josh and handed him his ID. "I'm going to need to make a phone call and verify that you're with the CDC. I rarely trust anything that's handed to me." He shifted his gaze and glared at Kohana, "to include stories about bear attacks."

Before John could speak, Josh said, "We at the CDC believe it to be a bear attack as well." Although he enjoyed pissing off the Native American standing next to him, he decided deflating the situation would be in all their best interests. "I'm here to find out what might be wrong with the bear. We know it isn't rabid. Now we have to find out what is wrong with it. And pray it's not communicable."

"Why wasn't I notified before you arrived?" Wagner asked.

"I'll accept full responsibility for that," Josh said. He sat up in the chair, hoping to convey confidence. If you have to lie, lie boldly. "I live in Dallas. As I read the reports of what happened, I immediately called my supervisor. He had me hop in the car and drive here as fast as I could. My official paperwork should've arrived this afternoon. It's probably in your email or on your desk as we speak."

Wagner glanced from John to Josh and back to John. He held up the folder. "These are staying with me until I can verify. I still don't know what a member of the US Forest Service needs with them. Good luck with that approval. I'll be right back. Will you two behave or do I need to have security babysit?"

"We're good," Josh said, not letting John answer.

Dr. Wagner hastily stepped down the hall. As he did, John glanced at his watch, prompting Josh to do the same.

"Nine o' clock already," Josh said. "Do you know of a good place to eat that's open this late? I hadn't expected to be here this long."

"Shit," John responded. He started down the hall. As he did, he shouted, "You and I are not done, *Dr.* Campbell." He increased his pace and jogged to the door. He smashed the button on the wall, waited the few seconds for the door to begin opening, and then squeezed through the smallest sliver of space as soon as it was available. The door wasn't even halfway open before he was through it and sprinting out of the hospital.

Campbell had a pretty good idea where Kohana was off to in such a hurry. He reached into his pocket, pulled out his earbud, and placed it in his ear.

"Dr. Campbell," Dr. Wagner said before Josh could warn the rest of the team.

Josh spun his chair as Wagner marched toward him. He held the x-ray folder in his hand, clutching it tightly.

"Yes, Dr. Wagner," he responded.

By the look on Wagner's face, he'd checked his email and found the one Josh had sent earlier that day. While Mike had been asleep on the bed, Josh had brushed off an old ID he had used a few times in the past. His fake CDC identity worked wonders to get information from medical personnel. The Center for Disease Control was such a large and well-known entity that most people just assumed if he had a badge, he must be employed there.

When needed, in case the badge itself wasn't good enough, as in Dr. Wagner's case, he would send an email confirming the visit. Timing was key, though. Send the email too early, and a suspicious individual might make a few more phone calls.

"Where did Ranger Kohana run off to?"

Josh shrugged his shoulders. "He looked at his watch and bolted out the door." Josh pointed at the folder. "Were you able to verify my credentials?"

Wagner nodded. "Yes, Atlanta sent a notification of your arrival about two hours ago. I will say, I'm relieved to know you guys are looking into this. When David was first brought in, I thought rabies, but he tested negative. However, his bloodwork did have some abnormal markings which concerned me. Then, there's what happened today. I've frankly never seen anything like that in my life."

"Can we take a look at the x-rays?"

"Yes, follow me."

Dr. Wagner led the way. Josh followed a few feet behind. He wasn't going to be able to warn the others just yet, so he slid his earbud back into its case. They turned the corner at the end of the hall, and the doctor stepped through an office door, clicking on the light switch as he did.

The room was empty except for a backlit x-ray film viewer on the wall. Wagner flicked a switch on its side, and the light within the box flared to life.

"A lot of hospitals are using digital files and high-definition monitors to review x-rays," Josh said as he positioned himself into the room.

"We'll get there, but a lot of us have used this since med school. There's a comfort level to old tech."

"There's been great enhancements to AI as well. You take a digital x-ray and run it through one of the new systems? AI will spit out the most probable diagnosis and the recommended treatment."

Wagner nodded his head. He slid the x-ray into a clip at the top of the viewer, shifted back to the door, and killed the room's overhead light. "AI wouldn't have any issue here. This is David's leg. What do you see?"

Josh wheeled closer to the panel. The x-ray appeared exactly as Josh expected it to. The dark picture showed a leg in white contrast. "A leg," Josh said with a smile. He hoped a little levity would get the doctor to be more forthcoming.

Sliding back in front of the viewer, Wagner slid another two x-rays into clips next to the one already on the wall. "These are his x-rays before and after surgery."

With the comparison, it became evident what Josh was supposed to be seeing. Each x-ray showed David's leg. The one before surgery showed the leg but with breaks in three places. Even though Josh didn't have a medical degree, the breaks were obvious. They weren't hairline fractures that would take a trained eye to see. The bone was completely shattered, and darkness held the space between pieces of bone that should've been connected.

The second picture, the after-surgery picture, showed David's leg with pins driven into the bone, holding it in place. The bone breaks were still obvious, but now the addition of the pins showed in bright contrast to the bone. Josh didn't count each individual pin, but he guessed close to a dozen of them held his leg together.

Josh shifted his gaze to the first picture the doctor had placed on the panel. That picture was taken not two hours before. The bone was solid. No breaks were visible.

"I see what you mean about AI not having an issue. I don't see a break," Josh admitted.

"There's not one. Within a week, David's leg went from shattered to the point of needing pins and extensive physical therapy to perfectly healed. His leg healed so fast, the bone violently expelled the pins from his leg, and then the muscle and skin healed almost immediately. I've never seen anything like this. It's supernatural. You'll probably want an entire team here when this animal is finally caught. Can the CDC explain what kind of disease can be passed from a wild animal to a human *and* cause this kind of healing?"

Josh wanted to say, "Lycanthropy," but knew better. Instead, he shook his head, and said, "I don't know of anything, disease or not, that can cause this kind of healing, much less be communicable." He gazed from one x-ray to the next. The healing was quite remarkable.

"Amazing," he finally said.

"That's a word for it."

"Dr. Wagner, I'd like to fill in some of my team. Do you mind giving me the room?"

"Not at all," Wagner said. He shuffled out of the room, pulling the door closed behind him as he did.

Josh grabbed his earbud back from its case and jammed it into his ear. "Mike? Nate? Niki? Can you hear me? This is amazing. David's leg... The bone completely healed. Oh, and there's a guy from the forest service. He's a werewolf, and I'm pretty sure, he's heading your way."

"WHAT DID HE SAY?" Niki asked.

"'David, bone, forest, werewolf heading your way'," Mike repeated. "I'm going to say the most important part is werewolf heading your way."

"Works for me," Niki said.

"I don't know how he knows, but I trust Josh. We should be ready."

Nate and Niki both drew pistols from their holsters and hunkered toward the back of the den. The stench of rotting flesh still gave weight to the air.

Mike wished they'd have been able to remove the bodies littering the ground, but that would've announced their presence. They needed everything to appear exactly as it had been, at least until the werewolf finally walked into the den. They just needed to let it get comfortable enough to come inside, so they could have a clean shot at it.

Mike positioned himself closer to the mouth of the cave. His job was to be their werewolf detector. Hopefully, he'd hear, smell, or feel it as it moved closer to the cave. Once the werewolf was inside, he would block the exit, trapping the beast within.

"You two had better not shoot me," he had warned.

"Love, if we shoot you, it's on purpose," Niki had responded jokingl y... He hoped.

Although he knew it was there, Mike touched the handle of the silver knife at his hip. To him, the blade emanated a cool heat. Nestled within its sheath, the silver weapon could inflict just as much damage on him as it could on the werewolf. He had to be careful handling such a weapon. Few things could harm him, and that exact substance was part of every weapon they had in their arsenal, from Niki's whip to the knife at his side to the bullets in their guns.

A vibration ran down Mike's spine. It was similar to what he'd felt as he had reached David's room. He breathed deeply through his nose, focusing on the smells. Hidden among the earthy tones of pine and oak and dirt, he picked up a musky scent. It was faint. If he hadn't felt the vibrations, he probably would've missed the smell. He backed against the earthen wall and bent down low to the ground. As he did, he turned to Nate and Niki, waved his hand, and pointed to the cave entrance. Both nodded their understanding.

Mike closed his eyes and focused his attention on what he could hear. The werewolf wasn't close enough for him to see it in the darkness of the forest.

The forest was silent. Nothing made a noise. Nate and Niki's heartbeats were louder than the forest sounds, yet, he knew the beast was close. He concentrated beyond the cave.

"Where are you?" he whispered.

Damp leaves shuffled across the ground. A single, guttural breath drifted his way. If it was a growl, it was extremely minute. A slight rumble deep within its throat. But that was all Michael needed to locate the werewolf, less than fifty yards away and heading toward the cave. The wet dog smell grew stronger. The vibration intensified. He wondered if the wolf sensed it as well. Based on David's reaction yesterday, he assumed it did, but the werewolf continued to draw closer.

Michael's body tightened. The vampire's predatory instincts hung on high alert. He was ready to pounce as soon as the werewolf stepped foot inside the cave. If this was the same one from last night, it wasn't getting away this time. If it was the other one, it wouldn't live long enough to tell its friend.

It was a dozen feet outside of the cave. Enough moonlight shone through the trees to cast the wolf's shadow across the mouth of the cave. It was on all fours with its head toward the ground; more beast-like than man. It stopped moving and raised its head. The elongated snout searched the air. Its nose sniffed deeply. All three of them had hoped the stench of rotting meat inside the cave would cover their scent. As the creature craned its neck from one side to the other, Mike suddenly doubted the smell was enough.

The werewolf stood up on its back legs. Immediately, its shadow appeared less like a wild animal and more like the formidable opponent he had fought last night. The shadow became a huge, hulking black mass silhouetted on the ground. It beat its chest and roared into the den. The sound echoed around the dark cave. The acoustics amplified the loud burst, making it almost deafening.

Mike kept still. So did Nate and Niki. They didn't appear intimidated at all. If the werewolf hoped to scare them out of the cave, its attempt failed. The Night Crew was ready for a fight.

The creature galloped on its legs, taking a few long strides, before bursting through the front of the den. The shadow vanished, leaving the actual werewolf standing in the center of the cave a few feet from the mouth. The werewolf was tall, but not as tall as the one last night. It stood just over six feet, only topping Mike by a few inches. Its fur was pitch black. The stark white eyes had yellow irises surrounding large black pupils. Despite it being shorter than the one Mike had previously fought, it looked wider. This beast was well fed and had come for a midnight snack. Instead, Mike, Nate, and Niki stood between it and its food.

Mike reached his hand to the silver knife. His fingers wrapped around the hilt. Slowly, he began to slide it out of its leather home. He needed the beast to step just another few feet into the cave. At that point, he could get behind it, blocking its escape. He knew Nate and Niki were drawing a bead on it, taking aim, and ready to unleash a barrage of silver bullets.

Before any of that could happen, though, the creature flashed its claws and back pedaled out of the cave. The moment it passed into the forest, it turned and ran.

"Shit, it knows we're here!" Mike shouted.

He immediately sprang from his crouched position and sprinted after the werewolf. A few steps later, he was outside of the cave and navigating around the trees. He knew Nate and Niki would be behind him and unable to catch up, but he didn't want to lose the werewolf.

"Mike," Nate shouted.

Mike heard him in his earbud. Being clear of the cave, he had signal again.

"I hear you, Nate," Mike responded. "I see him. Unless my bearings are off, we're heading toward the highway. Try to reach Josh. He can track."

"Josh, are you there?" Nate asked. "Josh, where are you?"

"I'm here. I'm almost back to the hotel, but I have my laptop. Did you guys hear anything I said earlier?"

"Not a word, love. Shitty reception inside of a hole in the ground."

"I'll fill you in later. Mike, I'm tracking your location. How far ahead of you is it?"

Mike felt his energy waning. It had been way too long since he'd fed enough to maintain a footrace. The werewolf pulled ahead of him. "Twenty feet, but I can't keep up, and I'm definitely not gaining on him."

"I should've taken the fucking shot when I had it," Niki said. "For a split second, I had a clean shot."

"Don't beat yourself up," Mike said. "It happens." He didn't know how far he'd run. The trees seemed to be nothing more than a repeating pattern. Every turn just offered more of the same. As far as he could see, the view never changed - shadows, darkness, and trees. It was like driving a long distance on a road at night in the fog. A winding abyss that never ends.

Mike dug deep, thinking back to all the times during his special forces training when he knew he didn't have anything left in the tank but couldn't give up. If he gave up, if he quit, people died. There wasn't anything different here. If he lost sight of this werewolf, if it got away, it'd kill again.

Out of the corner of his eye, Mike caught movement. He realized it wasn't just the two of them. It wasn't just him and the black werewolf. Something else shadowed their movements. He was being flanked. Just as the vampire figured out what was happening, a second wolf darted out of the trees.

ONCE HE PICKED UP on the second werewolf, Mike knew he was going to have to rethink his strategy. Nate and Niki were nowhere near him. It'd take them too long to catch up, and that was if they could maintain a sprint through the dark through the woods without slowing down. He gripped the knife tightly in his hand, realizing it and his speed and strength were his only weapons. Although with as fast and strong as werewolves were, he doubted if that would give him much of an advantage.

The second werewolf was brown and had a gash that ran across the upper part of its right arm. The cut had started to heal, but still appeared deep and red. It was the werewolf from last night; Mike was sure of it. That wound had to have been caused by Niki's whip.

The wolf matched Mike stride for stride but gained ground faster than the vampire. It pulled in front of him. At any moment, he expected it to spin around, blocking him from reaching the black werewolf. He prepared for the impact, braced for it, but it never came.

The werewolf accelerated and pulled away from Michael. It drew closer to the black werewolf. When it was almost on top of the smaller wolf, the brown werewolf leapt into the air, landing on the back of the black one.

Both wolves curled together into a ball and rolled along the forest floor. Dirt, branches, and brush flew into the air as the two massive creatures tumbled together as one. Their skid finally stopped when the huge fur ball crashed into a large oak tree. The werewolves broke apart, each sliding another ten feet apart.

Mike stopped in his tracks, his feet stuttering against the ground, as the two werewolves jumped to their hind legs, staring each other down. He kept his distance trying to figure out his next move. The brown wolf was larger than the black one by almost a foot. Its shoulder width was larger as well. He didn't know why the larger beast had tackled the smaller one, but he knew there wasn't time to have a meeting and talk it over. Something must've happened to put these two at odds.

The brown wolf stared down the black one. The massive size of both creatures was remarkable, but especially that of the brown wolf. Their yellow eyes blazed a vibrant hue, as if their very essence burned there. Both had their arms down by their sides and claws on full display, taunting the other to attack. They circled each other, never releasing eye contact.

The black wolf roared at the brown wolf. In response, the large werewolf roared back and beat its chest. It reminded Mike of documentaries he'd seen of gorillas trying to figure out who was the alpha. The brown wolf took a step forward, and the black one recoiled. In that single moment of weakness, the larger beast lunged forward, claws extended and gripped the black wolf around its side. As its claws sunk into the wolf's torso, the brown wolf lifted the other into the air. The black wolf screamed in pain, but the scream was cut off as the beast was violently slammed into the ground.

The smaller wolf, pinned to the ground, tried to fight and use its hind legs to separate the two of them, but the brown werewolf was faster. It pulled one hand away from the other's side, punched it across the face, grabbed one of the black werewolf's wrists, and pinned it to the ground. The other hand pressed deeper into the black werewolf's side, and the wolf cried out again in pain.

While watching, Mike realized the strength of the wolves, especially the large one who was dominating its smaller opponent. He doubted he'd win in a hand-to-hand battle with the larger one. He needed a strategy, and a blitz attack while the brown werewolf was handling the weaker black wolf seemed like a great time. It wouldn't see him coming.

If he could be quick enough, he could sink the silver blade into it, incapacitate the larger beast, kill it, and then take out the smaller one since it was already injured. He only had a short window to react, though.

Deciding it might be his only opportunity, Mike gripped the hilt of the knife tighter in his hand and bolted toward the two werewolves, locked in fight on the ground. The brown werewolf's back was to the vampire. Despite his waning strength, Mike sprung into the air. He turned the knife over so the blade extended out the back of his hand and cocked his arm out. He meant to drive the blade deep into the wolf's side.

A sudden shift of the black wolf's eyes betrayed Mike's plan. He saw his own reflection in the deep black pupils an instant before the brown wolf pulled its clawed hand out of the black wolf's side, twisted its back, and swung its now free arm toward Mike. The back of its fist violently collided with the vampire and threw him a few feet away.

Mike's entire side crumpled. He felt a rib break the moment the hand made contact. He'd been punched hard before. When Angie had thrown him through a wall in New Orleans, it had hurt. She had power behind her blows, but they were nothing compared to what he felt now. The pain rippled from his side and vibrated across his entire body. The wind left his lungs. A surge of heat exploded inside him. This was a fight he'd lost before it ever started. He fell to the ground, and his only hope, the silver blade, bounced out of his hand as he rolled and crashed into a tree.

Face down on the ground against the tree that had stopped his momentum, Mike knew he needed to move. Before he had a chance to do it on his own accord, two hairy paws gripped his shoulders. Sharp claws pierced his skin as the werewolf picked him off the ground and slammed his chest into the tree. Its rancid breath blew against the back of his neck. One hand let go of his shoulder and clamped around the back of his neck. Holding him tightly, pressing his face against the tree, it released his other shoulder and punched him in the side. Mike wanted to crumple into a ball, but since he was pinned to the tree, all he could do was hang there, suspended by the wolf's hold on his neck.

Mike was only barely aware as the black wolf ran past him, hunched over, holding its wounded sides as best as it could, before disappearing into the dark forest.

The other werewolf must've realized the same thing. It roared into the moonlit night sky.

A gunshot rang out, and the pressure on Mike's back immediately eased. He fell to the ground and scurried a few feet away. As he did, he spun around.

Niki held the pistol out in front of her. The brown wolf collapsed to the ground, gripping its leg, and scooting to the tree. Blood oozed from the bullet wound. The wolf growled in pain. It raised a hand in front of it. The claws were tipped with red droplets of blood. Mike assumed that was his. The bleeding puncture wounds on both of his shoulders reinforced the idea.

"Stop," the werewolf said.

Nate and Niki glanced at each other. Surprise shot across their faces.

Mike also peered at the beast. The voice didn't match the look of the creature, until it started to change in front of them. In a matter of seconds, the wolf-like features dissolved. The brown hair recoiled, and the snout pulled back. The claws retracted, the ears rounded off and lost their points, and the werewolf's frame shrunk. Where was once a large, brown werewolf was now a naked, older man with a long braid of hair.

"What have you done?" he shouted at them.

He still held his leg. Although, no longer bleeding, there was a bullet hole on the front of his thigh. The bullet must've gone clean through his leg. Mike was suddenly glad Niki aimed low enough that the bullet didn't go through the wolf and into him. Too many parts of him were damaged right now for him to need another wound, especially one that would've come from a silver bullet.

Niki repointed the gun at the naked man against the tree. She slowly approached with the gun trained on his chest. "We just stopped one of the fucking mutts that've been snacking on people in the woods."

"No, you fucking assholes," he shouted. "I almost did that. You let him get away!" As he spoke, spit flew from his mouth in rage.

"That one's injured. We'll catch up with it and put a bullet in its head also." Niki raised the barrel of the gun a touch higher.

"You must be the fucking Night Crew. Henderson, the Police Chief, told me he called you. I'm with the pack. I'm also hunting the two rogues. Get that fucking gun out of my face and help me up."

Nate stepped closer, standing next to Niki. "How do we know you're telling the truth?"

"He's telling the truth," Josh suddenly shouted into their earbuds. "I'm here with Henderson now. He's telling the truth."

35

"DID YOU HEAR SOMETHING?" Samantha asked, tearing her lips from Trevor's.

She laid across the backseat of Trevor's car. He hovered just over her, propping himself up with one knee on the seat cushion in between her legs, a foot on the floorboard, an arm under her head, and the other arm on the seat supporting his weight. She glanced up into his brown eyes. Sweat stuck the short, blonde curls she liked to run her fingers through to his head.

"Only you, sighing," he whispered, leaning in closer to continue their make-out session.

She raised her hand and placed it against his chest, giving enough pushback so that he knew she wasn't kidding. She was already nervous about being out this late.

The bear attacks were all over the news. Although she wasn't friends with any of the victims, her father hung out with Troy Johnson. The two of them spent a good bit of time at The Pit. Samantha had never been inside before. She had to be twenty-one to go in. But she knew that even in two years when she finally did turn that magical age, she still wouldn't. It was where most of the men over forty went to have a beer or whiskey, shoot pool, and throw darts while talking about that one year when they won state. She had always assumed every town had some version of The Pit. With her dad and Mr. Johnson being friends, she'd heard a good deal about what they planned to do if Henderson didn't get off his ass and kill that damn bear.

"Stop, Trevor," she said. "I really heard something."

He started to rise up and gaze out of the fogged over windows, but she grabbed his shirt.

"What are you doing?" Samantha asked. Fear and urgency invaded her voice.

"If you heard something, I need to take a look," he responded.

"You're a fucking moron, you know that? What if it's the bear? If it sees you, it'll break in here and kill us both."

Panic started to filter into her brain. Suddenly, she didn't want him on top of her anymore. She felt trapped, claustrophobic. She didn't want to sit up, but she also didn't want to be where she was. With him still hovering just over the top of her, she slid down onto the floorboard. It was a tight fit, but she made it all the way down, allowing Trevor to lay face down over her. Droplets of sweat glistened on the leather seat. She wasn't sure if it was his or hers, but at that moment, she didn't much care.

"It's not the bear," he said.

"How do you know?" she snapped back.

"Everyone says the bear is out in the woods. That's why we're not at a campsite or the RV park like usual. The football field is practically in town." He bent his arm and propped his head up. "You're sexy when you're scared." He reached down with his other hand and brushed a lock of brown hair out of her face and behind her ear.

"The mood's passed. Now, shut up for a moment and listen."

"What do you think you heard? And how did you hear anything with all that moaning?"

"If you don't shut up, it'll be the last time you hear any of that."

She shook her head while staring at him. Of course, he was only thinking with his penis. He was a guy. But she knew she had heard something, and with people actually dying, her nerves were on high alert. She placed her finger in front of her mouth and pursed her lips. "Shhhh."

The two of them laid still in the car, waiting, listening. Samantha's arm started to lose feeling as she stayed crunched on the floorboard. As the silence sat heavy around them, she began to hear two male voices. Trevor's eyes opened wider, and she knew he heard them too. Although the two men weren't arguing, their voices were raised.

"He did what?" the first voice asked.

"He tried to kill me," the second said. He sounded on the verge of tears. "Look at my side. He shoved his claws into my fucking side. It really hurts. He was going to kill me which means the pack has put a hit out on us. We're fucked."

"Stop bitching. You'll heal. It could be we've been put on a hit list, but could also mean that old fuck is acting out of line. It's not his first time taking matters into his own hands. Plus, there're two of us and one of him. Sure, he's older, but, also...he's older."

"What about the others? They were definitely hunters. One of them was a vampire. I felt it. We weren't supposed to be fighting hunters. The plan never involved hunters. What if we go back to the pack and beg their forgiveness?"

Confused, Samantha mouthed the word "vampire" to Trevor. He shrugged his shoulders, and both of them remained still and quiet, hidden in the car.

The two voices grew louder. They were moving closer to the car. Familiar with the layout of the parking lot, Samantha had a good idea where the voices were coming from. Trevor had parked on the visitor's side since that area was the darkest. Also, the back of the parking lot was Ouachita Forest. He had told her they'd have more privacy that way. His car was the only one there. The two men had to have come from the forest.

"We can't go back on our hands and knees begging for forgiveness. We're not showing weakness, especially to a group that has been nothing but weak for centuries. Do you remember what He said? We must rise up, instill fear in our food supply. We just have to be smart about it. What makes you think they were hunters?"

"The vampire had a silver blade. Why else would a vampire be carrying around silver?"

"Then we make sure we stick together. No more going off on our own for a snack. The den is obviously compromised. So we don't go back there for now. Fortunately, the full moon is in two days. We'll be at our strongest then and can take care of the hunters."

"What about Kohana? He'll be at his strongest then too?"

"Oh, little brother, I'll handle him. Plus, we'll have our third at that time."

Nothing the two said made sense to Samantha. It was as if they were rattling off a script to a low budget horror movie. Vampires, full moons, silver, hunters. What the hell was going on?

She glanced up at Trevor. His face wrinkled, and he scrunched his nose. Her eyes went wide, realizing what he was about to do. He took a deep breath. Although he tried to keep it as quiet as possible, he sneezed. It wasn't the full volume explosion that he usually did, but sound penetrated through his nose. Samantha breathed a sigh of relief. His normal sneeze would've been heard on the other side of the stadium. He had done a good job of keeping this one contained.

The voices outside stopped talking. She wished they'd start again so she could tell when they left. That way she'd know when it was safe for her and Trevor to leave. Maybe they already moved off, and that was why she couldn't hear them anymore. She twisted her numb arm, feeling the needles of that unmistakable tingling sensation travel up to her shoulder, and pushed herself up.

"Are they gone?" she whispered.

"I'll check..." Trevor whispered back.

He shuffled on the seat. The leather creaked underneath him. He kept his legs on the backseat and bent his back, raising his head like a snake. His head rose until his eye line barely cleared the paneling on the rear door.

The window shattered, and glass rained down on Samantha. She scrunched her head between her shoulders, dropping it to her chest. At the same time, she threw her arm over the top of her, hoping to shield her face from the falling glass. Two arms covered in black fur gripped Trevor's head.

36

Josh waited at the police station. He'd been there since he'd intervened and kept the four of them from killing each other. He had pushed the chair in front of the window out of the way and scooted up to the desk. Any minute now the door would open, and the team would stroll in. It was about time that everyone sat down together to come up with a game plan instead of operating individually.

The door opened. He'd expected there to be bickering, arguing, or even yelling, especially after the fight and Niki shooting John in the leg. Except there wasn't any of that. Niki stepped through the doorway first. Josh pressed the buzzer behind the counter, letting the door open into the bullpen. Once Niki came in, John limped through. He favored one leg, and Josh assumed it was the one Niki had shot.

Mike was next with Nate swinging around the door, having held it open for everyone. Each funneled through the front door and then the door to the bullpen with a somber look on their face.

Once Josh had met up with Henderson, the Police Chief had sent everyone else either home or out on patrol. He wanted the station cleared for their discussion. All the desks were empty, and the lights were off in every office but one: Roy's. With everyone in the bullpen, they fanned out. Niki sat on top of a desk. Nate grabbed a chair. Mike and John kept standing, sending deadly glances at each other.

"I just want to say," Josh said as Roy stepped out of his office, "that I fucking knew you were a werewolf. I didn't believe that a tree cut your arm. Not a chance."

"Don't start with me," John said. His voice shared the anger on his face. "I could've ended this tonight if it wasn't for you. Hunters are always getting in the fucking way thinking they're the heroes."

Roy stepped into the circle. "I called them. You weren't being helpful. Don't blame them for the fact that you waited so long to get here."

"We have rituals that we must follow. Just because you pick up the phone and make a call doesn't mean we immediately send someone to kill a member of the pack. Werewolves are civilized."

Mike raised his head, glaring at John and the implication the vampires weren't.

Kohana continued. "Once we had confirmation, I came right away. Even if we had known you were dealing with a werewolf, each pack takes care of their own. We had to verify the pack."

"I'm guessing you finally got around to doing that," Nate said. "It only took a dozen people. I'm sure their family members appreciate your bureaucracy. Apparently, the wheels of justice move slowly in the werewolf community."

"Easy coming from hunters. You murderers have no sense of loyalty or family. You get a call to go kill something, and you jump."

He took a breath before yelling, "Nothing but a band of fucking mercenaries!"

He placed his hands on the desk in front of him, leaning closer to Nate. "Do you have a wall of trophy heads or a punch card that you're trying to complete?"

"Oh, I have a wall, and it's filled with the heads of mutts. Keep it up, and I'll add yours right now."

"Like that's something that could ever happen," John shouted.

"Gentlemen..." Roy said.

Josh bounced his eyes from one to the other. At this rate, there was going to be a fight, and then it was going to take even longer to work out a plan.

Michael must've had the same thought. He started to move between Nate and John. As he did, Nate stood up. He reared back his massive arm and punched John in the face. John's eyes turned yellow, and he leapt over the desk. Mike hurried between the two of them as John reached his arm out to grab Nate. Instead, he grabbed Michael by the throat. Mike tried to bat his arm. Using his other hand, John grabbed one of Mike's arms and held it out. He picked Michael off the ground by his neck, holding one arm outstretched.

"Don't start with me, vampire!" Kohana said as if the word was a curse. "I'll rip your arm completely off your body, fledgling, and beat you with it."

Josh stared with utter disbelief at the scene in front of him. Niki and Nate simultaneously pulled their revolvers from their holsters and pointed them at the werewolf.

"This has got to stop, right now!" Henderson yelled. "This isn't helping." He pointed his arm, indicating the town of Mena, just outside the walls of the police station.

John held Mike, unphased by the guns trained on him. Instead, he pulled the vampire closer to him. "I could rip your throat out and drink your blood while you watch me."

He let go of Mike's arm and shoved him backward into Nate as he released the vampire's throat.

Kohana raised both of his arms in front of him as if surrendering. "Do you know what happens to a werewolf when it drinks a vampire's blood?"

Mike slowly shook his head, rubbing his neck as he did. Niki kept her gun steady, aiming directly at John; her finger hovering over on the trigger. She hadn't moved a muscle. With nothing more than the slightest necessity, she was ready to pull the trigger and put a silver bullet inside of John's head.

John continued. "Same thing that happens if a werewolf bites one of your kind. Not a damn thing. Creatures can't intertwine with each other. There's no crossbreeding vampires and werewolves. Once you're part of a blood family, that's your family. You vampires don't understand that. You share your blood with someone and leave them to fend for themselves. Sink or swim. But werewolves? We're a family. A pack."

John grabbed a chair, spun it, and sat down hard, as if his whole body crumpled.

Niki slowly lowered her gun, putting it back in the holster.

"Last September, a vampire, one of your kind," he pointed at Michael, "came into our village. Vampires don't usually come crawling into a town of werewolves, but this one did. Our pack leader knew him from years ago, so he gave this blood-sucker temporary refuge. He said he was just passing through, heading to Texas. Only thing, while he was here, when we ate or sat around the campfire, he only talked of an uprising."

"Silas," Mike said.

"So you know him also," John stated.

"Knew him. A long story. Short version. He made me, and then I killed him. That was last October, so just after he came to visit your pack. You said he spoke of an uprising?"

John nodded his head. "He said he was creating an army of followers and not just vampires either. He was recruiting from all kinds. Every group with representation on the Council. He said the Council would be no more, the Accords would be destroyed, and we would be free to kill or turn as we would like."

"Your pack leader just let him speak that way?" Henderson asked. "Sounds like this Silas character was inciting violence. I thought you were all about peace and controlling the animal within. At least, as long as I've known you."

"That is what we preach. We feed off the land. We eat wildlife, not humans. But Silas said he was changing how things are. No one listened to him, though. We've heard many people over the years talk about the same thing. Dissolve the Council! Return to the Dark Ages where we reigned supreme! We let him speak his peace, and then he left. But then October came, and word spread that the Council had indeed gone missing. We've heard rumors, of other groups ignoring the Accords and doing as they please, but we stayed true. Small skirmishes happen. The last time a council member was killed and there was a vacancy, there was infighting."

"What changed?" Josh asked.

Everyone in the bullpen stayed silent, listening to John Kohana talk. The animosity and aggression had been stayed, at least for now.

"Two of our pack, brothers, believed what Silas said. About a month ago, as rumors of more disruptions came, the brothers began reciting the vampire's words. They were reprimanded for it. Then, after the last full moon, they left. It's not uncommon for young men to want to explore on their own. They were seasoned wolves and knew how to control their change. Nothing about their leaving was suspicious."

"Not suspicious?" Roy asked. His tone oozed with agitation at that comment. "The missing hikers started shortly after the last full moon. Everything has escalated since then! The attacks have become more frequent. Those two are leaving a trail of bodies. Along with that, the people are ready to go all out on a bear hunt. The only problem with that is it's not a bear they are hunting. I can't exactly pass out silver bullets. If they go hunting for a bear and find your boys, it's going to be a bloodbath. No amount of shotgun slugs will put down a werewolf. We've got to get this under control. Anything else happens, and I won't be able to hold them off. God forbid that something happens in town."

37

As the creature gripped Trevor's head, holding it tightly, the glass on the other side of the car exploded in. Another pair of black fur-covered arms reached in. Hands (or paws, Samantha wasn't sure) grabbed Trevor around his ankles. The creature holding his feet pulled, and Trevor lifted off the back seat. He was suspended two feet in the air by his head and ankles.

Trevor screamed in pain. All Samantha could do was bury her head beneath her arms. She was trapped on the floorboard. She glanced up at Trevor floating above her. She tried to peer through the window at the beasts holding him but couldn't see past the large arms.

The conversation the two people outside had rushed into Samantha's head. Vampires, silver bullets, full moon. Through Trevor's agonizing screams and her own terror, her mind somehow made sense of what was going on. Two werewolves were attacking them. It wasn't a bear killing people. It was two creatures that shouldn't exist. She was in a real-life horror movie.

The two werewolves violently tugged on Trevor, fighting over who would get the spoils. Droplets of blood fell on Samantha's arms. Not realizing at first what was happening, she brushed them away, smearing bloody streaks down her forearms. She glanced up. The werewolf holding Trevor's head dug its claws into his neck. His screams became muted gurgling noises as blood began to drain from the punctures in his throat, as well as his nose and mouth. Stretched seams appeared in the skin of his neck. Trevor's eyes rolled into the back of his head. The small droplets became a fresh, hot river raining down on her.

As she stared up, Trevor's head separated from his body. His gurgled screams abruptly ended. His limp torso dropped to the seat. Blood gushed from his decapitated body. Then the werewolf holding his legs jerked the body toward the other window. As the body went one direction and the head the other, the backbone and portions of his carotid artery stayed with the head. The vertebrae pulled out of the corpse like a slithering snake leaving its hole.

Samantha, covered in Trevor's blood and random veins and tissues that had torn apart during the decapitation, sat frozen in fear on the floorboard. Her whole body stayed locked in place. She wanted to scream but knew that would just make her next. She wanted to run but there was no way she'd get out of the car without being disemboweled herself. Resolved, she clutched her arms around her chest and waited. She knew the beasts would come for her next. It was only a matter of time before they finished with Trevor's body and came for her. Slowly, she pulled her legs into her chest and curled into a ball behind the passenger seat. She wrapped her arms around her knees and pulled them tightly into her body.

"Dear Lord," she whispered. "Please forgive me for all the sins I've committed. Please accept me into your almighty arms. Please forgive me for all the sins I've done. Please accept me into your almighty arms." She kept repeating those two sentences over and over as though it was the only prayer she could remember, quietly praying so that when the end came, she'd be absolved.

"Do you hear that?" a voice from outside the car asked. It was one of the voices from earlier.

"I think she's praying," the other responded.

The two burst out in raucous laughter.

"Oh, pretty..." the first one said in an eerie whisper. "If we wanted to eat you, we would've. My brother needed some food to heal, and I wanted a snack. Your boyfriend was enough. Run away now. We know what you smell like. We'll come visit again in a few days."

"Put your clothes on, and let's get out of here."

Samantha didn't move. She couldn't. None of her muscles worked. From outside, she heard the sound of something being dragged across the gravel parking lot, the sound slowly diminishing until it disappeared completely.

There was no way for her to know how long she stayed behind the passenger seat, still clutching her knees as tightly as she could to her chest. It could've been five minutes or five hours. Time had no relevance. Despite what the voices said, she still waited, constantly repeating her two-line mantra over and over again.

"Please forgive me for all the sins I've done. Please accept me into your almighty arms."

Time ticked away. Slowly, she reached her hand up, gripped the door handle, and pulled. The door swung open. Samantha uncoiled her back, stretching her head and shoulders out of the car. She half expected for that to be the moment she died. That was when the sharp claws would tear into her flesh. Instead, she twisted her torso, placing her hands on the gravel and slithering through the opening. Trevor's blood had started to dry, leaving a tacky film across her body. She was certain no amount of showering would ever fully clean the blood off. His blood was a permanent stain on her. If not physically, it would forever be in her psyche.

The gravel dug into her palms as she placed one hand in front of the other, dragging her numb legs from the car. She'd held them so securely for so long, they'd fallen asleep. Tingling pains sparkled across them. A sign they were coming back to life, and that she wasn't dead yet. When she could, she bent her knees and dragged them over the small rocks, finally freeing herself from the nightmare inside the car. She flipped over. Pieces of gravel clung to her palms and her knees, and she violently swiped them off of her, slapping her hands together and hitting them across her legs.

She scooted across the gravel, backing away from the car as fast as she could, as if the car itself could attract the werewolves back. Something touched her back, and before she glanced at it, she screamed. Everything that had built up inside of her since this whole ordeal began just rushed out. She twisted her head and stared into Trevor's dead eyes. His head, atop his spine, lay in the parking lot. Its hair pressed against her back.

Samantha leapt to her feet, bent over, and vomited everything she had eaten. Between the screaming and the puking, she didn't know how much more her throat could take. The moment she could breathe she stood up and ran. Her feet slammed onto the gravel, propelling her forward as fast as they could. Later, she would be certain that she must've resembled the final girl in every horror movie, covered in her boyfriend's sticky blood, screaming and crying. But for now, she ran.

The moment she cleared the football stadium, she saw a sign hovering slightly above the houses. The sign had three letters in bright neon. "Pit".

It was The Pit. The bar where her dad and his friends hung out. She kept her eyes trained on the sign as she pounded her feet against the pavement and sprinted down the street.

38

Samantha stumbled across The Pit's parking lot. A dozen trucks and cars filled the asphalt lot. Because it was a weeknight, quite a few spots were empty. Out of the corner of her eye, she saw her dad's truck. *Good. He's inside,* she thought. She ran straight for the bar's door and slammed into it. It didn't budge. She backed up and remembered she had to pull. Staring at the door, she saw two bloody hand prints she'd left as well as a smudge from her shirt. The now dark brown stood out against the white of the door.

Trevor's blood.

She gripped the door handle and yanked it open.

Journey blared from a corner jukebox. A few pool tables lined the establishment. The bar counter and stools stood across from the entrance. Mirrors extended up to the ceiling, and an assortment of brown liquors sat on shelves in front of them. The place reeked of old beer, bourbon, oak, and the faint memory of cigarette smoke from a time when smoking had been allowed inside.

"Hey, Robert. Is that your daughter?"

"Sam?"

Samantha jerked her head toward the sound of her father's voice. Relief flood her, releasing the fear and anxiety she'd been holding on to, afraid she'd never hear his voice again. He stood on the far side of the room next to a pool table. He dropped the pool stick he held and ran to her.

Seeing him, knowing she was safe, the toll of the night finally took over. As he hurried to her, her legs gave out, and she collapsed. Robert managed to catch her just before she landed on the hardwood floor. He fell with her and wrapped his arms around her, holding her close.

"Sam? Are you hurt? Samantha? Someone call 9-1-1."

"Already on it," the bartender said.

"Samantha, where are you hurt?"

While cradled in her father's arms, all the muscles in her body went limp. Adrenaline had been all that had kept her moving. As he kept asking questions, she slowly shook her head. She needed to tell him. She'd made it this far, maybe she had the rest of it in her.

"Trevor," she whispered.

"Trevor? Did Trevor hurt you?" Robert asked.

She shook her head again. "No. His blood. Dead." She had to pause. Vocalizing it hurt, each word a chore. But she had to. She had to for Trevor.

"Attacked. Football field."

"Trevor's dead! You were attacked over by the football field?"

She nodded.

Someone else crouched near her.

"Was it the bear? Did that fucking bear do this?"

"Troy, we can figure that out later," Robert yelled. "We need to get you to the hospital."

"Bear," Samantha said.

She nodded her head but then tried to shake it instead. No, it wasn't the bear like they had all thought. Werewolves. Two of them. She needed to tell them. But how would she not sound crazy? Her mind wanted to work but with the adrenaline spike over, everything was shutting down.

She was crashing. It wouldn't be long before she woke up in a hospital bed. She had no doubt about that.

"Did she say bear?" Troy asked. "The bear killed Trevor. You three, put down the sticks and get in my truck. Put their tabs on mine. We're driving to the football field now."

"No," Samantha mumbled.

"Sam, don't try to speak," her dad said.

"Robert, ambulance is on the way," the bartender said.

"No," she repeated. "Not bear."

"It's OK, Sam. The bear can't get you. The ambulance is on the way, sweetie. Just stay with me, OK?"

Robert pulled his daughter closer to his chest. The two rocked on the bar's floor. Samantha tried to say more, but nothing came out. She wondered how much of Trevor's blood she'd transferred onto her dad's clothes. Probably a good bit.

She leaned her face into her dad's shirt. At the thought of Trevor, she wept.

MIKE HEARD A HANDFUL of trucks pull up outside the police station. At least three, possibly more. He glanced at Kohana and saw the ranger's eyes shift to the front door as well. They both had heard the same thing. As the truck doors slammed shut, Roy picked up his head as well.

"Henderson!"

Everyone turned to the front of the building. The yell came from outside. No one came through the front door. It reminded Mike of an old western. Whoever was outside was calling the police chief out, like a bandit calling out the sheriff.

"That's Troy," Roy said. "His son, Tanner, was one of the victims. He's become the de facto leader of the mob ready to hunt the bear. I wish I had never come up with that story."

"It bought time," Niki said.

"Do you need anything from us?" Michael asked. "I did my fair share of crowd control in the military."

"I appreciate it. They've probably been drinking and are blowing off some steam. I'll have a conversation with them." Roy strode across the bullpen, through the door leading to the waiting area, opened the front door, and stepped outside.

"I don't like this," Mike said, turning back to the room.

John stood from the chair. "I'm going to report to the pack leader real fast."

"He's not going to send another werewolf, is he? We don't need any more with the full moon right around the corner," Niki asked, more than a hint of disdain in her voice.

"I'll try not to take that as an insult," John said. He strode toward the back door.

"No, by all means, please take it as such," she continued.

He spun around on his heels. "I don't know what your problem is. We try to stay out of the Night Crew's way. We take care of our own issues."

Mike's attention was split between their argument and the ever-increasing volume from outside. He tried to hear what Roy told the crowd, but couldn't make everything out. As he drifted back to the argument between John and Niki, he smelled blood.

John's head shifted up slightly, and he audibly sniffed the air.

She pointed to the front of the station. "Oh, you mean like the issue we're here to fix? All you dogs are the same. Mangy mutts that should be put down."

"Listen, lady," Kohana shouted, marching back with his finger in front of him, pointing at her. "You don't see me throwing around names, and trust me, we have plenty. How about you..." his voice trailed off. "Do you smell that?"

"Yes," Mike said. The smell of blood had grown more intense. Everything in the police station became enhanced. He briefly caught his reflection in a window and saw the red hue in his eyes.

Nate squinted his eyes and curled his forehead, confused at what the two supernatural creatures were talking about. "Mike, your eyes..." he said.

The vampire leapt over a desk and ran to the door, leading into the waiting area. He bolted through it and out the front door.

Roy held his forehead in his hand while staring in the back of a pickup truck. A crowd of at least fifteen people stood around. Four different trucks had parked in front of the police station. Each had their headlights shining against the front of the station. The sting of the lights cut into Mike's eyes. He raised his hand in front of his face. He guessed he should at least be grateful the bright lights would conceal his red eyes.

Roy leaned back, flopping his butt into the truck behind him.

"Who the hell are you?" one of the crowd asked. It was the same voice which had screamed Roy's name earlier.

"I'm Michael," he answered. "You must be Troy. I'm truly sorry for your loss. My team and I are here to put a stop to all of this."

"Get in line. We're taking care of it. It's taken everyone else far too long. We aren't losing another member of our community to this fucking bear."

He yelled the last sentence as if a chant to the crowd. The group understood and uttered a collective, "Yeah", in response.

The tangy smell of blood wafted from the truck's bed. If he focused on it, he wouldn't be able to control his eyes. Instead, he opted to stay where he was. Mike glanced at Roy. Whatever he'd seen in the back of the truck had rocked him. It was obviously covered in blood. The truck wreaked of it. Mike surmised what happened without needing it laid out for him.

"As I'm sure Chief Henderson has said, we're here to help. Both my team and the U.S. Forestry Service can handle it."

"Well, as we told the Chief already," Troy said. His voice boomed in the open air, keeping everyone's attention. "We're going to handle this ourselves. Why don't you come over here and take a look at what the damn thing did? And this wasn't out in the woods. This was on the edge of town. This thing is killing our residents. Good people. Like my son who was just helping a fellow Boy Scout." Troy's eyes teared up. His mouth briefly quivered. He rubbed his hand over his face and shook his head, as if shaking off the pain. "Take a look," he demanded.

Mike, fully aware of the powder keg brewing, stepped toward the truck. He trained his eyes on Roy, trying not to focus on the smell of blood.

No red eyes.

He held the thought in his head, hoping he could overcome the urge to vamp out. If he could control himself within the hospital, he could do it here as well. Mike strode between two trucks. A large tarp lay across the bed of one of the trucks. Troy gripped it and pulled. A decapitated corpse, ripped to shreds, part of it eaten and gnawed, had been hidden underneath. The arms and legs had bite marks and chunks of muscle were missing. Morbidly, the head sat next to the body, staring out into nothing.

"This was Trevor Stone. Killed in his own car outside the football field," Troy continued. He stood next to Michael, yelling for the crowd to participate. "You say you're going to handle this. By the look of you, I'm guessing your military. Let me ask you, Mr. Military. Is this bear some kind of government experiment? Are you here to clean up your own mess?"

Mike shook his head. This was exactly what Roy was just saying they didn't need - another death. And this one in town. This may have just gotten beyond his control.

"You don't need to answer." Troy dropped the tarp over the body. "Don't worry, Chief, I'll take poor Trevor's body over to the coroner. I don't want his family to have to see him like this. Also, we, the people of Mena, we're going to handle your failure to serve and protect."

"Yeah!" the crowd cheered.

Mike glanced around. More vehicles had arrived on the scene - another two cars and three trucks. The crowd was growing despite it being almost midnight. Worse still, a few police officers dotted the crowd, participating in the uprising.

"Tomorrow afternoon, in front of the courthouse, there'll be a gathering in support of the families affected. I'm also doing a sign-up sheet for those who want to hunt with me. We won't come back until we're dragging the damn thing's dead carcass. Who's with me?"

"Yeah!"

Mike knew better than to intervene. Any attempt at quelling this mob had vanished. He also knew their job just became a lot harder. They had to kill the two rogue werewolves, and also had to make sure the werewolves didn't get to any of the townspeople.

Once the grieving father left, the rest of the crowd followed close-ly behind. Mike and Roy shuffled back inside the police station with their heads down. Worst case scenario on top of worst case scenario. This wasn't a trend that Mike was a fan of. They needed a win, but so far, nothing had gone their way.

Back inside, Mike surveyed the team staring at him.

"Oh, love, that didn't sound like it went well."

"No shit," Mike said. "This has slipped from a shitstorm into FUBAR really quick." He glanced at Kohana. "I thought you were leaving."

"I can give my updates later. They're going to be a problem."

"I've already said no shit once. I don't need to say it again. Chief, we're going to put an end to this. I also have an idea that may help you with Troy and his mob. I want you to agree with him and join the hunt tomorrow evening."

"Join the hunt? Why would I do some dumb shit like that?"

"You know what's really out there. We have silver ammunition you can use. Not to mention, we'll also be out there."

Mike leaned against a desk.

"John, you've got to give us something we can work with. The full moon is the night after next. Do you have anything?"

His eyes shifted to the ceiling. He paused, thinking. "The two rogues won't hunt tomorrow night," he said.

"How the fuck can you know that?" Nate asked. "They've done a good job of hunting every other fucking night."

"They're seasoned wolves. On the night of the full moon, they're going to want to make a statement. Every time we change, it's draining, exhausting. They know hunters are here. They know I'm here. They won't want to hunt tomorrow night and possibly have to fight while weaker. Instead, they'll lay low, conserve energy. That way, on the full moon, when we're at our strongest, they are at full charge, so to say."

"Two werewolves at full charge during the full moon," Nate said, nodding. He pursed his lips together. "Sounds fucking great. God, I fucking hate werewolves."

"Assuming you're right..." Mike chimed in. "Then we don't have to worry about Troy and his merry band tomorrow night. John, you and I will still be in those woods, just in case, and the Chief." He pointed at Nate, Niki, and Josh. "You three, keep your comm's handy. If John's right, then tomorrow should be quiet, and I'm really hoping he's right."

"We've got another problem," Josh added.

"For fuck's sake, Josh," Mike exclaimed.

"There's the other werewolf in the room. Let's not forget about David."

41

THE NEXT MORNING, JOSH and Niki pulled up to the hospital. Mike and Nate had stayed behind.

"Want me to give you a push?" Niki asked, shooting a playful smile to Josh.

"I should say yes, and then ride the brake on you. Give those scrawny legs a workout."

The longer they'd been a team, the more Niki reminded him of his sister. Not the whole Australian part, but her carefree attitude toward most of life and being an all-around badass. His sister had embraced that same take on life. She would've loved Niki. The two would've been inseparable... And a touch insufferable, as well, Josh assumed.

He tried not to think about his twin sister. Those thoughts often brought down his mood. He wasn't one to live in the past. He'd made peace with everything years ago.

"You're one to talk about scrawny legs, love."

"Oh, ouch. Kick the guy in the wheelchair, I see. Aren't you glad I'm not the sensitive kind?"

"Well, I can't talk about your arms. You've been getting buff. Muscling up to arm wrestle Nate?" She squeezed his bicep.

"I've got a ways to go before I have those guns. Heading in, let me lead. They think I'm with the CDC."

"You pulled out that old badge, huh? When was the last time you used that? The possessed girl in Wichita?"

"No, I've used it since then for the nurse witch in Sacramento. Remember? We got the files on everyone missing a kidney and noticed the same ER nurse on call."

"The nurse witch. She was an evil bitch."

Josh chuckled.

"What?" Niki asked.

"You've got your rhyming game on point. The witch was a bitch."

She laughed as well. "Whatever, DOCTOR Campbell. Let's go talk to the mutt."

The automatic doors slid open, and the pair strode to the front desk.

"We're here to see David Hall," Josh said. He held up his badge for her to see. "I was here yesterday and met with Dr. Wagner."

The same woman who had paid no attention to Niki the first time she had gone to visit David grabbed the badge, examining it. After flipping it in her fingers, she handed it back to him and sat back down.

"He checked out this morning."

"He did what?" Josh asked, his voice escalated, shocked at what she had said. The last time he'd seen David, just the day before, he had shot the pins holding his leg together out of his cast. How in the Hell could he be released already?

"He was examined this morning and cleared. Anything else, you'll need to talk to his doctor."

"I know where his office is. Is he available?" Josh turned to the door, waiting for her to buzz them through.

A moment later, the door clicked. "He may be finishing rounds, but go ahead."

Niki pulled open the door.

"Thanks," she said.

Josh wheeled himself though the door. Once it shut behind them, he craned his neck to Niki.

Before he could say anything, she said, "Already on it," as she raised her phone to her ear. "Nate, you and Mike need to find David. He checked himself out... Love, if I knew where he was, I wouldn't have said find him. Nathan Edwards, I don't care. Put up lost puppy posters. How the fuck do I know? You and Mike figure it out." She put the phone back in her pocket.

Josh slowed down as they approached Wagner's office. Fortunately, the light was on so he hoped the doctor was inside. He spun into the doorway and found Wagner behind his desk.

"Dr. Campbell," he said, standing up. He shook Josh's hand. His eyes glanced to Niki.

"Niki Davis," she held her hand out. "Dr. Campbell's research assistant." She gave a wide, fake smile, showing way too much teeth.

Wagner shook her hand as well and sat down behind his desk. "What can I do for you this morning?"

"I heard Mr. Hall checked out. After yesterday, I'm quite surprised. I thought you were running more tests."

"I wanted to. I insisted that he stay, but he refused. He didn't want any more tests. He had one hundred percent mobility in his legs and arms. There was no sign of any remaining contusions. If he had walked into my office fresh off the street appearing as he did today, I'd say there's no way he was involved in any accident or attack."

"And so he just walked out?" Josh asked.

"Hopped up on his own two legs. Legs that had pins holding them together until yesterday. And when I say hopped, I'm not exaggerating. He leapt out of that hospital bed. I had expected months of physical therapy, but the man literally jumped out of bed, landed on legs that were shattered not two weeks ago, and strode out of here. I've never seen anything like it before. A healing ability like that? I understand him not wanting to be a guinea pig but think of the medical miracles if we could understand how his body did that."

Josh nodded. He could sense the doctor's desire to want to know, but Josh doubted the man could accept the real answer. Lycanthropy wasn't a cure. "I agree," Josh lied. "Maybe I could have a word with him. Talk with him about the greater good that a few tests could mean for society. Did he give any indication where he might've gone?"

"He complained about being hungry. Said the hospital food was going to kill him. He wanted a burger."

42

David sat in a booth by the window. He stared at the back of his hands, watching the sunlight bounce off his skin. He'd never noticed how intricate a hand was, and not just the tiny wrinkles or the hair follicles, but also the slight discolorations. With each heartbeat, he sensed the blood flowing through the tiny capillaries.

Glancing up, the small diner exploded with colors, smells, and sounds. The white apron worn by the waitress appeared bright. Meat sizzled on the grill back in the kitchen. The smell of charred burgers, potatoes in the deep fryer, and even the hazelnut in the coffee bombarded his nostrils. The blue sky had a bolder blue than he'd ever noticed before. Every sound filled his head as if the volume had been turned up to eleven. Was this the rebirth after nearly dying that people had talked about? The fresh outlook on life?

All these sensations were part of the reason he had to get out of the hospital. He had thought the isolation, being stuck in that room, was driving him insane. The insanity was causing him to hear and smell things that weren't there. But now that he was out and the same sensations were overwhelming him, he knew it wasn't being trapped in the hospital bed that had caused it. This was a renewed chance at life. He'd survived the bear attack and being struck by a car. His body had healed in record time. He was alive.

Sadness accompanied the thought, though. Yes, he was alive. He had survived. But Rebecca hadn't. He never even had a chance to tell her goodbye. While he had been in a coma, her parents had cremated her. From what the police chief said, they blamed him for her death. Part of him understood. It was his idea to go camping, but it wasn't like he'd summoned the fucking bear. And it wasn't as if he'd left her to die. She had been dead before he escaped the tent.

His stomach growled. He wrapped his arm around his waist, hoping to silence the audible grumble emanating from it. The man a booth over glanced up, obviously hearing the sound. He'd already ordered and prayed it would be here any minute. Maybe his iron was low. He'd heard that when someone craves red meat, it was because of an iron deficiency. If that was the case, he must be extremely low because that was all he wanted. Red meat. He ordered his burger medium rare. Anything else felt too cooked. He couldn't bring himself to say raw but needed the burger to bleed a little.

His hunger consumed him, but so did his building anger toward Rebecca's parents.

You're just hangry. You'll be better after you eat.

As if on cue, the waitress came from behind the counter with a plate in her hand. She sauntered to his table and sat his dinner down in front of him. The moment it was within reach, he scooped up the burger and shoved a large bite of it into his mouth. The grease dripped down his chin and over his fingers.

"Need anything else?" she asked.

He hadn't bothered to pay attention to her name.

"Ketchup," he mumbled through a mouthful of burger. "And refill." He tapped his empty glass of tea.

She grabbed the glass and strode to the tea canister.

While she refilled his glass, he shoveled three more huge bites into his mouth. He had barely chewed before swallowing each one. The waitress returned with his tea. He took it out of her hand and promptly drained the entire glass.

"Shall I just bring you the pitcher?"

"Yes, please," he said, chomping on the last of the burger.

He didn't bother with a napkin and stuck each finger in his mouth, savoring the flavor. It was the best thing he'd ever tasted in his life. When the waitress had brought his glass of tea back to the table, she had also grabbed the ketchup bottle. He dabbed some of it on his plate, grabbed a few French fries, and swiped them through the red condiment. He ushered them into his mouth. Although he usually loved French fries, these tasted almost revolting, and he had to force himself to swallow and not throw up. They looked as fries should look. Felt as fries should feel. He was still hungry, but he couldn't eat these.

The brunette waitress came back with a pitcher of tea to leave on the table.

As she sat it down, David asked, "Let me order a second burger. Same way, but just the burger. No fries."

"No fries. Just the burger." She grabbed a notepad out of her apron and jotted that down.

"Two more."

"Two more?"

"Yes, two more burgers. Both the same way as the first."

"Need me to put them in a to-go container?"

David shook his head. "On a plate is fine. Thank you."

She turned and shuffled back to the counter, giving the order to the cook on the other side of the window before taking care of other customers.

His thoughts drifted back to Rebecca. He tried not thinking about what happened that night, but his mind betrayed him. Sadness washed over him again, as well as the growing anger. He needed to tell her goodbye, even if it was just to her ashes in an urn. David made up his mind. After he finished eating, he would march over to her parents' house and demand to be given that moment. He suffered too. It wasn't his fault that she was dead.

After ten minutes of stewing in his misery and fanning the growing embers of anger, the waitress slid another plate in front of him. This one had two burgers sitting side by side. Before she left, he handed her his credit card. "I'm done after this. Go ahead and ring me up."

"Will do," she said cheerily and strode to the register.

He took his time with his second order. Although still hungry, he didn't feel the need to cram the meat into his mouth. By the time, he shifted to the last burger, he pulled the bun off, grabbed the quarter pound patty with juices dripping from it, and ate it by itself. He didn't need the bun. The greasy beef patty eased his cravings. Maybe he did have an iron deficiency.

His meal finished, his stomach bulging from the three burgers, and everything paid for, David downed the last of the tea from the pitcher and slid out of the booth. With his phone in his hand, he ordered an Uber, typing in the address for Rebecca's parents. He had words for the woman he loved. As God was his witness, he was going to say them.

A few minutes later, the Honda Civic arrived. He opened the back door and sat inside. This was happening.

As the car drove off, a vibration traveled up his spine. The last time he'd felt that way, he had been in the hospital and thought he was having a heart attack. The Australian lady and her friend had come to visit him. Fortunately, as they drove away from the diner, the feeling faded to nothing. He smiled thinking how ironic it'd be if he survived the bear attack and getting hit by a car to then die from a heart attack after eating almost a pound of hamburger meat.

43

As in most small towns across the south, the courthouse sat in the middle. Mainly constructed of wood, it had large marble steps leading up to the large oak front doors. It was three stories tall, and the top of the building was a round dome with a small statue of Lady Justice uplifting her scale. It was easily the tallest building in the county. A grassy area surrounded the courthouse. Every four years, politicians stood on the lawn and gave their speeches on why their vision for Mena was better than the other asshole's vision. Every Fourth of July, the parade began in front of that same lawn, usually led by the Mena High School marching band. During Christmas, the courthouse and the lawn were decorated with lights and a nativity scene.

Today, it reminded Roy more of the election year setup. A stage had been carted in and constructed a few yards away from the marble courthouse steps. Close to fifty people milled around the grass, waiting. A lot of familiar faces peppered the crowd. Not surprisingly both Sergeant Lowell and a few of his other officers were among the group. They were just as upset about the killings as he was. Roy had struggled with letting them know what was really going on. On more than a few occasions, he almost had. Part of him still hadn't fully decided he wasn't.

He wondered if Troy Johnson and whoever else had organized all of this had secured the appropriate permits to hold an organized rally. He knew better than to raise that issue. It would only elevate the already high tensions.

A table sat on the other side of the courtyard. Occasionally, a person strolled up, grabbed a pen, and wrote on one of the pages taped to the top of the it. Roy marched toward the table, knowing full well what it would be.

"Good morning, Chief," Judy said. She had her long brown hair in a ponytail. He'd known Judy Daniel for a dozen years. She was a town council member.

Roy glanced at his watch. "Eleven o'clock. I guess that still counts as morning. How are you doing, Judy?" He glanced to the lady sitting next to Judy. He recognized her also, but never thought the two would be sitting next to each other as if they were friends. "Rachel."

Rachel was easily in her seventies. Her hair had turned completely white twenty years ago. Wrinkles etched into her face beneath her thick glasses. Anytime there was a call about someone disturbing the peace, Rachel was the one calling it in. She had raised a huge stink at a town council meeting two years back when Amazon had wanted to build a warehouse outside of town. Judy knew it'd bring jobs to the area. Rachel argued it would bring trouble and destroy the forest. In the end, Rachel won, and the council voted against the change in zoning. As far as Roy knew, the two hadn't spoken since.

"Town's in a world of hurt right now, Chief," Rachel said. "How do you think any of us are doing? I went over this morning to check on Trevor's poor parents. About broke my heart. I heard what happened to the boy. Troy told me how they found his body. It's made its way into town, Roy. Not just out there in the woods somewhere. In the town. What are you going to do about it?"

Henderson had expected this and more. He glanced down the table, eyeing the signup sheets lying in front of the two women. Two of them were food drives and donations for the loved ones of those who had been attacked or killed. The last one was the one he had come over there for. It was the signup sheet for the hunt. Roy grabbed a pen.

"This is what I'm doing right here, Rachel." He scribbled his name for the late-night group.

"Well, Chief Henderson," Troy said, strolling behind him. "I'm glad to see you're out here ready to serve and protect the town. Although, I'm pretty sure that's what we all hired you to do in the first place."

Roy reminded himself to breathe. Troy had lost his son a week ago. He'd obviously turned whatever sorrow he had into rage. Once this was all over, Troy would have to truly confront what happened. He wouldn't be able to hide behind his grief. Roy hoped the crash wouldn't destroy him. Troy and his family were good people in a bad situation. He realized he hadn't seen Troy's wife lately. She must be handling the funeral plans while Troy was plotting how to kill the beast. Each person dealt with pain differently.

"A few people have asked me to give a speech in a few minutes," he continued. "I'd love for you to stick around, Roy."

"That depends, Troy. How much of this speech is designed to criticize me or my department? Let me remind you, this hunt is for the bear, not for my head. I want the same thing as you."

Troy smiled. He clapped a hand on Roy's shoulder. "Since you've signed up to help and decided not to stand in our way on this, I'll go easier on you than I had planned. How's that? I've seen a number of your department in the audience. Am I to assume that we now have the full support of the police department to kill this thing?"

Roy wanted to punch Troy. He had become cocky and arrogant. Becoming the de facto mob leader had gone to his head. He'd bet his annual salary, Troy would be running for mayor at the next election. Troy had no idea what he was really after but was damn certain he'd kill it. Roy envied his confidence. He took a step forward, and Troy's hand fell from his shoulder.

"I'll be there tonight, and I'm not going to stop any of my officers from participating. Won't even consider it a personal day. Also, I'm not going to be checking for hunting licenses. From a support standpoint, that's really as far as I can go. It'll be like the opening day of deer season. Bring your own rifles or shotguns. I'm not loaning out any weapons. That's my only caveat. That work for you?"

Troy nodded. "You'll be right by my side tonight, Chief. That works great for me. Now, I need to hop up there."

He extended his hand, and Roy shook it. Troy Johnson jogged to the stage and hopped onto the platform. He waved to the growing crowd and sauntered to the podium at the front of the stage, as over one hundred people applauded.

Roy stayed by the table at the back of the audience. Every fiber in his body told him to leave. Troy wasn't going to say anything he needed to hear. They had a plan to keep everyone safe tonight and kill the two rogue werewolves tomorrow night. He strolled a few feet from Judy and Rachel and then turned back around, pacing.

"Good afternoon, Mena. Thank you all for coming out today," Troy said. He motioned his hands down, directing the crowd to quiet their applause. His tone became somber. "Today is not a good day in Mena. Actually, Mena hasn't been well for almost two weeks now. That was when we first heard rumblings of an animal in the woods. That was when Rebecca Summers was brutally killed. I stand accused, as do most of you, for not doing what we needed to do at that time. We should've done our constitutional duty and taken up arms to protect our town and our fellow neighbors, especially when those who were supposed to protect us didn't."

Roy stared at the stage and locked eyes with Troy.

"Then, a few days later, my young son..." Troy paused. He placed his fist in front of his mouth, choking back tears. "Tanner was a Boy Scout hiking with his troop. *He* was helping his fellow scouts earn the hiking merit badge. That evening started for his mother and I like every other evening. We ordered pizza, made sure he was dressed for the hike, and dropped him off with his troop, just a regular Tuesday night. If only we would have known. If only we would have known it was the last time we would have Tuesday night pizza before a scout meeting. If only we would have known it was the last time we would see our son, be able to tell him we love him, and he tell us back. If only we would have known there was a beast hunting people in the woods."

The crowd was silent. Roy watched on. The only sound came from the occasional audience member sniffling, holding back their own tears as Troy recounted his pain.

"I'm standing up here today, so that another father doesn't have to. Last night's brutal assault on Trevor Stone will never happen again." Troy changed his tone. The somberness in his opening dissolved into fire brand. He was revving up. "I was there when Samantha stumbled into The Pit, hoping to find her own father. It was only by the grace of God that she wasn't also attacked. I say that, though, knowing that her family is with her now. The girl has experienced so much trauma that her retelling of what happened has slipped into the world of fantasy. It's the only way her fragile mind is able to cope with the tragedy she witnessed. I pray, as should you, that God heals her."

Roy glanced over the crowd. Troy was doing a great job of keeping them engaged. He had a knack for giving speeches. If he did decide to run for mayor, he'd win in a landslide.

Off to his right, he heard a sound that was out of place for an event like this. He heard what sounded like someone snicker. He shot his head toward the sound.

A dozen feet to his right, two young men stood a few feet back from the crowd. Where everyone else was pressing closer to the stage, they kept themselves separated. One was a few inches taller than the other. Both had black hair and were Indigenous American.

Roy shuffled his way toward them, keeping his eyes on Troy as if he was inching closer to get a better view. He pulled himself into earshot of the pair.

What are you doing, Roy? If these are the two werewolves, you're going to get yourself killed.

Although he knew it wasn't safe, he needed to do something. If these two wanted to, they could turn on this crowd and leave a trail of destruction. There was no way to know how long it'd take for the team to stop their slaughter.

"Grace of God," the taller one whispered and audibly scoffed. If they were who he thought they were, then he was the older brother.

The younger brother leaned toward the older one. "Maybe that's what they're calling us," he also whispered.

That told Roy everything he needed to know. He dropped his hand to his waist and pressed on the snap holding his gun in place. The clasp gave a slight click as it released.

"That isn't a wise thing to do, Chief Henderson," the older brother said and turned his head to Roy. "John isn't around, and the Night Crew are chasing after Mr. Hall."

Roy took a deep breath. It was time for his bravado to do some talking. He stepped closer to the two werewolves. He stuck his chest out and pretended none of his fears existed. They were just two normal suspects. His hand still rested on the top of his gun.

"This is filled with silver, you know."

"We can sense it. But do you honestly believe you could pull your gun from its holster and fire not once but twice before your head is torn from your body? And once we've done that, well, what choice would we have but to continue through the entire town until — if — we are stopped. Most will die, but a few might end up like David. Is that what you want?"

Troy's cockiness had nothing on the arrogance of the older werewolf. The younger one didn't say anything. According to what Kohana said last night, he was the one John had almost killed. He did favor one side. Despite whatever wound he had, Roy knew the arrogant asshole was right. They were fast, and he was old. He wouldn't pull the gun in time.

He stared into the eyes of the older werewolf and slowly clicked the strap closed around his handgun.

"Wise decision, Chief." The brother's eyes flamed yellow around the dark pupils. "Let's go, brother. We should get some rest. Full moon is getting close." He tapped his brother in the stomach, and the younger one winced. He was still injured.

Roy paced back to the table as the two brothers hurried around a building, disappearing out of sight. He reached for his phone to call Mike, but it started vibrating before he had the chance. He recognized the caller ID immediately. It was the station.

"Henderson," he said as he answered.

"Chief, it's Dylan. I just had a call come in that I thought you'd like to be looped in on."

"What is it?"

"Disturbance call from the Summers residence. David Hall is demanding to come in and won't leave."

"Thanks, Dylan. I'll handle it."

Roy clicked over to his contacts and found the number he saved for Michael White. At least they now knew where David was. He hoped that would be the start of good things to come.

DAVID STOOD ON THE front porch. The big wooden door blocked his entrance. He pounded on it repeatedly sending reverberating thuds into the house. Then he pressed the doorbell a few times. This had been his pattern for the last ten minutes. "I know you can hear me!" he shouted. "I just want to tell her goodbye."

He rapped on the door again.

"It wasn't my fault. It almost killed me, too."

Quietly, from the other side of the door, he heard the faintest whisper of a voice. They were right behind the door. He knew they were. He could feel them there. Mr. Summers' cheap cologne lingered in the air just out of reach, but David could smell it. He stood still, listening.

"He won't go away..." the whisper said. It was Mrs. Summers' voice. David didn't know how he'd heard her whisper, but he did. She was typically a very soft-spoken woman and had a breathy tone that came across as almost fragile. He never heard her yell and doubted she could. "Thank you," she finished. "He said they'll send someone over right away."

"Who did you call?" David asked. "Did you call the police? Why won't you let me in so I can talk to her? That's all I'm asking."

David took a step back.

The Summers were one of the wealthiest families in Mena. Their house wasn't huge. It was only a single story, but the structure sprawled from one side of the oversized lot to the other. White stone facing provided the majority of its elegance. The door was solid oak. It provided the perfect focal point against the white stone. The covered front porch matched the door. Large white stone planters lined the front.

David leaned forward and pounded on the door again. Each hit echoed inside the house. From outside, David heard the sound bouncing around the interior. Just like being able to hear Mrs. Summers on the phone with the police, he wasn't sure how he heard the echo. The last hit created a small cracking sound. He glanced at his fist, unsure if the crack had come from the door or his hand. He extended his fingers, examining them. Once he was convinced it was the door, he balled his fingers into a fist again and continued to hit the door.

The frame rattled, and another crack appeared.

"David, you need to leave." That was Mr. Summers. Unlike his wife, he wasn't soft spoken. "The police are on their way, and I'm armed as well. If you step foot in this house, I'll be forced to take lethal action."

"You're going to shoot me? I'm not trying to rob you. I've been in a coma, and I woke up to find that you'd already cremated her. I loved her, too." The last came out as a desperate cry.

"If you hadn't taken our dear Rebecca camping, she'd still be alive."

Anger rose inside of him. Mr. Summers had vocalized his fears, his guilt. Everything he'd been tormenting himself with since waking up. If he hadn't taken her out, she'd still be alive. He leaned his head against the smooth wooden door. It provided coolness against his heated forehead. He placed his forearms against the door above his head. A searing pain burned into his fingertips as if each of his fingernails was being ripped away. He beared down on the door, pressing into the strain. Although the pain was agonizing, he didn't care. In fact, he relished it. The pain mixed with the anger, and he swallowed them both, letting them build a fire inside him. David dug the tips of his fingers into the door. The counter pressure alleviated some of the pain but not anywhere close to all.

He dragged both hands down the door. As he did, he picked his head off the door and peered straight ahead. Large gouge marks, one for each finger, trailed down the wooden door. It looked as if Wolverine had dug his Adamantium claws down it. He stared at the changes in his hands.

"What the fuck!"

He snapped his hands into fists, refusing to believe what he saw, burying the claws into the palms of his hands. As each one punctured its own track inside his flesh, he began to believe his eyes. Enraged at the stabbing pain from his own fingernails, he raised his fist in the air and ran at the door. He slammed his fist into it, and a large chunk splintered backward.

The tingling sensation spiraled up his spine.

What the hell is happening?

"David, if you hit the door one more time, I will shoot you." Mr. Summers emphasized his seriousness by chambering a round into the shotgun. The sound of the pump action was unmistakable.

David unclenched his fists and rubbed the back of his neck. Earlier, the sensation had died a few short moments but this time, it intensified.

"Mr. Hall," a voice from behind him said. The voice had a commanding sound to it, forcing David to turn around.

Two men stood on the front lawn. One was a tall, muscular black man. The other guy was pale in a gray hoodie. David couldn't make out most of his features as the hood obscured his face. That man continued to speak.

"We met briefly in the hospital, but you mainly talked to my friend. I'm Michael, and now we need to talk."

David glanced down at his hands. The fingernails that weren't fingernails had disappeared. His hands were back to normal. He turned them over, examining his palms. There wasn't a mark on either, as if he hadn't just dug an inch of each fingernail into them.

"I just want to say my goodbyes," David said. When he heard the sound of his own voice, it exuded defeat. That wasn't who he was. Now, even his own voice pissed him off. He wasn't defeated. He wasn't a loser. He wasn't a quitter. He was here for a reason. And he deserved that reason.

He took a deep breath and said it again but with conviction. "I need to say my goodbyes." He marched to the door, placed both hands on it, leaned his torso close, and pushed with all his might. The door broke free, shattering the frame, and raining broken pieces of wood onto his back.

In an instant, Michael stood next to him. David saw Michael at the same time as he saw Mr. Summers. Rebecca's father had the shotgun raised, and his finger on the trigger. David knew this was it, but before he could fire, Michael had grabbed the gun out of the old man's hand.

"There's no need for that," Michael said. "Chief Henderson sent me. Nathan and I are here to escort David home. But before we do, I would like to say I'm sorry for your loss. I lost my wife recently. Her memory is with me every day. More so than you can imagine. As she died, I had the chance to hold her in my arms and tell her goodbye. David didn't kill your daughter. At the time, no one even knew the beast was out there. He's grieving her loss, just as you are. Allow him a moment to say goodbye. Nate and I will make sure he says his piece, and then you won't ever see him again. The door will also be replaced. Please, accept our sincerest apologies."

David stood there as Michael talked. He spoke with the honesty of someone who had felt true and deep loss. He said he'd lost his wife, and David believed him. Obviously, so did the Summers. Mr. and Mrs. Summers backed out of the way.

"Be quick," he said. "Her urn is on the mantel." He placed an arm on his wife and escorted her out of the room.

"David, do them the honor of respecting their generosity by making it quick." Michael unloaded the shotgun and leaned it against the wall. He placed the shells on a table in the entryway.

David nodded and slowly strode into the living room. From the moment he saw the urn over the fireplace, his eyes never drifted. As he stood in front of it, he hesitated. He'd practiced over and over what to say, but now that he was here, he didn't know anymore. Finally, he just let the words flow.

"Hey, honey. It's me. I love you, and I'm really sorry. I wish it would've been me. You were always such a better person." The words became trapped in his throat, and he had to clear it to keep going. His eyes burned as the tears built. "Since I woke up, all I've thought about is you. What could I have done differently? They told me a bear's been killing people. We're going to kill it, babe. Going to kill it for you and everyone else it's killed."

David rubbed his eyes and cleared his throat again. "Listen, I'm going to go hunt this thing with everyone else. In the meantime, do me a favor. Can you put in a good word for me with the man upstairs? I've done some shitty stuff in my life. You were the best part of it. So, if something nice comes from you, maybe the Big Guy will think more fondly of me in case I make it up there in the near future. I love you. That'll never change. Bye, Rebecca." He leaned forward and kissed the urn.

David turned to Michael who had moved back to the broken doorway.

"Where do you want to talk?"

"My team is waiting for you at your place. Let's go there."

David nodded. "Sounds great. On the way, can we stop for a burger? I'm starving."

45

Dᴀᴠɪᴅ sᴀᴛ ɪɴ ᴛʜᴇ recliner in his living room surrounded by a bunch of strangers. He glanced from person to person. This felt like the set up for some kind of intervention. He'd seen each person at some point over the past few days, but never all at once. Until now, he wouldn't have guessed they all worked together.

If this was some kind of a meeting, he thought everyone would introduce themselves. Tell us your name and a fun fact about you. Except this didn't feel like that kind of situation. Everyone had already introduced themselves, well, re-introduced themselves, when he strolled in.

Now, he peered around the room, the center of attention. Chief of Police Henderson stood next to Park Ranger John. David remembered him from when he had come into the hospital room early one morning, not long after he'd woken up from his coma. From there Josh, who had stopped by the hospital yesterday when the pins shot out of his leg, sat in his wheelchair.

Niki, the supposed bear hunter, was on his couch next to Nate. Nate was the only one he'd just met today. Michael, whose presence sent tingling vibrations up David's back and smelled like death, stood behind the couch.

"I'm here," he finally said, breaking the silence in the room. David raised his hands in front of him before dropping them to the arms of the recliner. "I know something's wrong with me. I'm not an idiot. Since that night, I haven't felt like myself. No one heals as fast as I did to the point where the pins holding my femur together shot out of my leg. It's not natural. Same with how I smell you two." He pointed at Mike and then John. "And then there's what happened a little bit ago with the door." David shook his head and stared at the ground. Slowly, he lifted his head and asked. "What's wrong with me?"

John took a step forward and cleared his throat.

"You're a werewolf, love," Niki blurted out before John had a chance to say anything.

Kohana turned his gaze to Niki, the very definition of "if looks could kill."

"That was uncalled for. Over the years, we've learned the best ways to broach the subject with someone and deliver the news gently. I don't know how things work in the vampire world, but as I've said before, we look after our own."

"We don't have time for therapy sessions until he finds himself," Niki snapped back. "Plus, he already knew something was wrong. Might as well rip the Band-Aid off."

David listened to them bicker as if he wasn't in the room. He heard their words but didn't process anything. His brain was stuck on what Niki had said: he's a werewolf. As she said it, he felt the beast inside of him acknowledge her words. It didn't make sense. Werewolves weren't real. How could they be? Yet, as much as it didn't make sense, it did bind everything together that had happened to him so far. What did that mean going forward?

"A werewolf?" he finally vocalized. "So the thing that bit me... It wasn't a bear?"

"No, it wasn't a bear," John answered. "Two members of our pack have gone rogue. One of them attacked you and killed Rebecca. They've been the ones slaughtering people."

"Of our pack? Does that mean you're also a werewolf? It would explain the smell."

Niki audibly smirked.

John placed his hands on the arms of the recliner and leaned in close to David. David stared into his eyes and suddenly the Ranger's irises changed to yellow. A deep, guttural growl vibrated in John's throat. When David saw John's eyes, he recalled the eyes of the beast that had attacked them. They were the same color.

"Holy fuck," he said and slipped down into the recliner. "Holy shit. So I'm going to turn into that thing that killed Rebecca? The creature that everyone is hunting?"

"You will. Tomorrow night on the full moon." John pulled away from the chair and strode back to Roy. "Werewolves always turn on the full moon. Over time, you'll learn how to control the wolf and call it at will. For your first change, the beast will consume you. You'll have no control over it."

"Fucking fabulous," Niki said under her breath.

Both John and David shifted their gaze toward her.

She rolled her eyes. "Oh yeah, mutts. Of course you hear everything."

David glanced toward Michael. "You also smell off, but not like him. What are you?"

"A vampire," Mike said.

"Every time you were close to me, I felt it."

"From what I've been told, that tends to happen," Mike said. "I felt it, too."

"From what you've been told? How many werewolves have you met?"

"Just you four. I've only been a vampire for the last six months."

David nodded. "At least you get to be in control of yourself."

"When I first turned, I was so consumed with hunger, I nearly killed the rest of the team. I don't change into a wolf on the full moon, but every day, I fight slipping back into bloodlust."

David turned his attention back to John. "Does it hurt?"

"Yes."

"Just yes. Don't sugar coat that for him, love." Niki shook her head. "Where's your years of delivering the news gently on that one?"

"Thought you preferred the Band-Aid ripping technique?"

"I need you two to stop sniping at each other like children!" Roy shouted. "Those two are out there. They threatened me at the rally. They have something planned for tonight or tomorrow night. It's going to be bloody, and it's going to be bad. For us to stop them, we've got to work as a team. This divisiveness is going to get us all killed. Enough of it. Got it?"

Niki stood up. She marched out of the living room, threw open the front door, and slammed it shut behind her.

"If you'd been through what we have," Nate said, standing up as well, "you wouldn't blame her." He started for the door.

"Nate..." Mike demanded.

Nate turned with his hand on the doorknob.

"We need you," Mike continued. "Both of you."

He opened the door and followed after Niki.

David stared at Mike, as did John, Roy, and Josh.

After a moment weighed down by its silence, Josh finally spoke up. "They'll come around. Werewolves are hard for them. They have history. But don't worry, they'll come around. They always do."

"So, where do we go from here?" David asked.

Everyone shifted their gaze to Roy.

David knew an awkward pause when he saw one.

"Well," Roy said. "Your safety is a priority of mine. That being said, you're going to spend the next few nights in jail."

"In jail? Why?"

"For starters, there was the incident at the Summers' house. That would've gotten you a night in the slammer anyway. But beyond that, the station will be cleared out each night. I'll have officers joining the hunts to help keep people safe. When you...change, you'll be in a cell by yourself. I've already talked it over with John. He's confident the cell, plus a few chains around your arms and legs, will help keep you safe. You'll be mad as hell, but in the morning, you won't remember it."

David leaned back in the recliner. "I get out of the hospital, get told I'm a werewolf, and then get thrown in jail. Been a productive day."

46

"YOU'VE GOT TO BE fucking kidding me," Niki shouted. "Is this punishment for walking out? Is that it?"

She wanted to keep yelling, but by the look on Mike's face, it wasn't going to matter. That didn't mean she was going to stop, though. Fuck that.

Michael stood in the middle of the police station with his arms crossed as she paced from one side of the room to the other.

"John and I will be in the woods watching after the hunters. Josh is already at the hotel monitoring the drones, scanning the forest. That leaves you and Nate."

The smooth calmness in his voice made her angrier. Not to mention that he made sense.

Frustrated, she grunted, then said, "So, yes, this is punishment. I mouthed off to that mutt, so Nate and I are on babysitting duties. Fucking great!"

"It's not babysitting. It's a protective detail. You're being ridiculous, and you know it."

She stormed over to him. "Ridiculous? You know how Nate and I feel! You know what they did. You were there, in my head."

She wanted to punch him but knew it wouldn't have any effect. It'd probably hurt her hand more than it would his face. How could he not understand? This mission started fine. Kill a werewolf. Great, that sounded fun. She jumped at the opportunity any chance she got. Then, it was kill two werewolves, which was even better, but the cost was having to work with another one. She only stomached it because she'd already hit him with her whip and shot him in the leg. She'd doled out a little punishment in exchange for cooperation. Now, the mission had added a new element. Watch after the new baby werewolf who will try to kill you the moment he changes and loses all control of himself. You don't get to kill him; you just get to babysit him and make sure he doesn't hurt himself or others.

Lovely. Fucking A Lovely.

Great, fucking tell him not to kill me.

"You're right. I was there. I saw what happened, and the creature who did it. It was none of the ones who are here with us. We put a stop to those who are a threat, who have killed others. David's not hurt anyone."

"Not yet. But tomorrow night when he turns, then what?"

The door from the lobby into the bullpen opened, and Niki turned around. Roy escorted David inside.

"That's why he's going in the jail, and I have someone I trust as much as I do you and Nate to watch him. To make sure he doesn't hurt anyone when he turns." Mike shifted his eyes away from Niki. "David, how are you feeling?"

Niki eased herself onto the edge of a desk. She placed both hands on it. A small mirror sat on a desk in front of her. She saw her reflection and wasn't surprised at the flush on her face. Her cheeks were red, and her face had splotches of red and white. If Nate saw her, he'd turn and hide. Whenever she was that mad, he knew better than to stick around.

"I'm hungry," David answered. "I can't seem to eat enough right now. I had three burgers before you guys picked me up. I had another two a few hours after we talked, and a steak which was almost rare right before Roy brought me here."

"Nate's grabbing you guys food for the night," Mike said. He glanced at Niki. "Hopefully, you three eat and have a nice, quiet evening where you can get plenty of rest. Without issue."

"From your mouth to God's ears," David said. "I haven't had restful sleep since that night. Every time I close my eyes, I see it ripping through the tent."

"Any idea how much longer until Nate's back?" Niki asked. "I'm fucking starving."

"David and I passed him on the way here. He was in the drive thru line, so I'm guessing not long. In the meantime, David, let's get you stashed for the night."

The two marched through the bullpen and into the back room. A few minutes later, a large metal door rattled down a track and slammed into a metal frame. A clank rang through the station as the lock engaged.

"Get comfortable," Roy said, still in the jail room. "They'll bring you some food. Don't cause any trouble tonight."

Niki rolled her eyes.

Yep, babysitting. Security detail, my ass.

"I don't plan to be. At least this cot's more comfortable than the hospital bed."

Roy strolled out of the jail room, grinning.

"You know..." he said to Mike and Niki. "That's not the first time someone has said that. Guess we need to get some harder mattresses."

"Or the hospital needs to replace theirs," Mike said.

"You aren't lying. I'm heading to the courthouse to join up with Troy's group." Roy took his pistol out of its holster, ejected the clip, and checked the bullets inside it. "I'm loaded up with silver. To be honest, I really hope I don't have to use it. I don't want to come face to face with either of those two." He slammed the clip back in place and holstered the gun. "Makes me feel better that you and John will be out there with us."

"If we do our job right, you won't even know we're there."

"Am I getting one of those earpiece things your team wears?" Roy asked, heading for the door.

"No, it's best if you stay as natural as possible. Just, watch your six tonight."

Roy nodded and left.

Mike turned to Niki. The conversation with Roy had given her a few minutes to calm down. She'd already decided once Nate was there, she'd toss David a few burgers, close the door, and she and Nate would relax until morning.

"It'll be nightfall soon. John and I will be on comms if anything happens. Behave yourself."

"Don't worry, love. Nate and I won't kill him. At least not tonight."

Mike slow blinked a few times. She read the frustration on his face and enjoyed causing a little of the shared misery.

As he shuffled out the door, Nate strolled in carrying two large bags of food.

"You're in trouble," she said, sliding out one of the desk chairs and flopping into it.

"What did I do?" he asked. "I got your order just the way you like it. With extra pickles and no onions."

"You knew we were babysitting the mutt-to-be and didn't tell me."

The look on his face told her how right she was.

47

Niki lifted her legs and propped her feet on a desk, leaning back in the chair. Night had fallen. Everyone but her and Nate were in Ouachita National Forest hunting for a bear. Well, her, Nate, and David. He'd been stuck in the cell for a few hours now. Shortly after Nate had arrived with food, she had tossed him a burger. Another three sat on a desk by the jail room. She'd decided to ration them throughout the night so he didn't start complaining about being hungry.

She glanced at Nate. He had curled up on a small wooden bench against the wall. His snoring reverberated around the bullpen.

Her earbud sat on the desk next to her feet. She'd gotten tired of hearing nothing but breathing. Occasionally, Mike told Josh where they were. Niki didn't know why he did that. Josh tracked their location. He could probably tell Mike where he was better than Mike could. She reached across the desk, snatched the earpiece, and jammed it into her ear.

"Breaker, breaker one-nine. How 'bout ya, Good Buddy? Got your ears on?" she rattled off.

"In case you were wondering," Josh said, "Niki's bored. And I'm guessing that motorcycle sound in the background is Nate sawing logs?"

"You'd be correct, love. He's on the tiny wooden bench. I don't even know how he's fitting. If he kicked a leg out right now, he'd break an arm off of it. Poor thing's just so sleepy."

"How's our guest?" Mike asked.

"I haven't checked on him since tossing a burger in the cage a few hours ago."

"Poke your head in just to make sure."

"I just got fucking comfortable in this chair. I'll bring him another snack in an hour or so. Will that be OK?"

"Niki, it's nearly midnight. He could be asleep. In that case, you're golden."

"Sure, fine. See if I drop in on you guys again. I want to make jokes, and instead, you give me shit to do. Niki, out!" She popped the earpiece out of her ear and sat it on the desk. She let her feet fall to the floor, released an audible huff of air, and stood up.

She strolled past the bench where Nate's sleeping mass lay. She thought about kicking him but changed her mind.

"Ah, fuck it!" she said and moved past him.

She strode to the door to the jail room and poked her head inside.

David lay across the bed with a few pillows propping up his head. He held his phone in front of him, scrolling through whatever apps puppies liked.

Fuck, not asleep.

"Need another snack?"

David flatted the phone against his chest and sat up on an elbow. "I could eat."

"Of course you can," she mumbled and reached for one of the burgers, tightly wrapped in butcher paper from the diner.

"I can hear you. Super dog ears, remember?"

Niki suppressed a smirk at the corner of her mouth. With the burger in hand, she sauntered to the cell. She stuck her arm through the bars, holding the burger out for David. He rose from the bunk and stepped toward her. He grabbed the burger, started for the bed, but then headed to the wall and slid his back down it until his butt was on the floor.

"Didn't want to sit on the bed?"

"Change of scenery. Getting tired of staring at the same thing." David unwrapped a part of the burger, keeping the lower half tightly covered so the grease didn't drop onto the floor or his clothes. "Niki, can I ask you a question?"

"I was about to go back to the excitement of my feet on top of a random police officer's desk, but sure, ask away." Niki leaned her shoulder against the door frame and crossed her arms. She wanted to spend as little time as possible in here, but at the same time, there was nothing else going on. The night was turning out to be as quiet as John had anticipated.

"Will it hurt?"

"What's that, love?"

"When I change into a werewolf, will it hurt? In some movies, when they show someone change, it's painful. I'm thinking *American Werewolf in London*, for instance. Although *Twilight*, they seem to just morph into their wolf form."

Niki thought for a moment. "Well, if you're using *Twilight* as a source of reference, I'll point out vampires don't sparkle in the sunlight. If the vampires are wrong, it's safe to assume the werewolves are too."

David let his arms fall to his legs, still holding the burger, and his head leaned back into the wall. "Shit. That's true. It's going to hurt," he said, dejected.

Fuck, Niki thought and raised her shoulder off the door frame. She marched over to the cell and sat down on the floor on the opposite side of the bars from David.

"I honestly don't know if it'll hurt. That'll be a question for John when he's back. It seems like they've done this transition thing for new wolves before. I've never hung around to watch a new werewolf turn. It's not been part of the job before."

"It's your job to hunt and kill them... Well, I guess, to hunt and kill *us*, since I'm part of them now."

Niki nodded.

"Do you like your job?" David asked.

Niki opened her mouth to respond but then hesitated. She wasn't sure when the last time someone had asked that question. A year or two ago, she would've responded yes without thinking about it, but over the past few months, things had changed. The incident with Lilith, having to relive her worst moment over and over again, left a lasting impact.

After the pause, she finally said, "Yes, I like my job. I get to do it with Nate. The two of us get to help people and places like Mena."

"Makes sense. Another question."

"We've got all night."

"I saw how you blew up at John...and I've seen how you look at me. You work with a vampire, so it's not all monsters. Did a werewolf take someone from you? If you don't want to answer, I get it." David pulled the wrapper over the top of the burger and sat it down next to him.

A shot of pain hit her in the heart. She didn't want to think about it, let alone talk about it. And to top it off, she'd be talking about it to a fucking werewolf. Fucking hell. Sitting on the floor, she glanced down at her hands, as she rubbed them together.

"Our son. Mine and Nate's. Nate was at work, and I took Jamal to the park that evening. It was late. We had gotten bored waiting for Nate to get home. That kid loved the park, and it wore him out. He always slept good after playing. He got way ahead of me on the Playscape. This was before we knew about any of this." Her hand moved, indicating everything around them. "There was a werewolf. Before I could get to Jamal..." she trailed off.

She felt the tears well up and wiped them away before they could break free and slide down her face.

"I'm really sorry for your loss," David said. "Your son, Rebecca, Tanner. I know there are many others, but those are off the top of my head. I haven't even changed into one yet, and I already loathe what I have become."

Niki chuckled and shook her head. "You sound like Mike after he turned. Sad and brooding. It's ok. You don't need to apologize for what happened. It wasn't you in that park, and it wasn't your fault what's happened here. Don't blame yourself."

As Niki said the words, she realized she was projecting blame onto him, onto every werewolf she'd ever come across because of the pain one particular wolf had caused her. It would be like hating an entire race because of what one person did. David was also a victim in all of this. She'd been treating him like a burden and a willing participant.

She bit her lip and raised her head. "I need to apologize to you. I know you're scared, and all I've shown you, both Nate and I but primarily me, has been nothing but contempt. I probably owe Kohana an apology as well. Fuck, you know I shot him in the leg, right?"

David smiled. "I heard. How'd it feel?"

"Fucking great, of course."

She laughed. It was a raucous laugh from her stomach. She knew she needed it, and it felt purifying. She literally rolled on the floor laughing along with the werewolf only a few feet away.

"Did I miss something?" Nate asked, standing at the door. "You two look like you just heard the funniest joke ever."

Niki pulled herself together and sat back down. "Just reminiscing on how good it felt to shoot John in the leg."

Nate smiled. "I can see that. You two look like two peas in a pod."

"We've had a decent conversation, love. Did we wake you?"

"I wasn't sleeping that hard."

"Your snoring would say otherwise," David quipped from the floor.

Niki glanced over to David, then back up at Nate. "Don't listen to him, super dog hearing, remember? But Josh also heard you over the comms."

Nate rolled his eyes and shook his head.

The front door opened, and Nate turned his head. As the sound of shattering glass ripped through the station, Niki jumped to her feet.

48

MIKE STOOD IN THE shadows of the forest. The sounds of the night enveloped him. An owl hooted. A breeze ruffled the leaves in the tall trees surrounding him. It reminded him of relaxation tracks he'd heard. A few times, he felt like slipping into the memory of the vision. He wondered if doing so would turn into a memory or if he'd have another conversation with Valerie. Once this mission was finished, he wanted to learn more about her. How did she know who he was? How did she call out to him?

Footsteps drew close, so he silently melted further into the shadows. He had jostled between two hunting parties while John watched a third group on the opposite side of town. Once, Mike was far enough away that he wouldn't draw attention, he focused his attention on the two groups he was following.

"Dammit, Troy. Do you realize it's almost midnight?" Roy asked, as he leaned against a tree.

Based on the accelerated heart rate and breathing, Mike could tell he needed a break.

Roy was part of a four-man team that included him, Troy Johnson, and two others. They'd been scouring their sector of the woods for close to three hours. By the look of the other two, they were also wearing down. Troy was the only one who seemed ready to keep going. Mike noticed a look in his eyes that told him Troy had no intention of stopping until a bear hung displayed over the courthouse steps. It wouldn't surprise Michael if Troy had plans to have the bear stuffed and mounted in city hall.

Mike knew Troy wouldn't get his wish. They weren't going to taxidermy two werewolves. He tilted his head to the overcast night sky. Not a star shone through. The nearly full moon barely did. The whole area was pitch black. If not for Mike's vampiric power of sight, he wouldn't be able to see anything, let alone the four men standing thirty yards away. If only they knew whether Kohana was right about the two staying in and building their energy for whatever terror they had planned for tomorrow night. Mike would've loved to give the team a night off in preparation.

"Troy, we should start heading back," Roy said. "I don't think we're going to find it tonight."

"What's the matter, Roy? Worried we're going to kill it before that team you hired does? Robert? What about you? Are you ready to head back?"

Robert leaned his shoulder against a tree. "It is getting late. I'd much rather be home looking after Samantha. That girl is so traumatized from what happened, she doesn't want to move far from her mom or me. The doctor had to give her meds to sleep. She laid on my lap as if she was a little girl most of the day. I rubbed my fingers through her hair like I did when she wasn't feeling well. All day, she mumbled, 'No, bear,' in her sleep, as if trying to shoo it away. Once she even mentioned wolves. Poor thing is going through some stuff."

"Jeremy?" Troy asked, still not ready to concede and hoping to bully at least one of them into siding with him.

Jeremy, who was slim and in his mid-fifties with a graying beard, had a shotgun propped on his shoulder, as if marching off to war. "I'm kinda with the others, Troy. It's late, and if you're going to want us to do this again tomorrow night, I need to get some sleep. I gotta go to work in a few hours."

"You're all pussies, you know. Not a one of you man enough to take care of our town. That's fine. You three head home. I'll stay out here on my own."

Mike saw Troy's face flush with blood. The others' desire to leave angered him. He hoped Roy would at least stick around. He was the only one in the group who had the right ammunition to handle the threat.

"I'm not going to let you do that, Troy," Henderson said. "This is already dangerous. I can't let you wander around in the middle of the night by yourself."

"What are you going to do? Lock me up like you did David? I'm sure that'll go over well. There're a lot of people who want this thing killed before it mauls another one of our babies. I'll stay out here as long as it..."

Before he finished, a large clack echoed through the woods. It was the unmistakable sound of a rifle firing. Another two loud shots followed close behind. Mike stared in the direction the shots came from. They were close to him, so it had to be the other hunting party. The group was too far away for him to see, even with his superhuman vision.

"What happened, over?" Troy asked, holding a walkie-talkie in front of him. "Anyone there, over?"

The other three hovered around Troy.

Finally, the walkie-talkie blared to life. Sounds of cheering and excitement rang through the small speaker. "We got it," a voice shouted. "Did you read? We got it, over."

Mike didn't wait around to hear what Roy's group said. He sprinted toward the group on the other end. He knew they couldn't have killed one of the werewolves. They weren't packing silver bullets. He was afraid he knew what they killed, and more than that, he feared the fallout from it.

He darted through the woods, sprinting past trees and leaping over bushes, silently traversing the rugged landscape. As he heard the congratulatory acknowledgments, he slowed down.

"Anyone hearing me?" Mike asked in barely a whisper. "Josh, did your drones pick up anything?"

"I have one over you now," Josh said. "Picking up heat signatures. I see..." Josh exhaled audibly. "I see the five-person team standing around a fading signature. It looks like..."

"A bear," Mike finished. "They were hunting a bear, and they killed one."

The tone in Mike's voice matched Josh's. As soon as he had heard them say they got it, he had an inclination that was what had happened. He stood twenty yards away from the celebrating group. The bear lay sprawled on the ground. Black fur covered its body with the exception of the blood draining from the three holes in its chest. From head to foot, Mike estimated it was close to five feet.

He felt heat rising inside. He was angry at the group for killing an innocent creature, but what else were they to think? They'd been told to hunt a bear. These assholes just happened to find one foraging in the woods. The smell of the bear's blood filled his senses. In his anger, he realized he no longer saw the group as five people but instead saw five blood bags which he could drain in an instant. He could bury his teeth into them, rip out their throats, and feast on the sweet liqueur of their blood.

Bloodlust wasn't something he'd struggled with recently, but the combination of hunger, the smell of blood, and his anger broke down his inhibitions. His mouth watered.

"What are you thinking, Mike?" Josh asked.

"I think here in the dark, those five are an easy target. I could dispatch them quickly, retribution for the innocent."

"That's not a good idea, vampire," Kohana said.

Mike turned around to find the werewolf standing a few feet behind him. In his fixation on the hunters, he hadn't noticed the tingle down his spine.

"Go back to the hotel and feed. I'll deal with the bear. Others will be arriving soon as well. We've had enough death for tonight."

Michael turned and took a step forward toward the hunters, but the werewolf quickly shifted himself in front of him. He growled and stood his ground. "Do not make this a fight. Leave. I'll handle it."

"Josh..." Mike said. He had to force out the words he said. "Get a bag ready. I'll be there in short order. Have you heard from Nate or Niki?"

"Already have one ready for you. And no, she took her comms out, remember? They're having a quiet night."

Mike peeled away from the group and hurried out of the forest before he had a chance to do anything foolish. The further he separated himself from the bear and the group of five, the less he felt the descent into bloodlust. Somewhere inside of him, he hated that he still had the struggle.

49

"WHAT THE FUCK!" NATE exclaimed out of sheer sudden surprise.

Niki bolted into the bullpen, standing next to him.

A large cinder block landed on top of an officer's desk, cracking it. Pieces of shattered glass glittered across the bullpen. Niki glanced from the gray cinder block to the destroyed window and finally to the two men standing on the opposite side. Both were Native American with thick, black hair. Their eyes gave off a yellow tint. One was slightly taller than the other. Immediately, Niki knew who they were.

"You must be the hunters keeping our new brother in captivity," the taller one said. "That's unacceptable."

He leaned on the windowsill. As he placed his hand on the frame, pieces of glass crunched under his palm. He sniffed the air and turned his lip up, revealing sharp canines hidden beneath them.

"What's your name, beautiful?" he asked.

"None of your fucking business," Nate said.

"Aren't you testy. Will you have the same fight as I'm ripping your heart out of your chest and swallowing it whole? I'll do it so fast you won't even be dead before it's in my stomach." He leaned his head beyond the window and peered across the bullpen. "Just two hunters? Where's the vampire and that old fart from the pack? Did they leave you two all alone?"

Niki tapped her side, hoping her pistol was there, but instead she tapped her empty hip. The gun sat on the desk where she'd been comfortably relaxing earlier. Her whip sat next to it as well. Hopefully, Nate had something on him, but since he'd been sleeping not long before, she doubted it. The two of them were unarmed against two werewolves.

The werewolf stared back at Nate and Niki. He nodded his head toward the door behind them. "Is my new brother back there? I can smell him." In a louder voice, he continued. "David, can you hear me? We're going to have so much fun tomorrow night. You've never felt so free as you will when the moon is full."

He gripped the window and with a single bound from the floor, landed on the top of the desk within the bullpen. The other werewolf who'd remained quiet followed suit. Both of them stood tall, overlooking the police station interior.

Niki tapped Nate on the side. Without saying a word, he understood what she tried to convey. Both of them twisted their bodies and slid through the doorway, back to the jail cells and David as fast as they could. Nate gripped the doorknob and slammed the door shut behind him. A large, metal slide lock clung to the top of the door. As soon as it shut, he shoved the metal slide into its housing against the door frame, securing the door.

"Sounds like company," David said. He stood against the bars with his arms dangling through them.

"That door's not going to hold them for long," Nate said. "Do you have your comms?"

"Fuck. No. Do you?"

Nate shook his head.

"My gun, knife, and whip are all on the desk. Do you have anything?"

Again, Nate shook his head.

"Fuck, love. This isn't good."

From beyond the door, high pitch shrieking noises ripped through the bullpen. Niki glanced through the small glass pane in the door. The two wolves shoved desks to the side. Others they picked up and chucked across the room, scattering papers, pens, file folders, computer equipment, and other random office supplies across the floor. In a matter of minutes, the whole area looked as if a tornado had destroyed it. Raucous laughter erupted from the two werewolves as they demolished the police station.

Suddenly, a pair of yellow eyes stared back at Niki through the glass.

"I see you. Was that an Australian accent I heard? I've never eaten Aussie before, unless Outback Steakhouse counts." He laughed at his own joke.

Niki put her back to the steel door. "Any ideas? Now would be a great time to hear them."

Nate twisted his head from side to side, scanning what they had. Niki already knew the answer. Nothing. Nada. Zilch. Every weapon was out there. Inside this room were three jail cells. David was in the one on the far left. The other two sat empty.

The werewolf hit the door, placing a dent so deep Niki felt it against her back. The entire door vibrated on its hinges. Nate was right. This door wouldn't hold them for long.

Nate placed his hands against the bars. He turned to Niki and shrugged one shoulder.

"Ah, fuck it. Better than nothing," she said.

Nate yanked on the open cell door. Niki ran in, and Nate quickly followed. He pulled the door closed behind him and engaged the locking mechanism. Nate pushed on the door, making sure it was locked.

"Think that'll stop them?" David asked.

"Hoping it'll slow them down enough for us to find a way out of this..." Niki said.

Another thunderous hit reverberated across the door. The walls vibrated, and the door hinges bowed.

Niki stood waiting. Her heart raced. Nate gripped her hand. They were backed into a corner. She thought about the past few months, and all they'd been through since that final battle with Silas. They'd been in close calls before. It wasn't like being a part of the Night Crew didn't come with its own risks. But since they were almost killed by Silas at that forgotten school, it had felt like they were toying with death more and more, each time dancing a little closer to the edge. Silas had captured Jax, Nate, and her twice, and both times Michael and Thomas had to rescue them. In New Orleans, Lilith had her stuck in the nightmare loop. If not for Nate and Josh freeing Mike, and then Mike saving her from the loop, she'd have perished in that crypt.

But now, Mike was watching over a group of hunters, and Nate was next to her holding her hand. All they had was each other. She took a deep breath. If she had to die, at least it would be fighting by Nate's side. The two of them together against werewolves. Werewolves are what brought them into this world. She found it fitting they'd be what finally took her out.

A series of concussive blows dented the steel door and shook the hinges. With each one, Niki felt her resolve crack. The latch holding the lock in place finally gave way. The latch ripped off the door frame and flew across the jail room, clattering against the bars next to David. The door violently swung open, slamming into the wall behind it.

Niki glanced over to David's cell. He had backed against the wall as far from the bars as he could. His demeanor changed in front of her eyes. At first, he tucked his shoulders in, shrinking away from the incoming werewolves, as if cowering from their presence. But, as the older brother sauntered through the door, his stance changed, and he stood taller. His chest rose and fell as he took deep breaths. He turned his gaze toward

Niki and Nate, and his eyes blazed a bright yellow. Niki feared the wolf would burst out of him at that very second.

Once through the door, the older brother said, "It would've been a lot easier if you unlocked that for us, but that's all in the past." He turned his attention to David as the younger brother stepped into the room. "The wolf inside of you is ready to break free." He stepped to the cell door and ran his hands along the bars. "There's no reason why they have you locked up. You deserve to be wild."

"I don't want to hurt anyone," David said. His breathing had escalated. He huffed out air as fast as he could. He was obviously struggling with whatever was happening to him.

"Oh, brother, you will hurt people. You'll kill, and the beast inside of you will flourish with each one." He strolled to the cell with Niki and Nate. His hand trailed across the iron bars. "You'd be his first meal. What do you think, Aussie? Should he dine on you first or should I?"

"Leave them alone," David yelled. "They're keeping me safe so that I don't kill innocent people. I want to be in this cell."

"You might want to, but your wolf inside doesn't. He wants to be free. I hear him calling to me. 'Free me', it shouts, and that's exactly why we're here. We're going to free you, David. My brother and I can't wait to have you join us tomorrow night in your renewed form."

He slid back to the door to David's cell and placed both hands on the bars. His face contorted, almost turning into a wolf, but stopped just before a full transformation. His mouth and cheeks puffed out as if filled with elongated teeth. His ears shifted into points, and his arms and legs doubled in size. The cell door rattled, and the bars screamed from the pressure. The locking mechanism gave way, and the door came off the hinges. The werewolf turned and tossed the door into the bullpen.

With the door open, David rushed at the werewolf as his back was turned and grabbed him around the waist. He hoisted the older brother into the air and slammed him to the floor. With the werewolf on the ground, David kicked him in the stomach.

"Don't just stand there," the older brother said. "Do it now."

Niki shot her eyes at the younger brother as he pulled a syringe from behind his back. Before David could react, the syringe was in his neck, and the younger wolf had depressed the plunger. David tried to swat at the younger one, but his arms didn't seem to listen. He tottered on his feet and stumbled into the wall before falling backward onto the floor.

"What did you do to him?" Niki screamed.

The older brother picked himself off the ground and dusted off his pants and shirt. "We thought he might try something, so we gave him a heavy dose of tranquilizers with a little wolfsbane mixed in." He turned to his brother. "Destroy the other cells."

Nate placed his arm in front of Niki as if to protect her. The two backed against the wall. With David unconscious on the floor, it was the two of them against the two brothers. Niki felt her time drawing close.

The middle cell wasn't locked so the two easily removed the door and tossed it into the police bullpen. It clanged against the first door as it crashed onto the ground. Both of them stood in front of the last functional jail cell. With the two of them working together, they broke the lock and snapped the door off with a lot more ease than David's cell door. Nothing stood in the way of the werewolves rushing in and killing Nate and Niki.

The older brother sauntered up to Nate. Although Nate was almost a foot taller and six inches wider, Niki knew he wouldn't be able to protect her long. She held her breath, waiting for the end.

"You'd make a very large meal," he said. "But not for me or my brother." He turned and stepped out of the cell. He pointed at the three destroyed jail cells. "Good luck keeping David caged tomorrow night."

Both brothers left the room. As they shuffled through the bullpen, the older one tossed aside another desk, splintering it against the wall. Niki didn't exhale until the front door slammed shut. She stood behind Nate and placed her hand on his shoulder. He spun around and wrapped his arms around her, holding her tightly. She buried her face into his chest.

50

THE BROKEN GLASS CRUNCHED underneath Michael's shoes. He surveyed the destruction to the police station. Broken desks lay scattered about the entire bullpen. The offices had broken doors and windows. Office supplies, papers, folders, and broken computers littered the floor. One of the cell doors had been embedded into a wall. Another perched against the window of Henderson's office.

He continued his trek into the jail room. All three cells were now useless. The last door leaned against the wall. There was no way the cells could be repaired before that evening.

Mike brought his hands behind his head, interlocking his fingers. He arched his back, leaned toward the floor, and squeezed his forearms against his ears. He yelled. Frustration swallowed him. Every plan they'd made was falling apart.

They were running out of time. The full moon was just over twelve hours away, and Mike felt no closer to stopping the two rogue werewolves now than he did when they first arrived. How was he supposed to stop whatever terror they planned to wreak on Mena?

He wanted to pick up the phone and call Jax. Jax would know what to do. But he couldn't. Jax was lost.

According to Mike's vision, Silas's unknown accomplice had captured him while trying to bring about a monster uprising. So far, the accomplice wasn't doing such a bad job. Silas had sown the seeds, and he was doing the reaping.

Just as he felt the vibration in his spine, John walked into the room and up to him. Mike straightened up and dropped his arms to his sides.

"Don't blame yourself. We couldn't have known this is what they had planned." He clapped a hand on Michael's shoulder. "How are the other two doing?"

"Nate and Niki? As good as can be expected. Somewhat shaken, as you can imagine. But they've survived a lot, so I'm sure they'll be fine. I told them to go back to the hotel and get some rest. How's David?"

"He's resting as well. He'll be awake soon."

Mike placed a hand against the broken cell which had been David's. "Nate said they injected him with wolfsbane. Why would they do that? And why come here to destroy the cells and then just walk away?"

John nodded in agreement. He wore a thoughtful look, pondering the questions, and then finally answered. "We use wolfsbane to suppress a transformation. If a werewolf has an obligation away from a safe place and can't take a chance on turning, wolfsbane will keep it at bay for a few days. But, once one stops taking it, the wolf — well in most cases the pack — will have a well-secured place to finally change. The wolf demands to be let out routinely. The longer we hold it in, the angrier it is when it's released. Even those with the highest level of control have trouble once they stop taking wolfsbane."

"But David hasn't turned yet. That's not until tonight."

"His wolf has still been drugged and suppressed. When it comes out tonight, it'll be pissed. More so than usual."

Realization dawned on Mike. "They took a new werewolf, one who has never changed before, who will have no control, and pre-pissed it off before ever seeing the light of day. That sounds fucking awesome. Add in they destroyed the most secure place in town. Any thoughts on how we secure a freshly pissed off werewolf on a full moon without a convenient jail cell?"

"Chains. We'll need lots of chains. Big ones. With really big locks."

"Got it. I'll swing by the hardware store later and pick those up. Any word from Henderson?"

As Mike asked, the police station's door opened. Both he and John stepped out to greet him. Roy strode into the bullpen and placed his hands on his hips, pulling his jacket around his stomach.

"This looks fucking worse in the daylight," he said. "I don't have a clue how to explain this. Can't say a bear came in here and did this."

"I'll have Josh reach out to Intel. Hopefully, we have resources to assist in something like this."

"This is a cluster fuck," Roy said. "Avoid going down by the court-house. They have that fucking bear on display. That thing isn't anywhere near big enough to do all of this carnage. I can't help but blame myself. The bear story was convenient when all this started. But now... Now the townspeople believe it because it's easy to believe."

Mike had another concern that he needed to vocalize. "Before last night, the only people out were those hunting the bear. Everyone else honored whatever self-imposed curfew they gave themselves. But now they're singing the wicked bear is dead like they're the munchkins in *The Wizard of Oz*. Any chance we're going to get people to stay indoors now?"

"Are you fucking kidding me?" Roy asked. His voice took on a higher pitch in disbelief. "They're already planning a celebration party down Main. Whole fucking town will probably be out. There's a vigil at seven for all those killed. Once the sun goes down, the party starts."

"Once the sun goes down," John chimed in, "the full moon rises."

"I haven't seen a bear around here in months," Roy said. "That one wasn't a cub, but he wasn't full grown either. If I had to guess, those two took advantage of the bear story and lured one here just so the town would be lulled into a false sense of safety once they killed it."

Mike agreed. "Makes sense. Combine that with what they did to the jail cells and drugging David. Everything is escalating."

"What are we doing about Mr. Hall?" Roy asked.

"Chains," Mike answered. "Lots of really big chains."

51

NATE HELD NIKI'S HAND as they strolled past the large courthouse steps, heading back to the destroyed police station. Crosses were positioned on the lawn beside the marble steps. The picture of someone who'd been killed was tacked to the top of one cross. Niki glanced at her watch. The vigil for those killed would begin in an hour.

However, a few dozen people had already shown up and laid flowers in front of the crosses. Boxes of candles sat beside the crosses, ready to be passed out.

"There's a street dance and celebration after the vigil," Nate said. "Those two fuckers planned this beautifully. You've got to give them credit."

"Destroy the only place we can keep David safe, get everyone out of their homes and into the streets, and make sure it happens on the night of the full moon. For two mutts, it's some evil genius shit. Think they had help?"

Nate stopped and turned his head. "What do you mean?"

"It's just all turning up aces for those kids. You saw them. The oldest is maybe twenty, yet they are a step ahead of all of us, including Kohana. Maybe Silas's accomplice has a hand in this."

"I don't know. That's some conspiracy level shit right there. Doesn't matter. We need to get through this, get back to Dallas, and then get the great Xavier Morcos to tap into the steal trap Mike calls a brain. I'm more than ready to put all of this uprising shit behind us and get back to normal monster hunting. Silas was a virus, and although he's dead, his tentacles still seem to be popping up."

"It will be great to finally meet Xavier," Niki said with a coy smile on her face. The pair picked up their pace.

"Don't be getting any ideas."

"Oh, love, what happened to him being my hall pass?"

"That was before we were actually meeting him. I revoke said hall pass," Nate said, pulling her closer to him.

"I don't think that's how it works, but don't worry. I'll behave."

She glanced up at him, and he kissed her.

A couple of blocks later, they strode into the police station. The shattered window and broken door were a stark reminder of the previous night. Niki took a deep breath, preparing herself for the rest of the destruction on the other side of the wall. She followed Nate through the door and into the destroyed police bullpen. The whole place appeared as if a tornado touched down in the middle of the room. The two rogue werewolves had done a number on it.

Chief Henderson and Mike leaned against a wall talking to one another. Niki sauntered over to them.

Mike shifted his eyes her direction. "Get plenty of rest?"

"I'll sleep better after this is all over. It ends tonight, correct, love?" Niki nodded as she asked the question.

"If all goes as planned, yes," Mike answered. "Speaking of plans, here's the game plan for tonight."

Nate mulled about the room and picked his head up, listening. Niki thought he looked like a lost puppy. She smiled.

"Roy will be at the celebration. He's armed with silver bullets. John and I will be high, primarily on roof tops. Hopefully from there, we'll see them coming. I know you two plan to stay with David again tonight.

Although the cell doors are gone, the bars are still there. They're fastened securely into foundation. We picked up a shitload of chains."

"A shitload?" Nate asked.

"That's an accurate description," Roy answered. "Big, thick, heavy ones, too. Took Mike and John to load them into the back of the truck. I couldn't lift 'em." He pointed at Nate. "Pretty sure you'd have struggled with them also."

"We're going to wrap the chains around him and pray they hold. John thinks they should, but the wolfsbane was a wildcard we weren't expecting."

"Where's the little puppy?" Niki asked.

"I can hear you!" David shouted from the jail room.

"Good to know you're still with us, love. We'll be in there to shackle you to the wall soon enough," she hollered back.

She really wanted to be out in the field hunting the two brothers, but she liked the idea of making sure David didn't hurt anyone. She had a score to settle, but then again, so did most of the people and everyone participating in the vigil.

"Also," Mike continued, presenting two small cases from the pocket of his hoodie, "put these in your ears and keep them there. We'll all have them. John and Roy included. We need to keep each other in the loop. Josh is launching his drones now and will monitor everything from the hotel. Any questions?"

Nate and Niki shook their heads. They knew the assignment. Make sure David stayed chained to the wall. Mike and John would use their supernatural abilities to take down the two werewolves. She'd built a good rapport with David and didn't mind keeping him safe. She didn't want him to wake up to find he killed someone.

"Let's get this done," she said, grabbing her case out of Mike's hand and placing the earpiece in her ear. "I'll have my whip on me and a gun filled with silver bullets in case they decide to make a repeat appearance."

"I'm locked and loaded as well," Nate said, slipping the earbud in place also. "Silver slugs in the shotgun, and the pistol's loaded. For good measure, I've got one of Scott's silver nitrate grenades in my back pocket." He tapped his butt as he said the last part.

"Silver nitrate grenades?" Roy asked.

"I didn't realize we'd brought those," Mike said. "We used these against Silas. They're very effective against vampires, but I'm guessing they work great with werewolves too. Have any more?"

"Have a few more back in the hotel," Nate answered.

"Great. Roy, when we leave here, we'll stop by and grab a few. They'll do more harm than good to Kohana and I, but it'll be one more thing in your arsenal, should you need it."

"Fuck yes," Chief Henderson said. "Load me up."

Niki and Mike checked their watches at the same time. "Approaching seven," Mike said. "Full moon will be rising soon. David's waiting to be locked up for the night. Comms check."

"I hear you," Josh said. "Everyone hear me?"

"Loud and clear, love," Niki responded.

"These things have a helluva range," Roy said.

"These won't stay in my ear when the full moon hits and I change," Kohana said.

"Mike will just talk loud," Nate said, smiling. After a brief pause, he shifted his composure.

"Circle up!" he shouted, and the four of them shifted together in the middle of the decimated bullpen, surrounded by loose papers and manilla folders. "Lord, protect us from evil as we deliver Your judgment. Amen."

"Amen," the others said.

Mike and Roy headed for the door.

"Godspeed," Niki said as they left, leaving Nate and Niki alone in the police station with David.

52

David leaned against the bars of the cell. A pile of chains and a handful of heavy-duty locks sat on the floor next to him. Mike was wrapping up the conversation with the team, so he knew any minute now, Nate and Niki would waltz in to chain him to the bars, and for some reason, he was anxiously anticipating them doing that.

With a glance at his watch, David realized it wasn't long before he'd turn. He was about to become the very thing that had killed Rebecca. Sweat dripped down his forehead and back and caked his palms. He could feel the edge of a panic attack pressing in. He was certain that wouldn't help anything, though. Fortunately, Nate and Niki would chain him to the wall. He'd go through whatever pain was necessary and wake up sometime later hungry and glad no one was hurt.

Footsteps came his way.

Finally, Niki poked her head into the jail room door. "Ready, love?"

David couldn't help but smile and give a nervous chuckle. "As I'll ever be?"

She stepped into the room with Nate behind her. "I'm just here for moral support. Muscles will be the one strapping you in." She slapped a hand on Nate's shoulder.

"Those do look heavy," David said.

Nate bent down and grabbed the end of the chain. The muscles in his arms bulged from the weight. "They are," he said, dragging the end toward David.

"Where do you want me?"

Nate leaned to one side and then the other examining David's position against the bars. "Just stay where you are. I'll start around your waist and then wrap it around each arm and each leg. As many points of contact as we can get."

"Sounds like a plan," David said. He forced the words out of his mouth.

David licked his lips with a tongue that felt as dry as sandpaper. Sweat continued to pour down his body. As Nate hoisted the chain around his stomach and the bars behind him, the anxiety and panic attack David tried to quell kept forcing its way in. His breathing accelerated, and he felt his heart pounding in his chest.

"How are you feeling, love?" Niki asked, taking a step closer.

He tried to catch his breath to speak. Instead, he shook his head. Finally, he croaked out, "Think panic attack."

Instead of trying to comfort him, Niki grabbed the first padlock off the ground and rushed over to Nate. "We need to hurry." She attached the first lock to the chain, securing the loops Nate had made around his chest and the bars together.

Nate shifted to his arm, but David suddenly felt he didn't want his arm locked down. He violently shook his head back and forth. "No," he struggled to say. "Panic attack."

Niki stood directly in his line of sight. "No, love. Werewolf. You aren't having a panic attack. The change is starting. The wolf doesn't want to be locked down anymore and is starting to wake up."

David's eyes rolled to the ceiling. Consciousness began to slip away. His heart rate accelerated. Pain began to grip his stomach. A sharp and sudden pain ripped across his cheek, and he dropped his eyes back down to her. "Did you slap...?" he tried to say.

"Damn right I did. Stay with us. Fight it until we get you locked down. You aren't secure yet."

David's head flopped to one side, and he saw Nate had successfully wrapped the chain around his arm. The iron links traversed down his bicep and forearm creating a lattice formation. Niki attached another lock as Nate braced David's other arm. David tugged on his chained arm, but it didn't move. He was stuck, locked in, trapped against the cell bars.

Nate quickly looped the chain around the bars, pulling it to David's arm tight. Niki added another lock as Nate dropped to David's legs.

David stared at his hand. He twisted his palm facing his face and closed his hand. Numbness spread through the appendage. He squeezed and opened the hand, as if grasping for sensation. Moments later, a sharp pain erupted from each fingertip. He remembered that pain from the Summers' residence. This time, though, he watched as a budding nail burst from the end of each finger. It hurt more than anything he'd ever felt before. He could see why removal of fingernails was a form of torture in the movies. He didn't know if it happened in real life, but fuck, it hurt so bad.

David tried to hold in a scream, but as all ten nails grew, separating the skin and muscle of his fingertips, he couldn't take it anymore. He took a deep breath and cried out as loud as he'd ever cried before.

"Hurry, Nate," Niki said.

"I'm going as fast as I can. One more leg to go. Fuck, it's starting to grow. This wolf is coming."

Niki took a step back after attaching the final padlock to David's leg. The chain wrapped around his stomach, his arms, his chest, and his legs. Each loop secured him to the bars. Additionally, she had placed extra locks in multiple places to create points of resistance. David would have to break through all of the locks, against the weight of the chains and the strength of the bars in order to get free.

53

By the time Roy left the hotel with the silver nitrate canisters and arrived at the courthouse, the vigil had ended, and the celebration had begun. He wound up parking his truck three blocks away. It was the closest spot he could find, and even that was technically parking illegally. He hopped the curb and parked on the grass next to a tree. But who was going to give him a ticket? The thought brought a brief smile to his face.

As soon as he stepped out of his truck, he heard music playing. The sound of a fiddle and steel guitar streamed from the grassy area around the courthouse. Within a few minutes, he arrived at the celebration. He kept his pistol tucked into its holster. The four silver nitrate canisters were stuffed in a small drawstring bag he carried over his shoulder.

He estimated over a hundred people were in attendance. The stage that Troy Johnson had given his speech from yesterday now held the five-piece band. Instead of the small speakers he had used, towering speakers lined around the stage. Large black cables snaked across the courthouse grass and ended at a control board where yesterday's signup table still sat. The area directly in front of the band had become an open space, and a few couples danced across it.

Just beyond the stage, a barbecue food truck had parked. Across from it, The Pit had set up a stand selling water, sodas, and beer. Roy hadn't seen this much excitement since 2021 when the town celebrated its one hundred and twenty-fifth birthday. This had a similar feel.

"Roy!"

He quickly spun around as a grinning Troy approached with a plastic cup full of beer in his hand.

"Roy, are you on duty? If not, can I buy you a beer?" He clapped Roy on the shoulder with his empty hand, splashing some of the beer.

"Yes, I'm on duty. Gave all the officers the night off. I figured a night like this, I doubt anyone's going to cause any trouble."

Deep down, he knew the opposite. He had given everyone the night off to make sure Nate, Niki, and David had the station to themselves. Plus, the trouble that was going to be caused wasn't something his officers would be able to protect people from anyway. So many times he'd debated on filling them in on what truly was happening, but in the end, he'd decided against it. Knowing about the world of monsters felt more like a burden than anything else. Something he didn't want to worry his men with.

"Hell no. This is a celebration. Granted, earlier, it was sad as hell. The vigil was beautiful. Pastor Donahue did a great job. Proper dedication to all the victims."

"I'm glad to hear that. How's your wife? Is she here?" Roy leaned his head around Troy, not really looking for his wife, but scanning the crowd for the two brothers. At least he knew what they looked like, just in case. So far, though, he couldn't see them.

"No, she went home for now. Like I said, the vigil was sad. Very emotional. She'll be out later, though. How late are you sticking around? I'll make sure she says hi when she gets here."

Roy brought his eyes back to Troy. "I should be out as long as I need to be. I'd love to say hi and wish my condolences for everything. I know it's been tough lately."

"The bear is dead," Troy said, raising his beer-covered hand still holding the plastic cup as if making a toast. More sloshed out of it and onto his hand. "Time for mourning is over. Now it's time for healing."

"Amen to that. Now, if you'll excuse me, I'm going to wander around. Might get me one of those barbecue sandwiches."

He shuffled away from Troy, resuming his watch.

"Was he drunk already?" Josh asked.

Roy had nearly forgotten about the communication device perched in his ear.

"Knowing Troy, he's probably been drinking since last night."

"Pay no attention to the drone hovering above you," Josh said. Roy heard the smile in his voice.

"As loud as the band is, unless it drops onto their head, no one is going to know it's there anyway."

"Don't jinx her. She'll stay in the air as long as I need her to."

"Good to know. Guessing you aren't seeing anything suspicious?"

"No. I see vehicles coming down the streets toward you, and people walking along the road." Josh cleared his throat. "All in all, we're looking good."

54

"MIKE, HOW'S EVERYTHING ON your end?" Roy asked. "Where are you, by the way?"

A group of store fronts ran down Mena's main thoroughfare. All were connected together creating the appearance of one long building. Mike stood on top of the two-story structure, watching as much of the celebration as he could.

"I'm across the street, on top of the mechanic's shop."

"Sparks Auto. If you ever need a good tune-up, he does wonders. Everything looking good?"

"So far, but the night is still young. I really hope we're in the right place, that this is their intended target."

Mike paced the rooftop. The odor of oil and grease resonated up. Large air conditioning units dotted the roof. Mike guessed at least one for each business. The larger furniture store probably had a couple.

He flexed his hands, squeezing them into fists then stretching them back out. He was waiting again. Parts of this assignment had reminded him of his old army days. Hurry up and wait. His whole body was on high alert as it had been through every deployment. Except this time, high alert meant he saw crisper than ever before, smelled the faintest odor, and heard the quietest sounds. Although that last one was difficult with the band cranked up. He enjoyed country music and found himself tapping his foot along to the music, but it also drowned out his ability to zero in on noises.

A shudder ran down his back, and he twisted his head. John stood on the roof with him.

"The moon's full," John said. "We'll be turning soon."

Mike nodded. He reached his hand out and grabbed John's. With his other hand, he placed it on John's shoulder. John mirrored his movement.

"They'll be here soon. Those people down there don't know it yet, but their lives are in danger. They need us to protect them. Fight hard. Fight strong." The weight of their responsibility bored down on Mike.

"Of all the vampires I've met over the years, you aren't that bad," John said.

Mike smiled and laughed. He dropped his arms back to his side. "Shoo, mutt," he joked.

"Team," Niki shouted through the earbud. "It's starting." She sounded out of breath.

55

THE CHANGE BEGAN WITH David's fingernails. As he screamed in pain, she watched as sharp claws slowly broke from the tips of his fingers, shredding through his human fingernails and extending out. By the time she had finished locking him in, his legs had doubled in size. Stress splits appeared at the seams of his jeans.

She stood next to Nate on the opposite side of the jail room, already exhausted from fighting David while he resisted being chained.

"Team..." she said, after making sure her earbud was on, "it's starting."

"It hurts!" David screamed. "Make it stop. Everything burns."

Tears poured from his eyes, and spittle flew from his mouth. A ripping sound tore through the room, and David's T-shirt split down the front. Underneath, his chest was covered in black hair. To Niki's horror, his chest hair continued to grow; each strand wriggling like an earthworm trying to escape the soil. His entire torso continued expanding, and his shirt fell away in tatters, draping over the chain.

Nate had left a little slack in the chain per John's advice. He had warned him that as a wolf, David would be quite larger, and he hadn't lied. As David's chest expanded, his stature grew. Originally, he had been a few inches shorter than Nate and half as broad. Now, he dwarfed the hunter.

David's screams became almost unbearable as his body contorted. Cracking noises erupted from joints. His bones broke and reformed into a new shape. His jaw dislocated, and the skin of his face elongated. In less than a minute, his head went from his own to a disfigured nightmare to an unmistakable wolf's snout, covered with black fur. His lips curled back and sharp teeth, too large to be human, glistened within.

If he'd been wearing shoes, those would've been shredded. Fortunately, Niki had removed those ahead of time, and they sat untouched in the corner of the room. Niki watched as, what used to be feet, became large wolf paws with claws that matched the new fingernails.

David's pained screams changed from agonizing cries into a guttural growl. The tops of his ears became pointed, and his eyes took on a yellow glow.

The wolf had fully emerged.

Niki had never seen someone become a wolf. Frankly, she did not need to ever experience it again. She'd seen the reverse. Once a werewolf was killed, the wolf changed back to its human form. Even the other night, she witnessed John change back to a human after she shot him in the leg. That process was quick. Well, at least it had been for a werewolf who had changed countless times before. David's transformation was grotesque and obviously extremely painful. She felt sorry for him and couldn't imagine the pain he must've endured. Maybe she had some things still to learn.

Despite any camaraderie she'd built with David, the wolf standing before her now had none of the same misgivings. She stared into the wolf's eyes and recognized that look as one she'd seen in other creatures before. Ones who had wanted nothing more than to bury their claws in her or drain her blood. The beast's eyes contained only the desire to kill. David's humanity, any and all of it, was gone.

David's wolf growled at them and slammed its arms forward. Fortunately, the chains caught after no more than an inch and held the wolf in place. He tried again, shoving his arms and torso against the impromptu shackles, but he couldn't escape that one inch of slack. He roared in anger and then howled.

Niki glanced at Nate. "Think David would want a selfie?" She gave a nervous laugh and smile.

"Oh, I'm sure. He seems to be asking for one." He pointed next to the werewolf. "Go stand right over there, within reach, and I'll take it for you."

"Maybe next time." She flipped her braided ponytail at him. "I haven't done my hair, and my makeup is just atrocious."

Nate shook his head and smiled as a chuckle escaped his throat.

The sound of straining metal interrupted their playful banter. Niki turned back to the large werewolf. David's wolf had bent his knees as far as he could and flexed his quads. Every muscle fiber rippled and pressed against the chains, digging the links into fur-covered flesh. He maintained pressure on the restraints and bowed his back. The werewolf's biceps and chest bulged. He was trying to bring his arms together, despite the chains.

"Those chain and locks will hold, right, love?"

"According to John, but he also wasn't sure how much that wolfsbane shot was going to piss it off. I'm not sure how angry a new wolf can get, but this one seems pretty fucking pissed."

The wolf's head vibrated as he continued to press against the chain. The bars behind him held firm, giving Niki a vote of confidence. She let out a sigh of relief but immediately realized her mistake.

The first lock snapped and fell to the floor.

Niki held her breath. *How long before the other's lost the fight?*

With a loud ting and rattling to the floor, one of the leg locks snapped into multiple pieces.

Suddenly, David's wolf could step forward. The way Nate had interlaced them, every lock would have to break before the chain would fall away. It wasn't possible for the wolf to shake the chain off either leg with the other locks still engaged. But with two down already, Niki's confidence shattered.

A third lock, one keeping David's arms in place, snapped and clattered down the bars before scattering across the tiled floor.

"They aren't holding," she said with some surprise.

"No shit!" Nate replied.

"We've got a problem..." Niki said into her comms, hoping Mike or John would hear her. "David's breaking out of his chains. The fucking locks aren't holding."

She waited for a response, but none came.

"Any bright ideas?" Niki asked.

"I've got one, but it's not a bright idea. It's pretty fucking stupid actually."

Niki stared at him for a moment, letting silence hang between them. "How stupid?"

Nate shifted to the other side of the bars, behind the werewolf. He wrapped the slack in the chain around his arms, pressed his feet against the bars, and pulled back with all his might. David banged his back and head against the bars, not expecting Nate to pull him from behind. The wolf stood dazed for a moment before shaking off the confusion and resuming his struggle against the chains.

"Arrrr!" Nate grunted, trying to hold the beast in place.

The veins in Nate's neck stood out and every muscle strained. He pulled back as hard as he could, forcing David against the bars as if the wolf was a puppet. Nate was the marionette. As the wolf tried to pull free, Nate's arm moved simultaneously. As Nate pulled backward, so did the wolf's arm.

Although he had a grip on the wolf for now, Niki knew Nate wouldn't be able to hold for long. Despite Nate's strength, he'd surely give out before David's supernatural strength. She needed to figure something else out.

The beast continued to fight against his restraints. Another lock snapped and rattled to the ground, joining the others. As the wolf gained more freedom, Nate's grip waned. The beast had slack and could build up momentum. As Niki suspected, two more locks broke away in succession. Only two more locks remained, and Nate held the chain to them. She knew Nate would be the final obstacle and lone holdout. Once that happened, he couldn't help but lose the fight, and quickly at that.

The werewolf was stronger than she'd expected. The wolfsbane had done what the brothers had wanted. It had made David's werewolf impossible to hold back.

"Nate, we need to go," she hollered. "Maybe we can hold him at the door hopefully. Keep him in this room."

Drenched in sweat, Nate turned his head and nodded. He pulled back one final time. It gave Nate the slack he needed to unwrap his arms. The hunter dropped the chains to the ground. The wolf flung himself forward, immediately swallowing up all the slack as the chains flew through the iron bars. The final two locks snapped free, and the chain fell off the creature in a deep clatter.

Nate sprung to his feet and bolted to the door. Niki slipped through behind him, and the two slammed the steel door shut, holding it in place. Niki glanced through the small window embedded in the door.

The werewolf shook the rest of the chains off of it along with its tattered clothes. It snapped its head from one side to the other and then turned to the steel door. It ran headlong into it, crashing its shoulder into the barrier.

The door shook but held. Both hunters braced themselves against it, holding it firm.

The beast tried three more times to break free. Each time, the door shook and rattled on its hinges but held.

After the last attempt, it backed away and turned to the wall opposite the door. It was an exterior wall to the police station. The beast lowered its shoulder and sprinted at the wall. It crashed into it, leaving a large crack in the plaster, exposing the cinder block wall behind it. The werewolf shook off the dust and dizziness of the impact, backed up, and did it again.

Niki turned away from the door.

"Where are you going?" Nate asked, winded.

"Grab my whip and the gun. He can't get out. He'd rather be put down than kill someone."

He grabbed her forearm. "You really want to kill him?"

"No," she said. "But I can't let him have killing someone else on his conscience."

Another crash came from inside the jail room, along with the sound of falling bricks. Both Nate and Niki ran to the window and stared into the room. Instead of finding a wolf, they found an empty room with a huge hole on the opposite wall.

"Team, we have a problem. David's escaped."

56

A PIT FORMED IN Mike's stomach the moment Niki said David had escaped. Before he had time to process, the screams rang out from the crowd. They began to multiply and spread throughout the attendees. The audience dancing and celebrating in front of the band compressed, squeezing in on the stage. Those in the back of the swarm pressed forward, trying to escape. One by one, the band members stopped playing, confused by the audience's reaction.

Michael shot his eyes to the rear of the crowd. Behind the audience, by the soundboard at the back, two werewolves hunkered down on all fours, growling. Their large teeth glistened in the outdoor lighting. A body, bloody, its chest ripped apart, lay at their feet. Their claws were drenched in blood.

"John, they're here. We've got to hurry," he yelled as he bounded off the roof and crashed to the street below.

Screams increased. People scattered in sheer terror. Those on the extremities escaped and ran as fast as they could. Mike felt as if he was a salmon swimming upstream. People sprinted around the stage, trying to get away from the growling beasts.

Mike couldn't blame them. In another life, he'd like to think he'd have done the same thing but knew that wasn't the case. How many times had he run headlong into danger while in the service? According to the official records, Sergeant White was dead, and somewhere deep down, he was. Instead, a more lethal version of that man now existed.

Mike tried to see past the people streaming away in order to locate the wolves. He could've used his strength and forced his way through, but that would've caused other problems.

"Roy, what are you seeing? Where are they? John, are you close? Josh, I need information."

Josh spoke first. "I've got you on visual. They're by the sound booth. I see three down around them. They aren't in a hurry. A large group is trapped between them, the stage, and the courthouse. If you don't hurry up, they have a buffet to choose from."

Mike glanced to his right and saw the stage. The band's instruments littered the top. They'd dropped them and ran along with everyone else. The vampire shuffled to the stage and hopped on top. From his new vantage point, he saw everything happening.

A wolf leapt forward and pounced on one of the townspeople. It was a man who looked to be in his thirties. The werewolf sunk its teeth into the man's neck and ripped his throat out. Blood shot from the fatal wound as the man opened his mouth in a silent scream. The man collapsed to the ground.

The two wolves separated. They operated as two trained dogs corralling a herd of sheep. The crowd of over a hundred who hadn't been able to escape responded as if they were also being herded. They huddled into one large group. From either direction, there was no escape. Mike scanned the crowd. His eyes met Roy's. He was stuck in the middle trying to work his way closer to the front.

With the remaining stragglers rushing away and screams echoing down the road, the two wolves stood on their hind legs. They towered over the crowd. Both raised their head to the full moon and howled.

57

Roy needed to act and was tired of fighting against everyone in front of him. He saw Mike standing on the stage, but with the large group between then, Roy doubted even the vampire could leap the distance from the stage to where the wolves stood howling.

Unable to think of anything else, he did the only thing he could think of; he drew his sidearm and fired a shot into the air. "Everyone down!" he shouted at the same time.

The crowd ducked immediately and created some distance around him. Roy gained some mobility he hadn't had when everyone had crowded together. He dropped his hand into the drawstring bag he carried and pulled out a canister.

"Mike. John. You may want to stand back for a bit."

He cocked his arm back and threw the silver nitrate grenade like he was a football star. The canister hit the larger of the two werewolves in the chest and fell to the ground. A thick fog erupted from the canister and rose from the ground.

The werewolf dropped back onto four legs, sniffing the gas swirling around him. The moment his head dropped into the rising fog, he began to cough, gasping for air. He shot back up onto his back legs and raised his front paws to his throat. His yellow-ringed eyes bulged in his skull. He coughed and spat blood on the street. As his tongue dangled from his mouth, the tongue sizzled. The wolf released his throat and batted his paws, trying to fight the air itself.

"Courthouse!" Roy yelled. "Run to the courthouse!"

An opening formed by the distracted werewolf allowed the crowd to push their way up the steps. The first to arrive pounded on the large wooden doors, but they were locked.

"Give me room!" Chief Henderson shouted.

The group split in the middle, giving Roy room to maneuver up the marble steps. As he ran up them, he glanced at the two werewolves. The smaller one tiptoed close to the fog, but the moment the silver nitrate fog touched the wolf, he recoiled in pain. The larger one writhed in agony, completely engulfed in mist.

Finally up the stairs, Roy shoved the key in and twisted, unlocking the doors and shoving them open. He stepped away, helping the crowd pour into the courthouse while keeping an eye on the wolves. The crowd wasn't moving fast enough, though. Those at the front were stopping just inside the doors, blocking those at the rear who were still pushing, trying to get inside.

The smaller wolf backpedaled a few steps and then leapt over the fog. As he did, the larger one rolled out of the cloud and into a clearing. To Roy's surprise, when the two stood up, they were back to their human forms, naked. The older brother glanced at the younger one before turning to the courthouse. Both had vengeful rage in their eyes. Burn marks seared the legs and smoke rose from the skin of the older wolf. He coughed and spat a wad of blood-filled saliva on the ground. His arms outstretched, he roared at those still trying to get into the courthouse. It was a sound that Roy would never have expected possible to come out of a human's throat. But, then again, these two weren't exactly human anymore. They were werewolves.

Roy blinked, and the two naked brothers were gone. The two black werewolves had returned.

"Fuck me!" he said, trying to get the last forty or so people into the courthouse.

The smaller wolf fell back on all fours and jumped to the steps, tackling a woman and burying his claws in her back. Before Roy could react, the wolf bit into the woman's back and removed the part of her vertebrae running through her neck. Bone, spinal cord, tendons, and veins dripped from its mouth.

Roy pulled his gun free from his holster once again and fired, clipping the wolf in the shoulder. The wolf tumbled down the steps, and the last of the survivors scrambled inside the courthouse. The wolf spun around and rose back to its feet. Blood streamed down from the hole in its shoulder. A wolf's howl broke on the other side of the steps as Chief Henderson twisted his body. The larger brother bound up the steps directly for the Chief. He tried to adjust the angle of his gun and fire a second time but before he could, something slammed into the side of the wolf, shoving it off the steps.

"Get inside and lock the door!" Mike demanded.

Roy slammed the door behind him and twisted the lock.

58

As the larger wolf left the ground, claws outstretched and ready to bury into Roy, John Kohana, also in full werewolf form, jumped from the top of the building across the street, briefly touched the ground, propelled himself back into the air, hurdled the steps, and collided with the black beast. The two tumbled to the ground in a full embrace.

The pure athleticism of the werewolves astounded Michael. He knew vampires could do some amazing feats — he'd taken one helluva beating from a few succubi only a few months back — but had no idea if something like what John had just done was possible for him. At some point, he'd have to talk Thomas into giving him more skills training beyond how to control his hunger.

Mike jumped off the stage and ran for the smaller werewolf at the base of the marble steps. Roy's silver bullet had already weakened the mutt. As he drew closer, the wolf turned, and Michael no longer had the element of surprise. The two smashed into each other, neither giving an inch. Mike reached for the silver knife in his belt and withdrew it from its sheath. He held it in front of him, the blade extending from the rear of his hand. With his other hand, he motioned for the beast to attack him.

"Come on, fucker..." he said with a smile. "Let's dance."

The werewolf glared at the blade and sized up the vampire. He took a step back and charged Mike, swiping at the vampire's head. Mike ducked under the wolf's arm, pulled the blade across the wolf's thigh, and shifted around behind the beast. The knife sizzled against the wolf's skin as the blade tore through fur-covered flesh. Blood flowed from the wound, pouring over black hair. The wolf roared in pain and spun around to face the vampire again.

The werewolf tried to swipe at Mike again, but the vampire dodged the blows, using his forearms to block the strikes, before countering with another slash from the knife. Within seconds, three more cuts appeared on the werewolf's arm. Mike tried to deliver a lethal strike, but the wolf continued to evade despite his multiple wounds. For now, the former soldier realized he would have to resort to death by a thousand cuts.

A yelp sounded behind Michael, redirecting his attention. He saw the black werewolf pinning John to the ground and trying to nip at his neck. Both had dozens of slashes across their bodies, but John was at the losing end of the fight. The vampire knew he needed to help John before the larger wolf's teeth found their target in John's throat.

He shifted his head back to the smaller werewolf, but it was gone. It'd taken the brief moment Mike had turned his head to escape, probably realizing Mike would eventually win. As much as he wanted to run after his prey, John needed his help. The larger wolf was more the immediate threat.

Mike spun around, dropped his shoulder, and barreled toward the werewolf. Since both of its arms pinned John's to the ground, Mike had a clear shot. He collided with the wolf, wrapped his arms around it, and slammed it to the ground. Claws dug into the earth. Once the pair stopped moving, the wolf quickly adjusted and kicked Mike off. The vampire flew across the grassy area and crashed into the courthouse. His head slammed into the stone building, and Mike fell to the ground, dazed.

Slowly, Mike picked himself up. He wobbled a little but was able to finally stand straight. He raised his arms in front of him in a fighting stance and realized he'd dropped the silver knife somewhere along the way.

"Fuck..." he said.

The large black werewolf stood ten feet away. Its claws hung at its side. Ten sharp nails seemed ready to tear the vampire to pieces. Mike, unarmed, was undeterred. His mission was to stop these two rogue werewolves, corrupted by Silas's teaching, and save this town and future others.

Movement to Mike's left briefly caught his eyes.

John, still in his wolf form, strode next to Mike. The two stood shoulder-to-shoulder, ready to stand off against the killer werewolf.

Mike took a deep breath as the black, furry beast charged straight at him.

59

His back against the door, Roy Henderson scanned the faces of everyone locked in the courthouse with him. He took long, deep breaths hoping to slow his racing heart. As he glanced from face to face, he focused on meeting their eyes. Everyone was filled with terror. He pressed his back harder against the door. Feeling the solid oak against his spine brought him comfort. He knew he couldn't brace the door if the two werewolves decided to break through, but it still provided him a sense of security.

Stunned silence greeted him. A few sobs echoed in the courthouse rotunda. The space wasn't large. Usually, people didn't congregate here. Winding red oak staircases, one to his left and another to his right, traveled up to the second floor. Most of the offices were upstairs. The courtroom took up the majority of the first floor. A large metal detector sat unplugged and pushed to the wall.

As Roy looked them over, someone began pushing their way forward. After a few attempts, Troy Johnson finally broke into the front of the crowd.

"What the fuck were those things?" he demanded.

"Those things," Roy said, "are what have been killing people. It wasn't a bear, but two fucking werewolves."

"Werewolves?" The murmur spread through the survivors.

"Werewolves aren't real," Troy said. Anger sprang across his face as if Roy was intentionally making fun of him.

"Would you like me to open the goddamn door so you can inform them that they aren't real?" He glanced over the crowd. "Werewolves are real, and these two want to kill as many of you as they can. The people outside are trying to stop them. We need to be as quiet as possible. We should be safe inside here. The doors are solid."

"A werewolf killed my Tanner?" Troy asked. His voice went from angry to meek. His face turned pale.

Roy felt sorry for him at that moment. It was one thing to think that a natural creature, a bear, had killed his son. That was something that Troy could comprehend. But now the man had to process that it wasn't a natural beast but a supernatural one. His Tanner, along with all of the other victims, had come face to face with monsters right before they died.

"Yes, Troy," Roy said, nodding. He raised his head back to the crowd. The fear in their eyes had only intensified. "Listen, I know this is a tight space, but if we could move back away from the door, that'll help. Try to give others as much room as you can."

From the back, someone shouted, "What if those men out there can't stop the werewolves? Will they come for us next?"

Mutters and some brief sobs among the crowd broke out. The last thing Roy needed was for everyone to become more upset. Upset people panicked. Panicked people made dumb decisions. Dumb decisions could get a lot of people killed.

"Please stay calm. Believe it or not, they do this stuff professionally. I'm confident that as long as we all stay calm, we'll be safe."

As soon as he said those words, a window shattered on the second floor, and something large crashed into furniture. Roy's nightmare wasn't over. One of the werewolves had just broken into the courthouse.

MIKE'S SHIRT WAS TORN open, and blood streamed down his chest. Slash marks crossed his chest. If he'd still been human, he'd have been dead three times over. However, thanks to the excessive amount of feeding he had done earlier in the day, some of his wounds were already beginning to heal.

Mike and John continued to attack the large werewolf. The two landed some blows but were also kicked, clawed, punched, and knocked back. The wolf was stronger than either of them and also able to heal.

Frustrated by the lack of progress, Mike ripped off his tattered shirt. He preferred being covered, but his shirt held on by threads. The strips of fabric were getting tangled and in his way. In the dark, he couldn't really see how pale he was anyway, so fuck it.

The two werewolves were locked together. Teeth snapped, and claws dug in. As Mike headed back into the fight, another rippling sensation traveled down his spine. He shivered from his shoulders to his hips. Something else was coming.

Mike tried to ignore the sensation as a second werewolf came rushing into the courtyard. At first, he thought it was the younger brother ready to fight again, but then he saw the wolf's color and size. It wasn't the brother. It was David. All humanity was gone from the young man's eyes. Although David had to be in there somewhere, he wasn't in control. Only the wolf, staring and pissed off from wolfsbane, was present.

The newly-turned wolf ran on all fours. Paws slammed into the pavement, propelling him forward at a rapid pace, clearing the street in a single bound. Claws scraped the ground with each explosive push. His snout pulled back in a vicious snarl, and his pointed ears slicked back against his head. David was heading straight for them.

Michael knew he had to react. John needed his help. Without it, he would lose the fight with the black werewolf. The vampire also didn't want to hurt David. It wasn't that many months ago that he'd been in the same position. He had almost done terrible things to his friends. David was innocent. He hadn't asked to become a werewolf. At least Michael had known what he was getting himself into. By the time Silas had turned him, he'd known vampires were real and accepted the possibility of becoming one.

David had only wanted a nice night camping with his girlfriend. He hadn't known anything about werewolves. Now, with the full moon hanging over their heads, he had no control. It could be taught. John was a perfect example of that. David wasn't a lost cause. He could learn to control it. Mike needed to figure out a way to get David out of the way so he could help John finish off the older brother.

Now a few feet away, David leapt into the air. Mike jumped to meet him in the air, wrapping his arms around him. David sunk his teeth into Mike's shoulder, and the two landed on the ground.

The pain was excruciating. David's teeth pierced Mike's skin and ground against his collar bone. The comment John Kohana had made to him shortly after they'd first met flashed in his head as the werewolf's mouth filled with the vampire's blood. Creatures can't intertwine with each other. Once a werewolf is a werewolf, he can't become a vampire. The same was true the other direction, too. Since Michael was a vampire, he wasn't going to get infected with lycanthropy.

As much of a relief as that thought was, it wasn't going to be much help stopping David from gnawing his arm off. Mike punched at David's head, hoping the werewolf would release.

"Let go, you mutt!" he shouted, punctuating each word with a fist to the head.

With the wolf on top of him, Mike slid both hands up to the wolf's head and slammed his palms simultaneously onto David's ears. Immediately, the wolf released its grip on Mike's shoulder and jumped back.

"Don't like your ears boxed, I see. Well, my shoulder isn't a *CHEW TOY!*"

David stood on two legs and stared at the bleeding vampire. They circled as if in a standoff in an old western.

Mike shot a quick glance at John. He was pinned on the ground. His arms were outstretched, and the other werewolf gripped John's shoulders. He couldn't move. Mike was all out of ideas. He needed to help John, but he also needed to keep David out of the way. The empty sheath of his silver knife rested on his belt and pressed against his skin. It was a stark reminder of the weapon he wished he still had.

61

"GET IN THE COURTROOM. Now!" Roy yelled. He motioned quickly with his arm in the direction he needed the crowd to go.

Upstairs, the werewolf continued to slam into furniture. Roy assumed he was throwing chairs and desks against the walls, probably searching for a way out of the office and into the rotunda. Once the wolf found the door, he'd be on them in seconds.

The courtroom door thrust open, and the survivors shoved their way inside. It wasn't fast enough. They only had a few moments, if that. Slowly it seemed, people filtered through the door, but the crowd of about a hundred couldn't move quickly.

"Hurry!" he shouted. "Get your asses in there."

A door exploded, raining wooden shards onto the rotunda. Roy stared at the second-floor landing. As he did, the wolf marched to the railing and peered down. He locked eyes with the beast. The wolf tilted its head to the ceiling and howled. Roy pulled out his revolver and took aim. Just as he squeezed the trigger, the werewolf backed away, and the bullet missed its target. From the corner of his eye, he noticed the crowd pushing and shoving into the courtroom. As much as he didn't want that, at least it meant they were moving a lot faster. The group in the rotunda was at less than a dozen.

The beast moved past the railing and descended the stairs carefully on all fours. He seemed aware that the marble could be slick.

With the last of the group in the courtroom, Roy reached into his bag, pulled out another canister, and pulled the pin. He tossed it next to the stairs and hurried into the room. As he slammed the door behind him, it made a resounding deep boom.

Again, Roy found himself standing against a door with a werewolf on the other side, except this time, the Night Crew wasn't fighting said wolf.

The silver nitrate canister would slow it down, but he knew the fog would dissipate. The only thing standing between the creature and the hundred people trapped inside the courthouse was him.

He held the revolver in his hand and turned it over, pressing the cylinder release as he did. The cylinder dropped to the side. He had three bullets remaining. He would love to have more, but three would have to do. At least he prayed to God three would be enough. He slapped the cylinder back in place.

"Troy!" he yelled.

Troy muscled his way toward Chief Henderson.

"I need you to lead everyone out of here." He pointed to the back of the room. "The judge's chambers are back that way. Also, behind the jury box, is the jury's exit. It'll weave you through the back corridor and get you out on the other side of the courthouse."

"Wh-wha-what?" Troy asked, stuttering. All of his previous bravado leading up to that night had vanished. Being faced with an actual super-natural beast had snatched it right away.

"A lot of these people look up to you. They followed you into the forest at night to hunt a killer bear. They stood with you then, and they will stand with you now. They need someone to take the lead, and they need that someone to be you."

"Why not you?" He looked like a deer in the headlights.

"Because I have to go through this door and confront that thing."

"What about the professionals you hired?"

"They're fighting the other one. Plus there's a locked door between them and the one in here with us. You all hired me to protect this town, and that's what I'm going to do. You lead everyone out of here. Get them out of the building and to safety. Out of the square and behind as many locked doors as possible. We each have our calling. Yours is to do that. Mine is waiting for me on the other side of this door."

"I'm sorry for all the trouble I caused you," Troy said with deep sincerity in his voice. "If I'd have known..."

"Don't worry about it. Bear thing was my idea. I had no idea things would go the way they did. Now, get everyone out of here."

Troy nodded and shuffled past the crowd, around the large podium at the front, and onto the judge's bench.

"People of Mena!" he shouted. Roy thought he sounded a little more like the person from the previous days. "If you've been on a jury here before, you might remember the jury exit is back this way. Chief Henderson has volunteered to guard the front door and protect us from the beast on the other side of it. I need you to follow me out the jury exit and out the opposite side of the building. From there, we rush home as quickly as possible."

Troy hopped around the judge's bench and over to the jury box. He opened the door and poked his head in.

"There's a lot of us. We have to go quick but try not to shove."

Just before Troy ducked his head into the doorway, Roy caught his eyes. Troy nodded, and Roy did the same.

Before he could talk himself out of it, Roy slipped the door open and left the courtroom, easing the door closed behind him. He stood in the rotunda filled with gray smoke. Not daring to make a sound, he held the revolver close to him and prayed again that three shots would be enough.

62

MIKE SPUN AROUND DAVID. He dug his fingers into the werewolf's fur and jumped onto his back. He wrapped his legs around David's torso and looped his arm around the wolf's neck. Finally, he slid his other arm behind David's head.

Mike hoped a werewolf was susceptible to a sleeper hold.

"Sun's getting real low," Mike said, channeling Black Widow talking to the Hulk.

David thrashed and jumped, doing everything possible to throw Michael off his back. Pain seared across Mike's legs as David dug his claws into them. The pain was nearly unbearable, but Mike knew he needed to hang on.

If he could cut off enough of its oxygen supply, maybe the werewolf would eventually pass out. In all the movies Mike had watched, he'd never seen anyone try this before, but hell, he also hadn't seen any movies where someone was trying to protect the werewolf from himself. And in the only movies he could remember where vampires and werewolves teamed up, the vampires sparkled, so that was unrealistic.

Holding on like a bull rider, Mike continued to apply pressure to David's neck and forced his head down.

Looking over, John had been pinned on the ground but found a way to kick the rogue werewolf off him and into the courthouse wall.

John rushed forward at him with his arm cocked, ready to punch the other beast in the snout. As his powerful arm drove ahead, the wolf caught his fist, bent John's arm behind him, and quickly twisted. Mike picked up the crack and snap of bone. John screamed out. The sound was tired and defeated. Mike realized John had been beat, but with his arm still wrapped around David's throat, there wasn't anything he could to do help him.

John stumbled forward and dropped to his knees. His broken arm hung loose, useless at his side. Of course, after a few days of transforming from a werewolf to a human, the arm would heal unnaturally fast, but Mike knew John wouldn't live long enough to see that happen. He was on the ground, his back to his opponent. His head hung on his chest. The victorious werewolf roared into the back of John's head, exclaiming his dominance over the fallen elder.

Mike didn't want to watch, but he couldn't look away. He kept pressure on David, hoping the sleeper hold would eventually work. He realized David had slowed down and kicked less. Either he too wanted to watch what was about to happen, or the lack of oxygen had started to take its toll. As David stumbled one way and then almost fell the other direction, Mike knew it was the oxygen deprivation and intensified his grip.

Please, go down in time. I just need a second.

The black werewolf raised its arm in the air and brandished its sharp claws. Blood and skin clung to them. With one swipe, Mike knew it would slice through John's neck and remove his head.

Before the wolf could make the intended lethal blow, a silver chain wrapped around its throat.

The wolf howled in surprise, grabbed the chain, and tried to pry it from its neck, but Niki held on with an iron grip. Every time the wolf's paw touched the silver, it sizzled. Charred rings seared its neck. When he finally did grip the chain, he tried to tug Niki closer.

Niki's feet faltered, and she stumbled forward. Nate grabbed her waist and planted her feet back firmly on the ground in front of him. He held on tightly to her stomach, not letting the wolf drag her along.

"I don't think so, mutt!" Niki shouted. "You don't get to threaten me and my man and think you're getting away with it. Fuck no. You're my bitch now."

Her shredded arms straining, she pulled as hard as she could, making sure the chain stayed taut, not letting the wolf get its claws between the silver and its neck.

"John, *catch*!" Nate yelled.

He reached behind his back, pulled a knife from its sheath, and flicked it toward John. The knife made a beeline to the ground and stuck in the dirt, only a foot from John's leg.

Kohana gripped the handle, yanked the knife, and quickly spun around. With his good arm, he drove the silver-plated knife into the wolf's chest, burying the blade completely.

The wolf's arms dropped to flail at the knife's handle. The wolf dropped to his knees, still trying to remove the knife but missing it. His attempts grew weaker and weaker. With his head hanging low, the wolf's features began to change. The snout and teeth recessed back. The hair pulled back, and the claws retracted. Its entire frame shrunk until only the naked human form remained.

The brother wrapped his hand around the knife's handle and pulled the silver blade from his chest. The blade, dripping with blood, dropped on the ground. A deep hole gaped in the center of his chest.

As the brother transformed into his human form, so did John. He fell to his knees in front of the dying werewolf.

"You caused so much pain and sorrow in this town..." John said. "You and your brother have brought dishonor to your house."

"My brother," he spat out. "He still lives." A menacingly evil smile spread across his face. He weakly cackled a few times in John's face, but then the life drained from his eyes, and the brother fell to his side. Deep red blood oozed onto the courthouse's green grass.

As the older brother slumped to the side, Mike felt David stumble backward. His instincts told him to jump off before it was too late, but he was afraid to let go. Instead, he let David collapse onto the ground, falling onto Michael.

"Holy fuck, that worked..." Mike said. He tried to push David off of him, but he'd lost all feeling in his own arms. "Little help here?" Arms splayed useless on either side of him, the vampire stared at the night sky and the full moon hanging high above.

As he peered up, Nate's head came into view. The other hunter just stared at him, judgmentally.

"Are you sleeping on the job?" he asked, shaking his head. He placed his hands under David and started to roll the large beast. As he did, he teased Mike. "I'm going to report you to Intel. We need a new leader AND a new vampire. This one has some weird interspecies fetish where he likes to be the bottom to a werewolf's top. Damnedest thing I've ever seen."

With one final grunt, Nate rolled a sleeping David off Mike. He lowered his hand, and Mike somehow grabbed it.

"You're an ass, but thank you," Mike said.

John strode to David and bent down next to him.

"He's sleeping," John said. "Soon, he'll change back, but we have a bigger problem. Where's the younger brother?"

Mike glanced from Nate to Niki and back to John. Both Nate and Niki shook their heads and raised their shoulders.

"Fuck! We've got to find him."

63

"JOSH, ARE YOU WITH me?" Roy whispered.

Gray smoke surrounded him. He wasn't one who suffered from claustrophobia, but at that moment, he felt the dark interior closing in on him. His heavy breathing was the only sound in the open area. The revolver nestled in his sweaty palm.

"I lost you when you went inside the courthouse. Fortunately, your internet security sucks so I did some creative engineering. You're disconnected from everyone else, but I hear you. What's going on in there?"

Disconnected from everyone else? You have no idea.

"Well, Troy is leading everyone out the back. I'm still inside, currently trudging through a thick cloud of silver. This stuff isn't going to give me cancer or anything, right?"

At the suggestion, Roy's throat suddenly felt rough and scratchy. He needed something to drink. He didn't care if it was water, tea, beer, or whiskey. Anything would do.

A loud crash came from above his head, and he shot his eyes up, following the noise. The smoke must've driven the werewolf back to the second floor. He almost wished the wolf would've kept coming down the stairs. At least the rotunda was an open space with nowhere for either of them to hide. The second floor and all of its offices had plenty of space. He hoped he could use that to his advantage. He imagined he could hide easier than the massive werewolf could.

"Cloud of silver? You set off one of the canisters. Is a werewolf in there with you?"

"Yes. He's currently on the second floor." Roy, still operating blindly and on pure muscle memory, brushed his foot against the wooden stairs. He raised his leg, planted his foot on the landing, and forced himself to take the first step up. "He was heading down when I threw the canister. It forced him back up."

"What are you doing right now?"

Roy smiled, knowing how stupid his answer was about to sound. "I'm going upstairs." He hesitantly took another step, making sure his foot was steady before moving higher. In the darkness, surrounded by the thick fog, the last thing he wanted to do was miss a step and face plant. He could imagine the headline. "POLICE CHIEF KILLED BY OWN INEPTITUDE IN WEREWOLF FIGHT."

"The rest of the team is dealing with David and the older brother. It's chaotic. If you're dead set on going up there, stay sharp."

"I'm halfway up the stairs now. I've got a few silver bullets left. Might as well use them. And in the future, don't use the phrase dead set while I'm hunting a werewolf alone in a building. Gives a certain kind of connotation."

"Sorry. As soon as I can get the team inside the courthouse to back you up, I will."

As he rose higher, the fog began to clear away. Roy could see further in front of him. He glanced behind and saw he'd risen above the cloud. From this point on, he was on an even playing field with the werewolf. He quickly scaled the remaining steps. His heart raced and his breathing accelerated.

He switched the revolver from one hand to the other. Once he did, he wiped the sweat from his palm onto his pants and then placed the gun back in his dominant hand.

The second floor extended both directions. The County Clerk's office was to his right, and the City Utilities were on the left. He couldn't see very far either way, but he'd visited the building enough to have the floor plan memorized. A few solid brown doors dotted the hall. The men's room was on the County Clerk's side and the women's restroom was on the other. Both hallways only went straight for a few dozen yards before curving around the building. If he went through all the doorways and the back hallway, he'd eventually end up back where he was.

Another loud crash came from his right. With his shoulder close to the wall, he carefully moved toward the sound. With each step, he eased his foot onto the tiled floor. A glassed entryway with a door in the middle blocked the hall right where it began to curve. It had the words "COUNTY CLERK" stenciled on the top. At least, the glass entryway should've been there. As Roy traversed the hall, his shoes crunched on shattered glass. The werewolf had completely destroyed the barrier.

He placed his back against the wall and eased his head around the curve. Teller desks hugged the interior wall. The doors to three offices were on the exterior side. The werewolf growled, just on the other side of the teller desks. Roy assumed it was hiding, waiting for the silver nitrate to dissipate so it could go downstairs again. With the revolver gripped tightly, he raised his arm in front of him until he stared down the barrel of the gun. His hand shook. He braced his gun hand with his other, giving it some much needed steadiness.

"Come on..." he whispered, waiting for the beast to show itself. "Let's fucking get this over with. Show yourself."

As if on cue, a high back leather executive chair flew from the far end of the area over the desks and crashed into the hallway floor. It finally stopped when it collided with the wall. Two pictures fell off the wall and shattered on the tiled floor.

Roy glanced to the opposite end of the clerk's office where the chair took flight, but as he did, the werewolf leapt over the counter closer to him. Roy tried to twist his body and point the revolver at the creature, but he couldn't get there in time. The werewolf slammed Roy into the wall. Roy completely spun around. The gun crashed against the wall, firing off one shot before falling out of Roy's sweaty hands and sliding across the floor.

All the wind was knocked out of Roy. He tried desperately to gasp for air. While he struggled, the werewolf gripped him under his arms and picked him up. Roy stared into its black eyes. The sharp claws skirted against his skin. The pressure on his ribcage was excruciating. Roy felt his feet leave the ground as the creature lifted him higher.

Roy didn't want to wait around to die. If this wolf was going to eat him, he wanted to make it earn every single fucking bite. His shoes dangling inches from the ground, he pulled one leg back and swung it forward as hard as he could. He didn't know how many kicks he'd get in so he had to make it count. His leg split the wolf's legs and connected directly with its groin.

Immediately, the pressure from Roy's side disappeared, and he crashed to the floor. The wolf bent over in pain; its paws clutching its abdomen. Roy had a single instance to smirk that he'd just racked the fuck out of this werewolf. He turned his head and ran for the revolver.

As soon as he drew close, he leaned forward and reached out his hand, hoping to scoop it up on the run. He felt the cold metal against his fingertips when a bout of blazing red pain streaked across his back. His torn shirt stuck to him, plastered in place from the blood streaming out of the gashes. Instead of gripping the revolver, he kicked it, sending it sliding across the tiled floor.

As fast as he could, he sprinted for it. The wolf was on his heels. The chief doubted he could withstand another slash from those claws. Already, blood dripped down his legs. He was going to need medical attention soon. He probably had one more chance to grip the gun.

Instead of bending over to grab it, when he was a few feet away, Roy fell onto his stomach and slid. He had a brief memory of playing on a slip-n-slide when he was younger. It was a lifetime ago, but the memory brought him a moment of peace. Playing in the sun and water, sliding from one end of the slippery material until he splashed headfirst into a puddle of muddy water on the other end. Was there anything better?

With his hand outstretched, he snagged the revolver by the trigger guard. The moment he felt the grip in the palm of his hand, he flipped from his stomach onto his searing back. He fought to stay conscious. He flung his arm in front of him with the gun pointing straight ahead. As he did, his thumb drew back the hammer.

The werewolf, rushing on all fours, leapt off the floor, claws fully extended. It had every intention of ripping Roy to shreds.

Roy pulled the trigger as fast as his finger would let him. Two concussive explosions echoed down the hallway, and two matching holes appeared in the center of the werewolf's chest. Instead of falling on top of Roy, it landed on the ground next to him. Roy scooted backward, bringing himself even with the men's restroom back by the staircase.

The werewolf quickly transformed back to the young man Roy had seen the day before. He lay face down on the tiled floor, a growing pool of blood spreading underneath him.

"Josh, can you hear me?"

"I read you," Josh responded.

"Send a medic."

Roy fell backward and stared up at the ceiling. From somewhere far away, he heard loud pounding as if someone was trying to break the courthouse door down. A few minutes later, Michael's face stood over him. His eyes blazed red, and he ran off. Nate's and John's replaced Michael's.

Roy felt his mouth move but had no idea if he said anything at all. All he knew was that he wanted a nap. Sleep sounded good, so he closed his eyes.

64

He slowly opened his eyes. Harsh, bright white light blinded him, causing him to recoil and slam his eyes shut again. He pulled his arm over his face, trying to shield from the tormenting lights. His arm hit resistance, as if trying to lift too-heavy weights. The smallest pull of his shoulder sent radiating pain across his back and down his arm.

"He's waking up."

"About time, love."

"Told you he'd be fine."

He heard a flurry of voices and footsteps.

"Roy," a distant voice demanded. "Roy, can you hear me?"

Henderson slowly, oh so slowly, nodded his head.

Every movement hurt. He eased his eye lids open. He recognized the room. Mena Regional Health Center.

"How are you feeling, Chief?" Dr. Wagner asked.

"Hurt..." he croaked.

"I'm certain you do. I lost count of the number of stitches and staples holding your back together. We almost lost you a few times. You lost a staggering amount of blood. Don't worry, though. There's a wonderful little button next to you. I'll make sure it's in reach."

As a nurse relayed Roy's vitals to Dr. Wagner, Roy focused. His room looked like a flower shop was using it as excess storage. There wasn't a place on the counter or windowsill that didn't have some bouquet with a balloon flying above it. So many decorated the counters that at least a dozen had lined the floor. The room smelled nauseatingly like a spring day but not in a good way. The aroma was overbearing.

After the doc was satisfied with Roy's vitals, Wagner and the nurse started for the door. Roy watched him leave and noticed the group of people hovering around. Niki was the first to catch his attention. She stood in front of Nate, his arms draped under hers, squeezing her to him. Mike was next to them.

His face had a slight discoloration, the last remaining bruises fading away. John Kohana, arm in a sling, stood next to Mike. David stood next to the vampire. Josh sat in his wheelchair on the opposite side of Niki. The whole gang was there.

"How long have you all been waiting?"

"Love. You've been out for a month."

"A month?!" he said.

He forced out the exclamation, shooting unintentional sharp pains up and down his dry throat.

Niki's smile filled her face. Soon, the others followed.

"Sorry," Niki said, pointing to everyone behind her. "They made me." Her relieved smile turned into a grateful smirk. "You've only been out a day and a half. You look like shit."

"Like shit? Well, that's good. Means I haven't changed much." Roy smiled. Despite the pain radiating down his body, it felt good to smile. A nice dopamine hit.

He decided to add to the hit and depressed the button next to him. A few moments later, he lost feeling in his toes, and the pain in his back throttled down to a low throb.

Euphoria must've shown across his face. "The drugs just hit," Mike said. "I know 'high as a kite' when I see it."

"Did we win?" Roy asked.

"We're all here, yes," Nate responded. "And so are a lot of people in Mena thanks to you. You saved a lot of folks."

Roy's smile widened more. He wasn't sure if it was from Nate's flattery or the drug high. Probably both.

"If you can't tell," Josh said, motioning to the abundance of greenery and balloons in the room, "everyone is quite grateful. There was a fruit bouquet also, but we ate it already." He shrugged. "We didn't know how long you'd be out."

"Besides the fruit basket, what did I miss?" The words slurred out of his mouth.

His cheeks and lips were numb, and his tongue fought him.

"It's a long story," Niki said, "but I'll hit the highlights for now. John's arm was broken. It's starting to heal, but he's being a baby and keeping it in a sling. Mike looked like he got in a fight with Freddy Krueger, but he'll heal as well."

"I've taken possession of both bodies," John said. "I'm taking them back to the pack for burial. They went wrong. They knew better than to do what they did, but in death, they still deserve to be at peace. Hopefully, their lesson will help to undo some of the damage. Maybe others who might've been persuaded by Silas will turn back."

"Silas had a persuasive tongue on him," Josh said. "He was an expert deceiver."

"This was a hard lesson," John continued. "But I'll work to spread it among the packs. Just because the Council is gone, doesn't mean it's time for a new world order. Our ways have kept us safe for hundreds of years. Sticking with them may keep us safe for hundreds more."

Roy glanced over at David. The chief tried to form words, but nothing came out. He wasn't tired or sleepy, but the pain meds had numbed enough of his body that none of his muscles listened to his brain.

Fortunately, he didn't have to speak.

"David is going with me to meet the pack."

"They're going to train me to be a werewolf," David said. "I'm pretty sure I never expected those words to leave my mouth — ever — but yet, here we are. I have nothing left for me here in Mena. The pack can teach me control." He turned his head and peered past John at the rest of the team. "Who knows. Maybe after I learn what I'm doing, I can join the Night Crew. Help you guys hunt monsters."

Niki stared up at Nate, and then said, "Have to run it by our supreme vampire leader, but I wouldn't mind having a werewolf around. What do you think, my Nubian dream boat?"

"Once you figure out how to control yourself, I'm game," Nate added. "Niki, Josh, and I should probably stick with one monster at a time with control issues. Might be good to have a dog around. You can fetch the newspaper, bring me my slippers," Nate said, smiling.

"But no barking at the mailman," Niki finished off.

Roy started to laugh and ended up in a painful coughing fit. His nerves woke back up with a start. He gripped his stomach and leaned to the side, hoping to ease some of the radiating pain off of his back.

"You two are assholes," Mike said, stifling his own laughter. "Let's get out of here and let the chief get some rest. Don't want him to bust a stitch or shoot out a staple. That shit hurts."

"Get better, love."

Everyone filtered out, leaving Roy there with nothing but his thoughts. He had so much to think about, and so much still to find out. He was happy that everyone had made it out alive, and that they were able to stop the two rogue werewolves from decimating his town, but so much death had happened. He decided he'd make it a point to attend each and every funeral that he could when he got out. On top of that, the whole town knew about the existence of werewolves. He wondered how they were taking it. How was his little town going to cope with the knowledge that monsters were real?

Roy closed his eyes. He needed to take one thing at a time. Thing one: get better.

65

MIKE MARCHED OUT OF the hospital; the others close behind him. The midday sun set high overhead. There were no clouds to cast shadows on the ground. Just the suffocating sunlight cascading down. He longed for night.

Standing by the parking lot, Mike turned to John and extended his hand. "I know we started out on the wrong foot, but I'm glad we ended up on the right one."

John gripped Mike's hand. "I feel the same way."

He cocked his head toward Nate and Niki. "After listening to those two talk about werewolves, I had a completely different take on your kind. Plus, the only other werewolf I'd ever seen was in a mind trap. Long story. But that one was sickly. Looked like a dog with mange. Definitely not the creatures you actually are."

"Sickly?" John asked. "We don't get sick. We can't. Are you certain it was a werewolf? Or an accurate vision of one?"

"It was a werewolf," Niki said, obviously overhearing the conversation. "And it was sick. But I've judged an entire race of creatures on the actions of one, and I shouldn't have. It was a pleasure working with you, and I'm glad we were here to help. You take care of Mr. Hall. Teach him well."

John nodded. "I will."

He and David turned to John's truck. Two wooden coffins sat in the bed. The two men opened the doors, hopped inside, and backed out of the parking lot.

Mike turned to Nate, Niki, and Josh. As he did, Troy Johnson strode up the sidewalk toward them.

"I heard he's awake," Troy said.

Troy's tone was absent of the arrogance that had infected it only a few days before. Now, a more somber appreciation resonated through.

"News travels fast," Mike said. He glanced at the others. "Hop in the car. I'm coming."

Nate nodded at Mike, and he joined Josh and Niki in the car, leaving Mike alone on the sidewalk with Troy.

"I'm sure I'm violating HIPAA, but yes, the doc put on blast that he's awake. I hurried as quickly as I could to speak with him and then help with crowd control. A lot of us owe him our lives."

"You stepped up as well. You led everyone out of the courthouse."

"I wouldn't have been able to if not for Roy. Assuming we'd have even made it out of the courtyard and into the courthouse to begin with? Once inside, that thing would've certainly found us and killed us. If the chief hadn't stayed behind to fight, we would've been goners."

A thought occurred to Mike. "How is everyone handling the realization that werewolves are real? I didn't see panic."

Troy nodded and licked his lips. "You're right. There wasn't. I'm actually a little surprised myself. I've talked with a lot of people over the last two days. Well, all day yesterday and this morning. Turns out, most people in town at least believed in the possibility of werewolves. There've been stories for decades about weird creatures in the woods. A few of the old timers said it used to be common knowledge. Go figure. Knowing there are people who make sure we stay safe from the bad ones helps as well."

Mike smirked. He realized the town was going to be alright. Roy was a lucky man. He pointed to the hospital. "He's going to need some time to heal. Take care of him."

"You don't have to tell me. By the end of next week, he'll probably have a school named after him."

66

AFTER THE LONG DRIVE back to Dallas, Mike released a relaxed sigh as he stepped out of the SUV.

"Never a better sight than coming back home," Nate said.

Both Niki and Josh nodded their agreement.

"How long do you think we'll have between missions this time?" Mike asked.

"Prior to you coming along, we usually had a week or so of R&R before the next assignment," Josh said as he rolled to the door, fumbling with the key. "Your control is getting better and better. If I had to guess, we probably won't be sidelined long."

Josh gripped the doorknob, and it turned in his hand. He paused, hand still on the knob, and glanced at the others.

Nate and Niki hurried to the back of the SUV and opened the trunk.

Mike understood their urgency to arm up. It hadn't been that long since Silas had ambushed them. At the time, the weapons had been with him and Scott. It had almost cost the others their lives, including Jax and Thomas. Nate and Niki weren't going to be caught unarmed again. With the disruption in the world, anything could've broken in, waiting to pounce the moment the door swung open.

"Mike," Niki said, "head's up."

She tossed a machete, and he snagged it by the handle. Nate marched from behind the SUV with a machete tucked in his belt and a shotgun in his hand. A belt with a holstered handgun dangled across his shoulder. Niki held onto her own machete and had a pistol tucked in the small of her back.

"What about me?" Josh asked.

Nate slid the black leather belt from his shoulder as he walked toward the door. He dropped it in Josh's lap. "I didn't forget about you."

"Thanks."

Mike moved next to Josh. If anyone was going in first, it would be him. He wasn't going to let the others rush in. "Slide back," he said, and Josh eased his chair away from the door.

Mike placed his hand on the doorknob and slowly turned. He gently leaned on the door, opening it just a crack. He searched the gap, looking for any kind of trigger wire. Once he was certain it was clear, he pressed the door, swinging it wide. His eyes quickly adjusted to the dark hallway. Nate and Niki's footsteps echoed on the flooring, inches behind his own. The trio quickly scampered down the corridor ready for whatever attack might come.

Mike turned the corner into their main meeting area and immediately stood up, halting the others behind him.

Thomas sat at their conference table sipping on a wine glass filled with blood. His long black hair draped his shoulders. His leather jacket wrapped around him like a cape. A stranger sat next to the vampire. The man had light brown hair. Based on his olive complexion, Michael guessed he was either Mediterranean, maybe Greek, or Middle Eastern. His face was long and angular with well-defined cheekbones. He wore a loose-fit white shirt, looking like he'd just come off a cruise boat.

"Fuck, Thomas," Mike said, directing his attention back to his mentor. His shoulders relaxed, and he lowered the machete. "We thought you were an intruder. We were ready to kill."

"I see that," Thomas said, pointing to the three of them. As he spoke, Josh came in the room as well. "We only arrived this morning."

"Holy fuck, you're Xavier Morcos!" Niki said, pushing past Michael and nearly crashing into the table.

Her whole face flushed. Even in the dark room, Mike saw the blood rush to her cheeks.

Xavier stood up. He was six feet tall, and although slender built, he was toned with staggering muscle definition. If he was in a movie, he'd surely play a Greek hero. Xavier extended his arm across the table, grasped Niki's fingers, and placed a kiss on the back of her hand. "You must be Niki," he said in a baritone voice. The words rolled off his tongue, almost lyrically. "Pleasure to meet you. Thomas has told me much about you." He angled his eyes to the others. "All of you." He glanced to Michael, releasing Niki's hand. "But you, especially."

Mike reached over the table, shaking Xavier's hand. "I've heard a bit about you as well. I've never met a real-life Harry Potter before."

Xavier let go of Mike's hand, smirked, and rolled his eyes. "Yes. That never gets old." He eased back in his chair and leaned back, propping one foot across the other knee and resting his hands in his lap. He laced his fingers together.

Niki shoved a chair from under the table and sat down. Her face still beamed. Nate stood behind her and placed his hands on her shoulders, grounding her. Josh rolled over to his desk, turned on his computer and the multiple monitors around the room, and then spun back around to the table.

Thomas stayed in his chair the whole time sipping his glass. Once the awkward pause set in, he asked, "All the celebrity fawning done?"

"Yes, love. Sorry," Niki said.

Thomas smiled. "It wasn't unexpected. Especially since Xavier is your hall pass."

Niki's eyes took up half of her face. The remaining portion turned a shade of red Mike was certain he'd never seen on a human before. Nate snickered. Mike glanced over to Xavier, but he didn't appear fazed. Mike guessed it wasn't the first time he'd met a fan.

"Everything in Arkansas turned out well, I see," Thomas said.

"It could've gone better, but we're still here to fight another day," Mike responded.

"While you were gone, we briefed Xavier on your vision. He has some thoughts. Xavier?"

The warlock maintained a very casual posture, still leaning back in his chair. "Yes, well, I will first fill you in on what we know. We had tasked Jax and Thomas with finding the missing council members, utilizing whatever means necessary. Their team has been scouring the country, following up whatever leads they could find, over the past few months."

Mike listened intently, waiting to hear what this had to do with his vision. If Xavier was there, there must be some correlation. He did have a question, though. Something that had been bothering him for a few weeks. This was a good opportunity to bring it up.

"Mind if I ask a question?" Mike inquired.

Xavier uncrossed his fingers and raised his hand to Mike, giving him the floor.

"You said scouring the country. Did the Council reside here? Don't creatures exist all over the globe? And how do you know they're still here in the US and haven't been moved somewhere else?"

"We aren't at liberty to answer some of those," Thomas said.

"Don't give me that shit, Thomas. Who can give you liberty to answer? Austin?"

Thomas shifted his eyes to Xavier, and Mike followed his glance.

Xavier's stoic face cracked a slight smile. "Very good questions. At this point, we can answer some of them." He paused and glanced at Thomas. Mike thought he was waiting for an objection, but none came. "The Council was meeting here in the States when they were abducted. It was the first time they'd all been in the same place at the same time in close to one hundred years. In the past, meetings had been held through intermediaries; each sending an envoy and relaying information and decisions through telephone. With the dawn of remote technology, the meetings changed once again. They usually still spoke through an intermediary but at least were also present on the calls."

"So why did they get together then?" Nate asked.

As Mike surveyed the room, everyone hung on Xavier's words. Only Thomas appeared agitated. His dynamic with Xavier seemed odd to Michael. Thomas was the one entrusted to find the Council. Xavier was a powerful warlock and a celebrity in the creature world.

Why was Thomas deferring to Xavier?

"The death of a Council member," Xavier continued. "Madame Marie Luc. I know you three know who she was, so for Mike's sake, Madame Marie was the magic wielder representative on the Council."

"Why wasn't anyone informed?" Josh asked.

"For continuity reasons, it was decided to keep it under wraps until a successor was chosen. She died under extremely suspicious circumstances considering."

"Was a successor chosen?" Nate asked.

"Yes," Xavier answered. "I was chosen as her successor."

That answered Mike's question. Thomas deferred to Xavier because Xavier was truly the one in charge. The revelation did pose another question, though.

"Does that make you the only member of the Council that wasn't taken?" Mike asked.

Xavier nodded. "Unfortunately, yes. Whoever secreted away the other members, knew the Council was meeting and where, but didn't know about my elevation."

The warlock can unlock the secret.

Valerie's words from his last vision echoed in his head. Mike was convinced now more than before that Xavier was the warlock she referred to, and Mike said as much. "Valerie told me you'd be able to help."

Xavier dropped his leg to the ground, leaned forward, and placed his hands on the table. A surprised look briefly flashed across his face before he regained his composure. "You spoke to Valerie?"

"While we were in Mena, I had another vision, but it was different. She spoke to me, called me by name, and said I was known to the Council. The last thing she said was 'The warlock can unlock the secret'. At the time, I assumed she meant you, but now that I know you're on the Council, I'm certain. What secret can you unlock?"

"Once you and I dive into your head, I'll be able to tell you. As I was saying before our detour, we've had to break up teams into two groups: those on Council duty and those on control duty. As an example, Jax and Thomas have been on Council duty. Your team has been on control duty. The control teams are running thin. We've had pockets of uprisings all across the globe."

"The werewolf issue we just handled was caused by Silas," Niki interrupted. "He'd visited their pack and planted seeds of unrest in the younger members."

"That's been a consistent story. Silas or his lieutenants spread his message of revolution. Although he's dead, the message has lived on. Our control teams have been mainly successful, but as I said, they are running thin." He eased back in his chair. His shoulders relaxed as he fell back into his monologue. "The Council teams have not had much luck. Only one team has seen promise, and that was Jax's team. But now the entire team is missing, including Jax. Michael, prior to your vision, we thought the worst. We had lost communication a week before your conversation with Thomas."

"Thomas said the vision could have something to do with a blood tie."

"Yes," Xavier said, nodding. "That's part of why I'm here. If the vision is truly because of a blood tie with Silas's bloodline, it may lead us to Valerie's location or the identity of Silas's accomplice."

"Let's do it," Michael said.

Xavier glanced at Thomas. Thomas shrugged his shoulders as if saying, "Told you he'd be ready."

"Good. I'll begin the preparations."

67

INSIDE MIKE'S BEDROOM, HE sat on his bed, his back against the wall. It was his usual meditative posture. With no windows, the door shut, and the lights off, Michael was encased in darkness. He closed his eyes and waited.

Xavier stood next to him. Michael heard his heart beating and his breathing.

"Are you relaxed?" the warlock asked.

"Getting there," the vampire answered.

Michael breathed in deeply, waited a few seconds, and then slowly exhaled. He repeated the process multiple times. Each reiteration, he found his body relaxing. He focused his mind on individual muscles, starting with his neck and shoulders, forcing each one to release the tension locked within. He slid his thoughts down his back and across to his chest. He continued relaxing stiff muscles throughout his entire body.

"As I speak, you will feel certain sensations," Xavier said, "such as heat and possibly vibrations as I focus my own powers on your mind. As you drift into a dreamlike state, I will push your mind's eye to the direction of your vision. Once the blood tie is established, I will be able to follow your journey and join you. It is important you stay focused and do not let your mind wander. Doing so, can create false memories, derailing us, and leading us into an altered state. One that is not based in reality, but a dream realm. Follow the vision."

With his eyes shut, Mike pulled the image of the cabin into his head. His UltraNet, the vault where all his memories stayed locked away because of his highly superior autobiographical memory, conjured the most intricate details of the dilapidated house in the open field.

Follow the vision.

Don't let my mind wander.

He replayed Xavier's instructions.

As he slipped further into the vision, he felt his body flowing through the air as if wind had picked him up and carried him. Waves of radiating heat washed over him. The hairs on his arm sizzled. The heat was so intense he could have been lifting the lid off a grill.

His vision came to a stop in the field outside of the log cabin, but this time it felt different. He wasn't an observer in someone else's body. It was his own, but this time he also felt nauseous. He gripped his stomach and bent over. He readied himself to vomit, but nothing came out. Just a gripping pain like a wrench tightening around his stomach.

"Xavier, are you here?!" he shouted.

What he heard was wrong. Everything sounded muffled, as if his ears were stuffed with cotton balls or full of water. A warbling noise echoed across the field, distorting everything he heard. Even his vision warped around the sound as if he was stuck in a fishbowl.

"Xavier?" Michael shouted.

Loud cracking sounds ricocheted across the trees. The wolves he'd heard howling the last time were no longer there. The snapping and cracking sound grew louder as if something very large ran through the trees, knocking them over.

Michael watched the tree line as the trees shook. When the sound became unbearably loud, the trees on the edge of the field collapsed.

Their roots pulled from the ground as the whole series of trees toppled over and crashed onto the grass.

Michael anticipated a massive creature but instead a large gust of wind slammed against him, and he flew into the air once more.

He flailed his arms. It was the only thing he could think to do, hoping somehow he'd sprout wings and gain the ability to fly. He glanced to the ground, seeing the cabin fifty feet below him. The wind stopped blowing, and Michael plummeted back down.

As he fell, he closed his eyes tightly, readying himself for the impact. He doubted the fall would kill him, but being a vampire wasn't going to stop it from hurting.

One final time, he yelled, "Xavier!" as the ground rose up to meet him.

68

JOSH WAITED WITH THE others inside the conference room. He hadn't left his station at one end of the table. Instead, he stared across the large, wooden table at Thomas. Thomas had known Xavier Morcos had been elected the magic wielder representative on the Council. He'd known and kept it from the others.

Not only that, but Thomas had known of Madame Luc's death.

According to Thomas, he hadn't found out until after the group went missing. He hadn't been read in until it was need to know.

"Of the twelve members, we know two are alive," Josh said. "Valerie and Xavier."

"Xavier for sure," Thomas said. "Valerie, assuming Michael's vision is real."

"What else could it have been? He didn't guess Valerie's exact description. It was a vision linked through a blood tie. Silas created whoever has the Council." Josh was convinced that was the truth. It was the only thing that made sense in a crazy world of magic and monsters.

Thomas leaned back in his chair and glanced up at the ceiling. Almost to himself, he said, "Benjamin, what were you doing?"

"Michael!" Xavier's shout echoed throughout the house.

Immediately, Thomas, Nate, and Niki shot up from the table and sprinted down the hall. Josh followed as close behind as he could. Nate reached the door first and tried the handle, but it wouldn't budge.

"*Move!*" Thomas commanded with an urgency Josh hadn't seen before.

From the other side of the door, Josh heard Xavier say weird mumblings in a language he'd never heard. Whatever it was had the cadence of a spell.

Thomas gripped the doorknob to Mike's room, leaned away from the door, then slammed his shoulder into it. The door broke away from the frame, splintering, and raining wood and plaster shards on Thomas's trench coat. He shot his hand to the wall and flicked the light switch on.

Nate and Niki pushed into the room, and Josh crowded in.

Xavier stood over Michael's bed. Both arms were extended in front of him. Ripples of heat emanated off of his body. The waves distorted the air around him.

Josh rolled his chair around the group so he could see Michael. Mike laid on the bed as if asleep. Xavier had one hand on Mike's forehead and another on his chest. Although the vampire was typically pale, his body appeared stark white, nothing more than a chunk of marble lying on the bed.

Xavier continued chanting.

"Morcos, what's wrong? What's going on with Michael?" Thomas asked.

Xavier rattled off a few more phrases and then stopped. Before anyone could react, Xavier collapsed onto the floor. Niki dropped to the floor and cradled his head.

"He's burning up. Nate, grab some water."

Nate rushed from the room.

Josh moved closer to Michael. "Mike's in some kind of a trance."

Thomas stepped next to Mike. He placed his hands on both sides of his young protege's head.

Nate returned with a glass of water. Niki stuck the tips of her fingers in the glass and flicked droplets of the cool liquid onto Xavier's face. As she did, his eye lids fluttered and slowly opened. She eased his head a little higher, and he started to come to.

"Here, sip," Nate said, bringing the glass to Xavier's lips.

The warlock sipped from the glass and sat up on his own power.

"Thomas, stop!" Xavier shouted.

"We have a blood connection. I'm going to wake him," Thomas said.

"You can't. I lost him," Xavier said.

"What do you mean? What's that mean?" Niki asked.

"It means, he's trapped. I tried to reach for him but couldn't." Xavier danced his eyes from person to person. The look on their faces must have showed their confusion. "He followed the vision to the cabin. I saw it along with him. Then something changed. The vision went off course. He's stuck somewhere else. Some time else."

"Some time else? What the fuck does that mean?" Niki asked.

Josh was stuck in a stunned silence. He didn't say anything. Instead, he wheeled next to his friend. He reached for Michael's arm. Vampires were usually cold. It made them stand out when he did drone flights. The team always showed up in red because of their heat signatures. Vampires in blue. But when Josh touched Michael's arm, it was hot. The heat was a stark contrast from the stone white color of his skin. Again, Josh thought he looked like a marble statue, but this time, one that was on fire.

"What does that mean?" Niki asked again, a notch below yelling the question at the newest and only remaining Council member.

"Blood has memory, especially vampire blood. Somewhere deep inside their DNA exists all the memories of the vampires who've come before it. Thomas inherited the memories of the vampire who turned him. Whoever Thomas turned would have Thomas's memories along with those of Thomas's sire. It's there, locked away. When I joined Michael's vision, it boosted his own special strength. I haven't experienced anything like that before, not on that level. The memories unlocked, creating a crack.

He fell in. Trapped within his own mind, down a memory spiral the likes of which I never knew existed."

"What can we do?" Thomas asked.

"Pray and hope," Xavier answered. "He has to find his own way out."

THE NIGHT CREW Will Return

Acknowledgements

I'm forever humbled by the love and support I've received for The Night Crew series. When I wrote the first book, I never could've anticipated the amount of support my little band of monster hunters would receive. With each book, even as we move closer to the inevitable conclusion, this is a world I continue to look forward to returning to. I have my favorite characters, and I'm sure you do too.

None of this would be possible without the support of my family. As always, thank you for listening to my ramblings and helping make each story better and better.

Thank you to Joe Mynhardt and the Crystal Lake Publishing team. I'm honored to be part of the Crystal Lake family.

Thank you again to Maarten van Vuuren for another truly amazing cover. Your work is magnificent.

And, as always, thank you to the readers for spending time inside my head and with the Night Crew. There are more adventures to come.

Be sure to follow me on Facebook or TikTok at @BradRicksAuthor, and follow The Night Crew Podcast wherever you listen to podcasts. It's where shadows breathe and monsters listen.

Until next time.

About the Author

Brad is the author of *Fear Not The Dead, To Hell with Hallmark,* and *The Night Crew* series. He draws inspiration from legends, folklore, and masters of the genre like Edgar Allan Poe and Stephen King.
A lifelong resident of Central Texas, he spends his nights listening to the little voices in his head and jotting down the stories they tell him.
Brad is also the host of *The Night Crew Podcast,* where he dives into all things monsters. You can find his podcast wherever you enjoy listening to podcasts.
Website: https://BradRicks.com
Email: Brad@BradRicks.com

JOIN BRAD RICKS'S BOOK CRYPT

THE END?

Not if you want to dive into more of Crystal Lake Publishing's Tales from the Darkest Depths!

Check out our amazing website and online store or download our catalog here.
https://geni.us/CLPCatalog

We always have great new projects and content on the website to dive into, as well as a newsletter, behind the scenes options, social media platforms, our own dark fiction shared-world series and our very own webstore. Our webstore even has categories specifically for KU books, non-fiction, anthologies, and of course more novels and novellas.

Readers...

Thank you for reading *The Night Crew III Hunting Ground*. We hope you enjoyed this novel. If you have a moment, please review *The Night Crew III Hunting Ground* at the store where you bought it.

Help other readers by telling them why you enjoyed this book. No need to write an in-depth discussion. Even a single sentence will be greatly appreciated. Reviews go a long way to helping a book sell, and is great for an author's career. It'll also help us to continue publishing quality books.

Thank you again for taking the time to journey with Crystal Lake Publishing.

You will find links to all our social media platforms on our Linktree page. https://linktr.ee/CrystalLakePublishing

Follow us on Amazon:

Mission Statement

Since its founding in August 2012, Crystal Lake has quickly become one of the world's leading publishers of Dark Fiction and Horror books. In 2023, Crystal Lake officially transitioned into an entertainment company, joining several other divisions, genres, and imprints, including Torrid Waters, Sinister Smile Press, Crystal Lake Comics, Crystal Lake Games, Crystal Cove Press, Crystal Lake Kids, Memento Mori Ink, and The House of Shadows & Ink on YouTube.

While we strive to present only the highest quality fiction and entertainment, we also endeavor to support authors along their writing journey. We offer our time and experience in non-fiction projects, as well as author mentoring and services, at competitive prices.

With several Bram Stoker Award wins and many other wins and nominations (including the HWA's Specialty Press Award), Crystal Lake puts integrity, honor, and respect at the forefront of our publishing operations.

We strive for each book and outreach program we spearhead to not only entertain and touch or comment on issues that affect our readers, but also to strengthen and support the Dark Fiction field and its authors.

Not only do we find and publish authors we believe are destined for greatness, but we strive to work with men and women who endeavor to be decent human beings who care more for others than themselves, while still being hard-working, driven, and passionate artists and storytellers.

Crystal Lake is and will always be a beacon of what passion and dedication, combined with overwhelming teamwork and respect, can accomplish. We endeavor to know each and every one of our readers, while building personal relationships with our authors, reviewers, bloggers, podcasters, bookstores, and libraries.

We will be as trustworthy, forthright, and transparent as any business can be, while also keeping most of the headaches away from our authors, since it's our job to solve the problems so they can stay in a creative mind. Which of course also means paying our authors.

We do not just publish books, we present to you worlds within your world, doors within your mind, from talented authors who sacrifice so much for a moment of your time.

There are some amazing small presses out there, and through collaboration and open forums we will continue to support other presses in the goal of helping authors and showing the world what quality small presses are capable of accomplishing. No one wins when a small press goes down, so we will always be there to support hardworking, legitimate presses and their authors. We don't see Crystal Lake as the best press out there, but we will always strive to be the best, strive to be the most interactive and grateful, and even blessed press around. No matter what happens over time, we will also take our mission very seriously while appreciating where we are and enjoying the journey.

What do we offer our authors that they can't do for themselves through self-publishing?

We are big supporters of self-publishing (especially hybrid publishing), if done with care, patience, and planning. However, not every author has the time or inclination to do market research, advertise, and set up book launch strategies. Although a lot of authors are successful in doing it all, strong small presses will always be there for the authors who just want to do what they do best: write.

What we offer is experience, industry knowledge, contacts and trust built up over years. And due to our strong brand and trusting fanbase, every Crystal Lake book comes with weight of respect. In time our fans begin to trust our judgment and will try a new author purely based on our support of said author.

To date we've published around 300 books, and with each launch we strive to fine-tune our approach, learn from our mistakes, and increase our reach. We continue to assure our authors that we're here for them and that we'll carry the weight of the launch and deal with third parties while they focus on their strengths—be it writing, interviews, blogs, signings, etc.

We also offer several mentoring packages to authors that include knowledge and skills they can use in both traditional and self-publishing endeavors. This includes Shadows & Ink Creators on our The House of Shadows & Ink YouTube channel and our Crystal Lake Academy.

We look forward to launching many new careers.

This is what we believe in. What we stand for. This will be our legacy.

Welcome to Crystal Lake Publishing—Where Stories Come Alive!

Thank you for purchasing this book